Jack Vance

The Fox Valley Murders

Jack Vance

The Fox
Valley Murders

John Holbrook Vance

Spatterlight Press Signature Series, Volume 21

Published by Spatterlight Press

Cover art by Howard Kistler

ISBN 978-1-61947-138-2

Spatterlight Press LLC

Spatterlight
P R E S S
340 S. Lemon Ave #1916
Walnut, CA 91789

www.jackvance.com

THE MAN, THE MAP, THE MOTIVE

The Man: Familiar Stranger, or Strangely Familiar

A successful TV show launched in 2012 bears a strong resemblance to a truncated novel series of the 1960s. The successful show is "Longmire," based upon seventeen books to date; the truncated series is Jack Vance's Joe Bain, with two books and an outline.

Consider the similarities. Walt Longmire is a sheriff in a contemporary rural area, such that his story is a blend of modern police detective with Old West frontier lawman. Joe Bain is likewise, albeit he is only the acting sheriff. Longmire has an election coming up, and this tension continues through case after case for the first two seasons. Joe Bain is also facing a looming election, and this through two novels.

Both sheriffs were born and raised in their respective counties, and both returned after military service, but this seems rather typical for a genre hero. What seems extraordinary is that both men are single fathers of only-child daughters.

I cannot think of a series where the lawman-hero has a daughter. The TV show "Gunsmoke" ran for a couple decades, but Marshal Matt Dillon never married Miss Kitty, let alone formed a family with her. Even the more recent TV series "Castle" (2009-16), which I interpret as a gender-flipped remake of Nick and Nora from the "Thin Man" movies, has the daughter as the offspring of the writer, not the cop.

For story-telling purposes, a sheriff's daughter can be either a helper or a person to be rescued. Longmire's daughter Cady is in her twenties, a lawyer who can offer skills and insights. In *The Fox Valley Murders*, Bain's daughter Miranda is sixteen years old, a high school student, and as the novel opens up the area is abuzz over the return of a man who had been convicted of raping and killing a 13-year-old girl. This parallel between the victim and Miranda sets a powerful tension of a visceral sort, giving the reader a taste of the simmering revulsion felt by members of the community.

Both sheriffs are operating as heroes of modern Westerns. A common theme of Westerns is that of the Closing of the Frontier, the pushing aside of the old ways for the new, and the hero usually resists the change. For Longmire this trope manifests as a new casino being developed by a corrupt alliance between business and government; for Bain it is the plan for a shiny new courthouse, the signature symbol for a countywide modernization pushed by a vocal minority made up of businessmen and politicians.

Because both sheriffs are single, a certain amount of romantic tension is present.

The first Walt Longmire Mystery was published in 2004 and the TV series came eight years later. In contrast to that long lead time, Jack Vance won an Edgar for his 1960 mystery *The Man in the Cage* and it was made into an episode of "Thriller" in 1961.

Still, Longmire is a success, and Bain was cut short.

Perhaps in the mid-Sixties a reader wanted a modern mystery or an old Western, but not a hybrid of the two. Maybe a sheriff with a teenage daughter was off-putting back then: too much "baggage" for an action hero.

It might be that Joe Bain was just forty years ahead of his time.

The Map: Fixing the Location(s) of San Rodrigo County

Granted that Joe Bain's fictitious "San Rodrigo County" is said to be situated in Central California, south of San Jose, where exactly is it? Or more correctly, where might it reside?

Answering that simple question is like mapping a mirage.

Start with northern San Benito County and cut it off before Hollister. This provides a shape close to the map of San Rodrigo County, with San Juan Bautista as analog to San Rodrigo County's "Mission San Rodrigo de Luz."

But this chunk of San Benito County seems too small for all of San Rodrigo County, suggesting additional land carved from Santa Clara

County to the north. The San Rodrigo County map shows a chain of settlements along a road from the Mission toward San Jose similar to the way Highway 101 connects San Juan Bautista to Santa Clara's Morgan Hill. On the San Rodrigo County Map this road is called "mission highway," which is a term for Highway 101. So there is a suggestion that the fictional town "Aurora" might be Santa Clara's Gilroy or Morgan Hill. (In fact there is a faint clue that "Pleasant Grove" might be Gilroy, since Gilroy's pre-incorporation name was "Pleasant Valley.")

Although there are hints locating San Rodrigo County in northern San Benito County, there are contrary details pointing to the southern end of the county. For one provocative example, the town of "Panoche" on the San Rodrigo County map (thus north of Hollister) has the same name of a real town, but one that is located 35 miles south of Hollister. Nearby the real Panoche is Mercey Hot Springs, which seems the likely inspiration for San Rodrigo County's "Hicks Hot Springs." The natural waterways stretching east to the Central Valley is a third case that seems transplanted from south to north: "Genesee Slough, part of the intricate system ... linking the San Joaquin River to the Sacramento River and eventually San Francisco Bay" (Chapter II).

San Rodrigo County seems to be a chimera made up of southern Santa Clara County (Morgan Hill, Gilroy) and northern San Benito County (the shape of the map; the position of the Spanish Mission), with details of southern San Benito County folded in.

The Motive: Why It Was Done

It is obvious that Jack Vance designed Joe Bain to be his Sherlock Holmes, a recurring hero in a set location. From the mid-Fifties Vance had expanded his reach into the mystery genre with six stand-alone novels, including three ghost-written books for Ellery Queen, and no doubt he felt the time had arrived to establish a franchise of his own.

For this project Vance desired a professional detective rather than an amateur sleuth, yet also one who was relatively new to the job. He conjured up a lawman and brought in elements of the Western, but softened it by making this macho hero a single father of a teenage girl. For being an action hero Joe Bain is like Kirth Gerson, avenger against the Demon Princes, but Bain is also a family man, rather than a loner;

and he is an honest lawman rather than a rogue agent pursuing his own obsession.

In addition, the Joe Bain series would be open-ended, in contrast to the five book limit for the Demon Princes and the four volume limit for Tschai. Instead of concluding with the killing of the last galactic gangster or with the successful escape from the planet of adventure, life would go on at its own usual rate: Bain would face the sheriff election, sooner or later; his daughter Miranda would have her remaining two years of high school and then the decisions beyond that; Bain would continue searching for a new wife; the county would continue to grow and change with the years of the tumultuous Sixties. There is enough solid world-building here to support many novels, certainly more than three: in his reviews of the Joe Bain novels, Anthony Boucher compared them favorably to Cunningham's "Sheriff Jess Roden" novels of the 1940s, and a little research shows that series grew to twenty titles.

As for the setting, Vance had written mysteries set in real California locations like Berkeley, San Rafael, and Fresno; but he had also penned puzzlers occurring in imaginary California places like "San Giorgio," north of San Francisco (*The Flesh Mask*) and "Bird Island," off the coast from Monterey. So he could go either way, and he chose imaginary this time.

In the Bain novels, Vance seems to be drawing from his life experience of growing up in the delta of the rivers Sacramento and San Joaquin. But rather than set it in this obscure area, he shifts it over to San Benito County. Which is next door to Steinbeck country. And I suspect that is why Vance did it: he was gunning for Steinbeck, winner of the 1962 Nobel Prize in Literature.

Consider the Joe Bain books as a response to *Cannery Row* (1945). Take Steinbeck's treacly neighborhood of a heroic abortionist, a whorehouse of practical women, and those precious bums with their hearts of gold; set up years and decades of bad blood and gossip; then add a murder. Examine pretensions of urbanity in rural settings; acknowledge rural insecurities and bellicosity; ethnic tensions and class frictions; question the corruption among the agents of change as well as among the heroes of the status quo.

The Joe Bain project produced two novels and a developed outline for a third. The third book should have appeared in 1968 or 1969. Instead 1969 brought a stand-alone mystery, *The Deadly Isles*, the last of Vance's mass-market mysteries (since *Bad Ronald* of 1973 is more a thriller, and was written in 1955).

So what happened? The reviews of *The Fox Valley Murders* seem strong. Were reviews of *The Pleasant Grove Murders* so bad as to sink the series? They seem strong. It appears, therefore, to come down to two different possibilities that are not mutually exclusive: the sales might have been disappointingly low; and Vance might have lost interest in the project.

A conclusive clue is found in two lines of commentary regarding the outline for *The Genesee Slough Murders*: "Robert Ockene, editor at Bobbs-Merrill, died after publication of *The Pleasant Grove Murders*. Successors at this house expressed no interest [in continuing the Joe Bain series]" ("All Title Index" from VIE volume 44*).

This seems a very likely answer to what happened. The sponsoring editor died; the publishing house pulled the plug; the series was scuttled. While low sales may have been a factor, Vance losing enthusiasm is clearly not. Any attempt to find a publisher for *The Genesee Slough Murders* would involve the baggage of republishing the whole series.

It looks like this setback turned Vance away from mystery writing so that he returned to science fiction and fantasy. If Joe Bain had been successful, perhaps the Demon Princes would remain unfinished, and the Alastor series un-started, to say nothing of Lyonesse, Cadwal, et cetera. It might be a relief then that the mystery series was abruptly halted; even so, it is hard not to wish that Vance had published at least a few more Joe Bain novels.

— *Michael Andre-Driussi*

---

* "All Title Index" from VIE volume 44 as presented on Foreverness website, archived by web.archive.org. Accessed 13 Oct 2016.

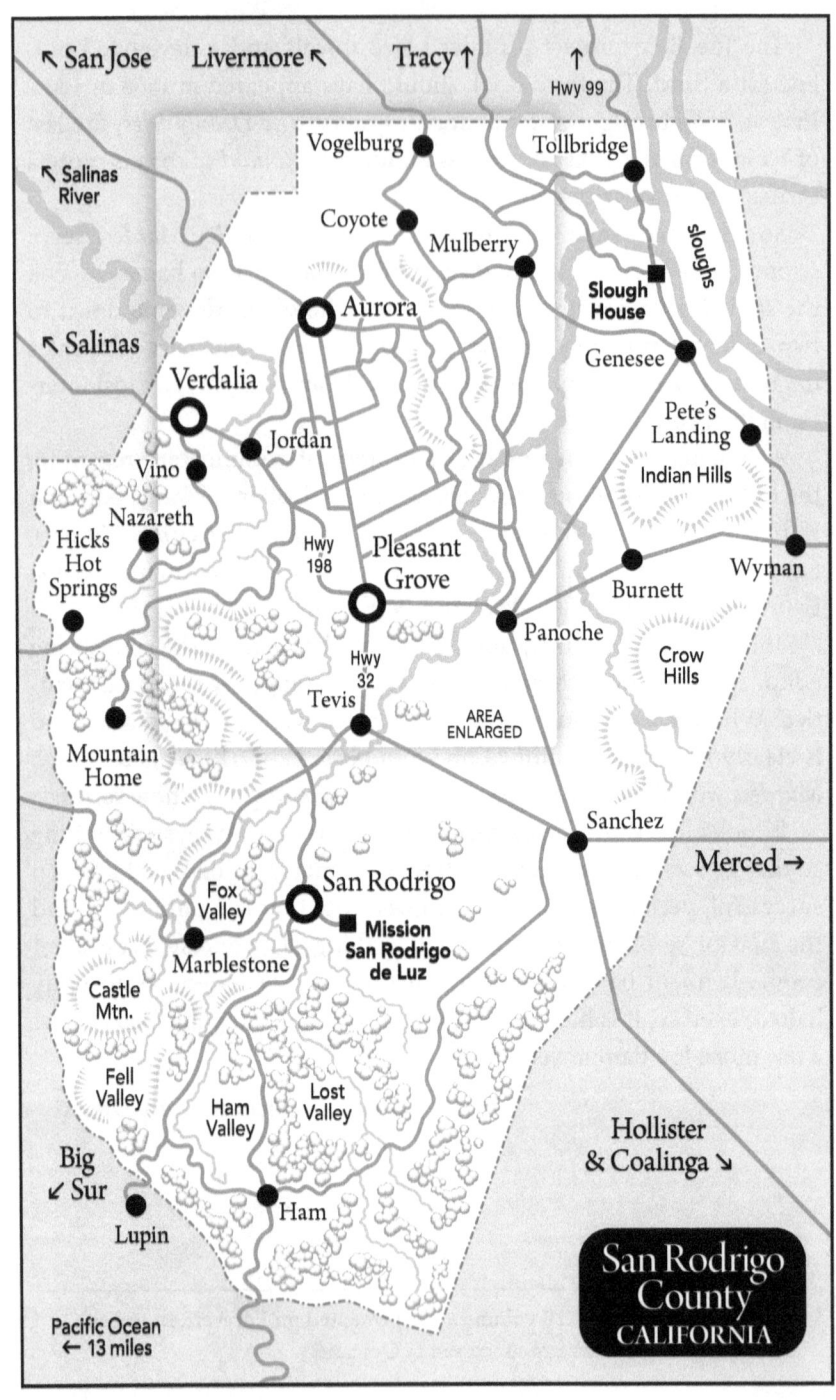

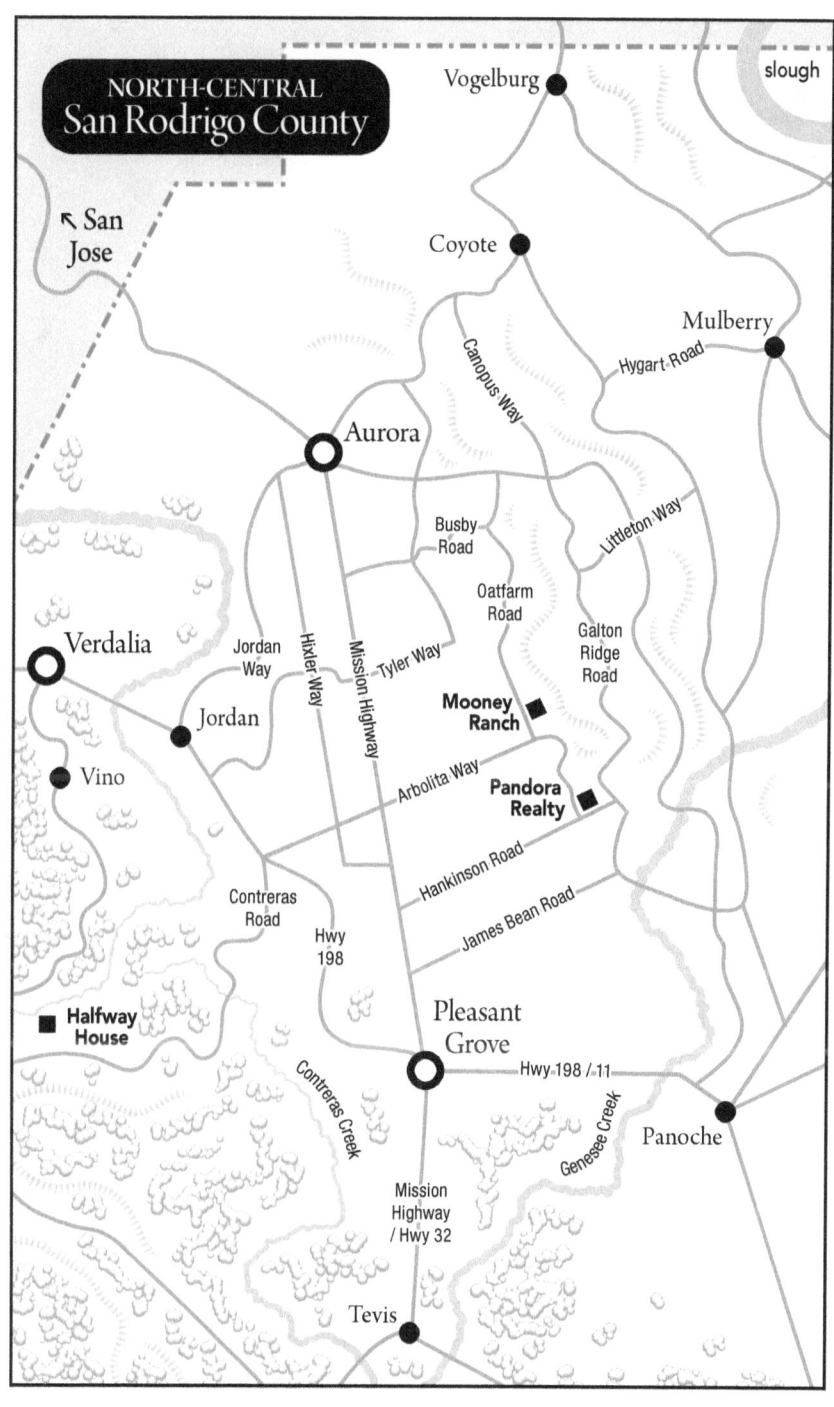

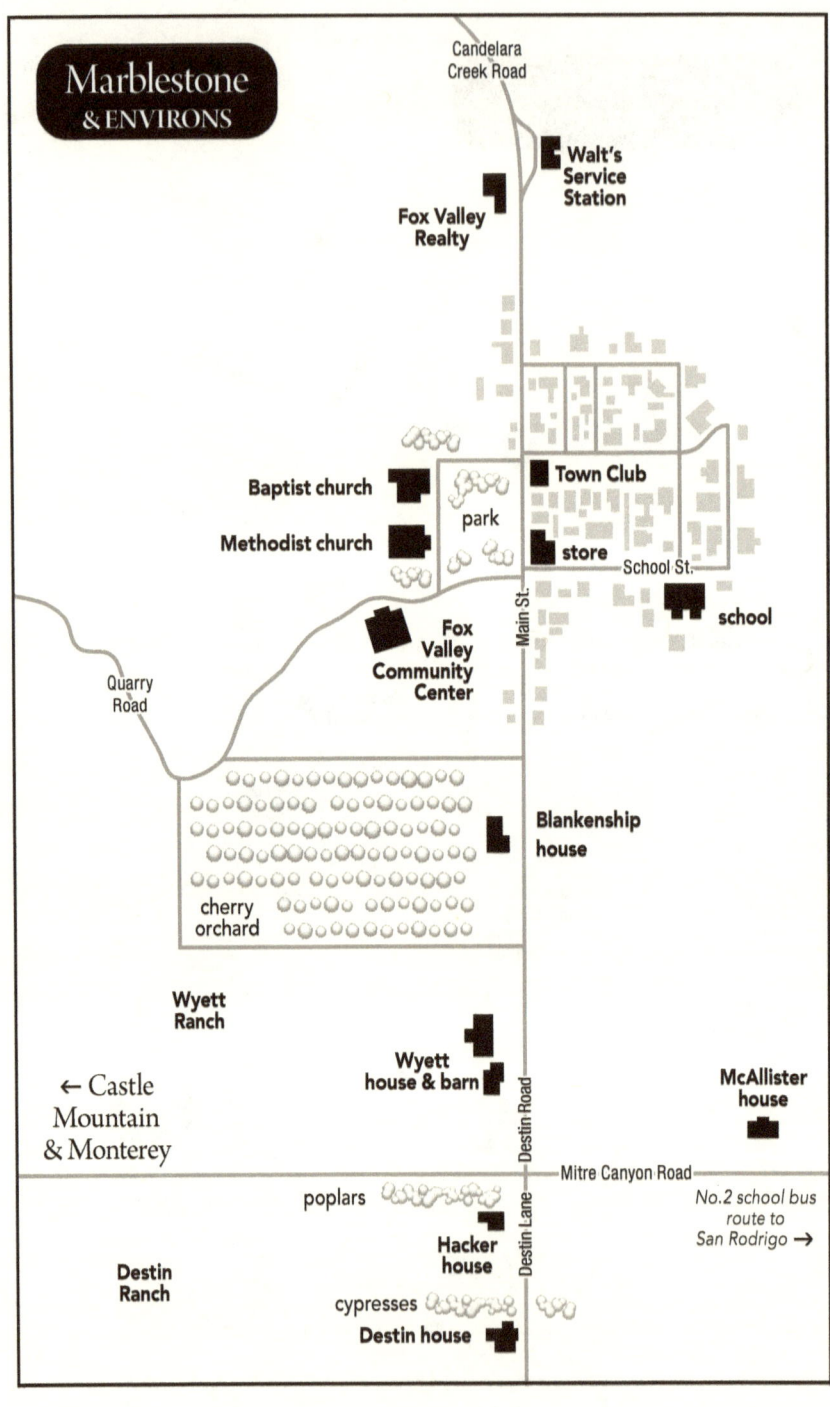

Marblestone
& ENVIRONS

Candelara
Creek Road

Walt's
Service
Station

Fox Valley
Realty

Baptist church

Methodist church

park

Town Club

store

School St.

school

Main St.

Fox
Valley
Community
Center

Quarry
Road

Blankenship
house

cherry
orchard

Wyett
Ranch

Wyett
house & barn

McAllister
house

← Castle
Mountain
& Monterey

Destin Road

Mitre Canyon Road

poplars

Destin Lane

No.2 school bus
route to
San Rodrigo →

Hacker
house

Destin
Ranch

cypresses

Destin house

CHAPTER I

ARRIVING AT THE OUTSKIRTS of Marblestone, Joe Bain swung into the driveway of the service station operated by his old school chum Walt Hobius. Walt, relaxing in his office with a newspaper, jerked erect, clearly startled at the sight of the black and white patrol car. He put down his newspaper, stepped outside, peered into the car with a quick intent glance which instantly noted all there was to note. "Hey, Joe. I thought Cucchinello had got awful skinny."

"Cooch has had it," said Joe. "Died night before last. I'm acting-sheriff. For a while anyway."

"I'll be damned," said Walt in a soft marveling voice. "Joe Bain, Sheriff. Well, well, well." And he gave his head the slow skeptical shake of one who marvels at the incomprehensible vagaries of fate. "I guess I should say congratulations."

Joe alighted from the car, looking down at the gilt emblem which read, *Sheriff, San Rodrigo County, State of California.* "Thanks. Not that I wanted the job, or anything else, at old Cooch's expense."

"That's the way it goes," said Walt with intense conviction. "One man's gain is another man's loss. You can't get around it, that's the law of life."

"Yeah, maybe so," said Joe. "What's new around town?"

Walt turned Joe his characteristic sharp quick look, as if for every overt act he suspected a deeper more important meaning which in the name of sanity and self-interest must be elucidated. "Nothing much of interest. Ausley Wyett's back. The girls are wearing iron pants."

"You seen anything of him?"

Walt gave a short resentful nod. "He's got himself an old Jeep station wagon and comes in for gas. That's all I see of him, that's all I want to see of him." Walt's eyes glittered as he warmed to the subject. "He's got real gall coming back here in the first place!"

"I guess he got lonesome for home," said Joe. "Sixteen years is a long time."

"Not long enough! Not for what Ausley did!"

Joe refused to argue Walt's perfervid opinions. "The main thing is, he's out, legal and otherwise, and there's no use raking up old scores."

Walt tilted his head to the side. "I suppose Ausley feels the same way?"

Joe shrugged. "As to that, I can't say."

"Which is maybe why he watered Bus Hacker's gas tank?"

"Eh?" demanded Joe. "What's this?"

Walt pointed to an old brown Plymouth sedan. "There she sits. About a gallon of water in the tank. Now I got to drain it off, blow the line, clean the carburetor." Walt's small tender mouth quivered with rage.

"If you're real busy, I better get along," said Joe. "Now that I think of it, you looked pretty peaceful when I drove in."

Walt gave a sour grunt. "Cranky old barstid, let him wait. He's always wanting something or other."

"There's ingratitude," said Joe ingenuously. "Seems to me you broke into the garage business working on the old No. 2 bus. Bus Hacker has been the making of you!"

Walt once more inspected him sharply, then turned away as if the conversation no longer were interesting. He grumbled, "I've got better things to do than clean up after Ausley."

"Somebody catch Ausley in the act?"

Walt held out his hands. "Who else would pull a trick like that?"

"Why should Ausley?"

"Revenge." Walt seemed surprised that Joe should ask. "What else?"

Joe looked off up the road. Ausley was acting strangely, no doubt about that…Peculiar. Very peculiar.

"A lot of people around here don't feel too Christian about Ausley Wyett," said Walt. "I'll give you a hint. You'd be doing Ausley a big favor if you got him to sell up and leave."

"You know better than to say a thing like that, Walt," replied Joe in a mild voice. "Ausley is a free man. There's nothing I can do."

"Give him the word! You're sheriff, aren't you?"

"Acting-sheriff."

"Same difference. I'm telling you facts. Ausley just isn't liked around these parts. If he goes mooching around like nothing happened, he might just run into an accident. At least, that's the talk I've heard."

Joe turned back to the patrol car. "You tell these talkers they better keep things on a conversational level; otherwise there'll be big trouble for all concerned."

Walt turned away, marched to the lube rack. Joe got into the car. Walt called across the graveled driveway: "You'd be doing him a favor!"

Joe started the motor and continued into town.

Marblestone, to the south of San Rodrigo County, in the shadow of the Coast Range, centered on a eucalyptus-shaded square known as 'the Park', in deference to a half-dozen benches, a few clumps of oleander, a decaying band-stand. Opposite, across Main Street, was the business district: Olin's Drug Store, the Town Club, the post office, the Ace Barber Shop, the general store. West of the park were Marblestone's two churches: the Methodist, patronized by the gentility of Marblestone; and the Baptist, preferred by the mountain folk. Down School Street was the Fox Valley Elementary School; along Quarry Road, just south of the park, was the Fox Valley Community Center.

Joe Bain parked in front of the general store and sat for a moment. The town was quiet: a warm summer silence disturbed by not even a voice nor the hum of another car. Joe alighted and stood on the cracked concrete sidewalk under the massive old oak tree, which was something of a town landmark. Nothing had changed, not even the blue EDGEWORTH CUT PLUG advertisement nailed to the trunk; the years which had passed were dreams. Joe looked along Main Street which upon leaving town became Destin Road. A quarter-mile south began the white-washed fence enclosing Charley Blankenship's cherry orchard. A line of poplars in the distance indicated the intersection of Destin Road and Mitre Canyon Road, whereupon Destin Road became Destin Lane, terminating at the old Destin mansion. Behind the poplars glinted Bus Hacker's white cottage. In Joe's memory the distances were longer, the air more limpid, the leaves a brighter green, the sunlight a richer gold — but essentially nothing had changed. Sixteen years ago Tissie McAllister, age thirteen and a half, had walked that road, on just such a day as this. She was later than usual, having stayed after school to rehearse a scene from the commencement play; and there were no other children on the road.

On that bright afternoon Tissie McAllister had not a care in the world. She loved her parents and was loved in return. Her hair was a glossy golden brown; she had long-lashed gray-green eyes, a cute pug nose, a mouth that seemed always on the verge of twitching into a grin. She was the prettiest girl in the eighth grade, and daily was becoming more aware of her attractions. Today she wore a pleated green skirt with a white blouse, white shoes and white bobby-socks. On her left wrist swung a charm bracelet, the latest ornament being a miniature hourglass, with real sand, a present from her boy-friend Tommy Hobius. At a party last Saturday Tommy had kissed her five times and somewhat more after the party. Tommy's older brother Walter had tried to kiss her too, but he'd been drinking beer, and Tissie had avoided him, though rather thrilled that she had attracted his attention. Walter's reputation was not good. He was a friend of the even more notorious Joe Bain, the tall hell-raising lad from Castle Mountain, who had run away from home and now lived in San Rodrigo where he consorted with Mexicans and fruit tramps. Tissie secretly admired Joe Bain, who was romantically wild and gallant. She also had a crush on Cole Destin, who was engaged to her sister May. Cole was blond and proud, and drove a blue convertible. He and May went everywhere together, arriving home at all hours, and Tissie sometimes wondered what they had been up to. Tissie felt that her parents were over-tolerant; but then Cole Destin was a great catch for May, as everyone, including Cole Destin, was well aware.

Another week of school — then commencement, and the whole glorious summer ahead. Lazy mornings, swinging in the hammock, swimming in the quarry, long twilights. And boys. Tommy mostly. He was a sophomore at San Rodrigo High, which Tissie would attend next year, riding the No. 2 school bus, driven by Bus Hacker. She'd have preferred to go by the No. 1, which Tommy and Walt and the Marblestone kids rode, but that was out of the question, since the No. 2 bus passed directly in front of her house.

Tissie passed the cherry orchard, and Mr. Blankenship peered owlishly at her from the verandah of his house. Tissie disliked Mr. Blankenship; he reminded her of a big white worm. She had none-theless eaten many of his cherries. It was a dangerous sport, as Mr. Blankenship kept handy a shotgun loaded with rock salt and had been known to use it, notably on his nephew Walt, causing an enormous family row.

Beyond the Blankenship orchard was the Wyett property — the pig farm, as it was known locally. Poor silly Ausley. He always had been tall and awkward, with lank brown hair, knobby knees and wrists, a good-natured, if somewhat moony, face. Tissie's sister May couldn't stand the sight of Ausley. One time at a Community Center dance, May had been trapped into dancing with Ausley, who — according to May — had done something unspeakable out on the dance floor. May refused to particularize, and referred to the event only through the medium of grimaces and shivers. Tissie had never quite understood the nature of Ausley's offense. She herself found Ausley rather amusing. Whenever he came upon her in the store he bought her candy or an ice cream bar, which Tissie was forced to accept, rather than seem rude.

The Wyett place was vast, extending a mile up Mitre Canyon Road and far back into the hills. The old marble quarry with the pond where young folk sometimes swam was on the Wyett property.

The Wyett house was fifty yards back from the road: hardly more than a large cabin built of unpainted boards, with a roof of tar-paper. Here Ausley lived with his half-crippled father who occasionally could be glimpsed hobbling between house and barn and pigstyes. Tissie often thought that if she owned the Wyett property she'd burn the house, barn, and styes to the ground, plant trees on the site, and then build a beautiful home up by the quarry. Whoever married Ausley would own lots of land, and perhaps be rich as well, for popular rumor imputed a miser's wealth to Jake Wyett...To be married to Ausley would be utterly weird, thought Tissie. She toyed with the idea, laughing to herself at her own nonsense. If she were Mrs. Ausley Wyett, she wouldn't let Ausley in the house. He'd have to eat outside under the trees, except on his birthday and Christmas and Thanksgiving, when he could come in. Married people usually slept in the same bed, and, Tissie supposed, did that. Sleep in the same bed with Ausley? Tissie gave a little amused shudder. No, thank you. He was nice, though.

As she passed the driveway Ausley looked out the barn, and seeing her, loped down to the road. "Hey, Tissie!"

Tissie paused. She really didn't want to talk to Ausley, but her parents had trained her to be polite. And also, she was a kind-hearted girl who didn't want to hurt anyone's feelings. "Hey, Tissie," panted Ausley. "Six kittens. Mother cat bust loose last week, and now everywhere you look — kittens."

Tissie was stirred. She loved kittens, and was appalled by the probable fate in store for the newcomers. "Are you going to keep them?"

"Nope. I'll drown 'em in the horse-trough. Pa said to give 'em to the pigs."

"Oh, *Ausley!* How terrible!" Tissie's heart contracted. "The poor little things."

Ausley grinned. "They're no good for nothing. Just yell and fight. The old man had to go to the hospital at Pleasant Grove, otherwise they'd be gone already."

Tissie was far less concerned for Jake Wyett than for the kittens. "Why don't you try to find homes for them?"

"You can have 'em. Take the lot."

Tissie deliberated, the tip of her pink tongue between her teeth. Ausley cocked his head, looked at her with an intent appraisal. Tissie moved a little away.

"Well?" asked Ausley. "You want the little varmints?"

"I don't know. I couldn't keep all of them. My mother wouldn't let me."

"Why don't you pick out two or three you like?"

Tissie hesitated. "Where are they?"

"In the barn."

"Well — I'll look at them." She turned in through the gate, walked with prim determined steps toward the barn. The doors were open, sagging on rusted hinges. Tissie heard the sound of an engine; standing in the dark aperture, she turned to see Cole Destin drive by. "Cole!" She called and waved, but Cole apparently did not see her. She looked after him a moment. The school bus from San Rodrigo High was coming up Mitre Canyon Road, still a long way off.

Ausley went into the barn. Tissie followed him in. "Where are they?"

"Over here in the manger, with mama cat."

Tissie looked down at the kittens, who were nursing, nuzzling, toddling back and forth, eyes still glued shut.

Tissie sighed, bent forward. "Oh…They're so cute."

Ausley stood behind her. "You want 'em?"

"I'd love them. But they're too young. I couldn't take them now. They'd die. Won't you take care of them, just for a while?" She looked pleadingly up into Ausley's face.

"All right. If I can keep the old man away from them. I guess I can. He won't be back for a few days."

"Thank you, Ausley." Tissie turned to leave the barn.

Medical testimony at the trial was to the effect that Teresa McAllister had been savagely raped, with resulting hemorrhage. The hemorrhage was not the cause of death, though it might well have been. Teresa McAllister had been garroted with a length of baling-wire.

Charles Blankenship testified that he had seen Teresa McAllister walk past his house at approximately four o'clock. She had been alone; she had not returned along the road. Sometime later — twenty minutes? half an hour? he could not be sure — he had heard a scream from the direction of the Wyett barn. At first he had been alarmed, then decided that he had heard one of the Wyett pigs squealing.

During cross-examination the defense attorney asked: "You heard this sound, which you decided was a squeal?"

BLANKENSHIP: A scream, I decided it was.
DEFENSE ATTORNEY: At the time you heard it, you thought it was a scream?
BLANKENSHIP: That is correct.
DEFENSE ATTORNEY: When did you change your mind and decide it was a squeal?
BLANKENSHIP: Right away. That is, I thought that it must be a squeal.

DEFENSE ATTORNEY: Then the cry actually might have been the squealing of a pig?

BLANKENSHIP: No sir. As I think about it now, no pig ever squealed like that.

Cole Destin testified that he had driven past the Wyett house a few minutes after four and had noticed Ausley Wyett and Teresa McAllister walking toward the barn. She was going of her own volition, without any evidence of duress, otherwise he naturally would have stopped his car and intervened. He was sorry he hadn't done so; he'd regret his negligence till the day he died. The judge ordered the last comment stricken from the record.

Bus Hacker came to the stand and was sworn. He stated his name: Clarence J. Hacker; his residence: a house at the corner of Destin Lane and Mitre Canyon Road, leased from Philip Destin; his occupation: retired.

DISTRICT ATTORNEY (*puzzled*): Isn't it true that you own a bus, that you are employed by the San Rodrigo High School District to transport students between Marblestone and San Rodrigo?

HACKER (*truculently*): Half-true. It's just a side-line with me, not an employment.

DISTRICT ATTORNEY: How do you mean 'half-true'?

HACKER: There's two buses for Marblestone. Bill Giacometti drives the No. 1 route, by Magnus Way. I drive the No. 2 route, down Mitre Canyon Road and into San Rodrigo by Bosco Road.

DISTRICT ATTORNEY: I see. Do you recall the afternoon of May 22nd?

HACKER: Very well indeed.

DISTRICT ATTORNEY: You drove your route as usual?

HACKER: I did.

DISTRICT ATTORNEY: Where is the end of your route?

HACKER: The corner of Mitre Canyon Road and Destin Lane. That's as far as I'm paid to drive, and that's how far I drive.

DISTRICT ATTORNEY: There are students who live farther up Mitre Canyon Road?

HACKER: Three. Two Bazely kids and Henrietta Micklebarth.

If there was five, the county would have to furnish transportation.

DISTRICT ATTORNEY: What happened on the afternoon of May 22nd?

HACKER: Well, I drove the route as usual, let off the kids, and backed the bus into my driveway. I was having trouble with the engine — sticky valves; in fact I am getting an overhaul right now. I lifted the hood to check the distributor points, standing where I could look out on the road —

DISTRICT ATTORNEY: Excuse me, Mr. Hacker, to make matters clear, could you see the Wyett house?

HACKER: No. The poplar trees at the corner cut off my view. But I could see the crossroads. Tissie McAllister definitely did not walk past.

DISTRICT ATTORNEY: Did you see anyone at all?

HACKER: Cole Destin drove past in his car.

DISTRICT ATTORNEY: Did he continue south along Destin Lane to his home?

HACKER: No. He turned up Mitre Canyon Road, to the west.

DISTRICT ATTORNEY: He was alone?

HACKER: So far as I could see.

DISTRICT ATTORNEY: I see. Did anyone else pass?

HACKER (*hesitating*): Not while I was standing there.

DISTRICT ATTORNEY: Specifically, did Teresa McAllister pass across your line of vision?

Here Bus Hacker turned a malevolent glance toward the somber Ausley Wyett, who leaned forward and back, cracking his knuckles. "She did not walk past. If Charley saw her and —"

The defense attorney sprang to his feet, but the judge's gavel forestalled him. "We don't want any speculations, Mr. Hacker."

Later, in his closing statement, the District Attorney emphasized that

A. Cole Destin had seen Tissie walking toward the barn in the company of Ausley Wyett.

B. Charles Blankenship had seen Tissie walk past and sometime later Cole Destin drive by in his car, and no one else.

C. Clarence Hacker had seen Cole Destin pass, but no one else.

Hence, declared the District Attorney, no person other than the defendant had had opportunity to commit the crime.

After an ineffectual cross-examination of Bus Hacker, the next witness for the prosecution was called: Oliver Viera, a stocky pugnacious young man of twenty, with a swarthy skin and a vigorous growth of sleek oiled hair. He sat stiffly on the witness stand, and answered questions with an air of reluctance.

DISTRICT ATTORNEY: You are — I should say, were — a schoolmate of the defendant?

VIERA: Yes sir. We were in the same class.

DISTRICT ATTORNEY: So then you know the defendant well?

VIERA: All my life.

DISTRICT ATTORNEY: He would be likely to consider you an intimate friend?

DEFENSE ATTORNEY: Objection!

DISTRICT ATTORNEY: Let me put it this way…Well, on the morning of May 22nd, did you see Ausley Wyett?

VIERA: Yes.

DISTRICT ATTORNEY: What did he tell you?

VIERA (*in embarrassment, not looking toward Ausley Wyett*): He told me that it was his birthday, that he was twenty-one years old. I said congratulations. He said he'd decided he'd been missing out on a lot of fun: girls, cars, parties, and he was going to turn over a new leaf, starting today. In fact since his father was away, he was going to give himself a birthday present.

DISTRICT ATTORNEY: Did he say what?

VIERA: No.

DISTRICT ATTORNEY: Now then, Mr. Viera, did you see the defendant later the same day?

VIERA: Yes, I did.

DISTRICT ATTORNEY: Please describe what you saw.

VIERA: Well, I came down Mitre Canyon Road, heading east. It was about sundown, maybe a little after. A car passed me going lickety-split, back toward Castle Mountain. I recognized Ausley's Chevy pickup, and it looked like Ausley driving. I continued the way I was going. At the corner of Destin Lane I saw Mr. McAllister standing in the road beside his car looking up and down. I stopped, and Mr. McAllister asked me if I'd seen Tissie. I said no. He told me that she hadn't come home and the family was getting worried. He told me that she'd been seen talking to Ausley Wyett.

DEFENSE ATTORNEY: I'm finally forced to object, Your Honor, this conversation is all —

JUDGE: Sustained. Mr. McAllister can testify to his own conversation, Mr. Viera. You just report what you told him.

VIERA: Can't I testify to what I heard? I heard Mr. McAllister —

DISTRICT ATTORNEY: Just what you yourself said and did. You see, there might have been a misunderstanding. Mr. McAllister can supply his own testimony.

VIERA (laughs): I told Mr. McAllister that I had seen Ausley Wyett driving up Mitre Canyon Road, and Mr. McAllister took off up Mitre Canyon Road himself. I was late for night school so I went home...

The fifth witness was Willis Neff, a hard-faced man of thirty, stocky, with long arms and burly shoulders which stretched the seams of his blue suit. His hair was thick and yellow, his eyes china-blue. During the whole of his testimony he stared at Ausley Wyett, who grimaced uneasily, shuffled his feet, and, finally, hunching his shoulders, sat looking down at his hands.

Neff testified to the effect that at approximately seven o'clock on the evening of May 22 he had noticed a gray Chevrolet pickup proceeding west up Mitre Canyon Road. Shortly afterwards, a car driven by Paul McAllister had pulled up. In response to McAllister's question, he stated that he had noticed a gray Chevrolet pickup proceeding west. McAllister explained his interest in the pickup, and Neff, whose oldest daughter Gertrude was a classmate of Tissie's, immediately jumped into the car with McAllister and they continued westward, up into the twilight, the ridges now dark against the sky. Two or three miles farther along they noticed a car approaching, which they stopped. The driver of this car had passed no such gray Chevrolet pickup; McAllister and Neff went

JACK VANCE

back the way they had come. At the bridge across Candelara Creek, a dirt road, hardly more than a set of tracks, led up into the primitive area; examining the road with a flashlight they saw fresh tracks, and parking the car proceeded on foot, McAllister now frantic with worry.

The creek wandered into a little meadow overgrown with cat-tails; here the pickup was parked. They stopped to listen and heard noises through the gloom: "puffin' and gruntin'," so Neff described them. Advancing, they came upon Ausley Wyett digging a hole, with close at hand the body of Tissie McAllister.

McAllister, screaming in agony, ran forward, Ausley Wyett looked up with a sick grin. He backed around the grave and McAllister in his frenzy fell headlong into the hole. "Just a minute, fellas," said Ausley. "Just a minute. Be reasonable, give me a minute to —"

But Neff was on him. Ausley stumbled and fell and Neff, to use his own words, "kicked hell out of him".

They tied the unconscious Ausley hand and foot, tossed him into the back of his pickup. McAllister carried the body of his daughter back to his car. They drove to Marblestone, where they telephoned Sheriff Ernest Cucchinello.

Sheriff Cucchinello was called to the witness stand. He testified that he had searched the Wyett barn and there had found torn underpants (subsequently identified as those worn by Tissie), as well as a number of rags soaked with blood.

The prosecution rested and the defense attorney, rather despondently, so it seemed, presented the case of Ausley Wyett, which consisted almost entirely of Ausley Wyett's protestations of innocence.

"What did you mean when you told Oliver Viera that you were going to give yourself a birthday present?"

"I just went into Fritz's and got me a big steak and a box of candy, then I went into the Town Club and bought a pint of whiskey. That's all I meant."

Fritz Hunsacker, proprietor of the Marblestone General Store, and Shorty Olson, bartender at the Town Club, verified the purchases.

Ausley fervently denied lascivious intent when he took Tissie McAllister to the barn. "All I wanted was to show her these kittens; otherwise they was about to be drowned."

"And what happened after Tissie looked at the kittens?"

"I told her I had some candy in the house, would she like some? She said no and went out, and I went off up the hill for the cows. That's the last I saw of her until I went back into the barn to bring milk to the mama cat and found her lying there."

"And when was this?"

"Just before sundown."

"About two hours after you had last seen her?"

"Close to that."

"Now, another question. Did you see anyone as you departed the barn?"

"I didn't look real close. But I kinda noticed somebody walking, coming down from Hacker's corner toward town. Beyond this I can't say. I've tried to figure out who it was, but it was just a glimpse. Somebody. I can't be sure."

"Did you see a car along the road?"

"Not after Cole Destin went by. But I couldn't see much of the road. The house and tank-house cut off the view."

"Whereupon you became frightened and panicky?"

"I sure did; I lost my head and did the foolishest thing I could have done."

During cross-examination the District Attorney said, "You've heard the testimony of the witnesses for the prosecution. If you are as innocent as you claim, who ravished and murdered Teresa McAllister?"

"I can't figure it," said Ausley, frowning and shaking his head. "Unless someone was on the road. One thing for sure, somebody isn't letting on all they know. When I get out of this mess, I'm gonna find out a few things."

The jury, ten men and two women, was out three hours, the only point at issue being the state of Ausley's sanity. One of the women said, "It's well known that Ausley Wyett is crazy and has always been crazy. My nephew knows a boy who went to school with him, and the things he's heard about Ausley Wyett!"

One of the men grunted. "Crazy. Maybe so. But a mad dog is crazy and you shoot a mad dog. A man like that isn't any more use than a mad dog."

The other woman said, "I certainly believe society must protect itself, but insanity is a sickness, and you don't kill people just because they're sick. We're not barbarians yet."

The verdict was "Guilty", with the foreman of the jury reading a statement. "We feel that there is an element of doubt as to the sanity of Ausley Wyett, and therefore recommend that he should not be sentenced to death."

The judge took cognizance of the recommendation and sentenced Ausley Wyett to life imprisonment. Ausley grimaced sadly and was conducted away to jail.

Joe Bain, with troubles of his own, had been only remotely aware of the circumstances of the trial. Immediately upon graduation from high school he had married Lucy Martinez, the daughter of a packing-shed worker, already several months pregnant. Lucy, who was vivacious and nervously active but far from tractable, refused to live at the remote Bain ranch. Joe moved to Verdalia, and for two years worked in lettuce fields and packing sheds. One evening he took Lucy to a dance at the IOOF Hall in Verdalia, with music by Lefty Harkins and his Oklahoma Ranch Boys. Lucy was entranced by the glamour of the evening, to such an extent that two days later she eloped with Gil Sears, the long-legged guitarist of the band. Joe came home from work to find his nineteen-month-old daughter Miranda standing in the play-pen, diapers dripping, milk-bottle empty, quietly philosophic about the whole sad situation.

Joe took Miranda to his mother and joined the army. He saw action in Korea, transferred to the Military Police and wound up as sergeant.

After his discharge he used his GI benefits to attend the Chapman Institute of Criminology in North Hollywood. Then, visiting his mother and Miranda in Pleasant Grove, where they had moved upon the death of Joe's father, he spoke with Sheriff Cucchinello and accepted a job as deputy-sheriff, which job he had held until Sheriff Cucchinello's death.

About a week before Sheriff Cucchinello fell into the swimming pool, Joe came into his office to protest regarding Mrs. Rostvolt, the matron and office manager. In Joe's opinion Mrs. Rostvolt's tendency to throw her weight around had passed the tolerance level and he wanted a line laid down. Sheriff Cucchinello made soothing noises, puffed out his cheeks, became interested in the morning mail. Joe turned to leave. If by some chance he and Mrs. Rostvolt got into a big dust-up, old Cooch could never say he hadn't been warned...Sheriff Cucchinello looked up from an official form letter. "You're a Marblestone man, Joe. Remember Ausley Wyett?"

Joe nodded. "Ausley's a hard man to forget."

Sheriff Cucchinello frowned at the letter. "Sixteen years he's been in. Damn lucky he didn't get the chair. The jury thought he was crazy."

"He never did have good sense. I wouldn't say he was crazy. I never thought he was vicious either."

Sheriff Cucchinello leaned back in his big black leather chair. "He's going back to Marblestone to live. To me that sounds like lunacy."

"One thing for sure," said Joe, "they won't meet him with any brass bands."

A week later Sheriff Ernest Cucchinello attended a Saturday night smoker and through circumstances never quite clarified fell into a swimming pool. After being hauled out he drank whiskey to ward off the chill, but the ministrations were futile. Sheriff Cucchinello contracted pneumonia and four days later was dead.

The County Board of Supervisors met at Pleasant Grove, and without any particular ceremony appointed Sergeant Joe Bain Acting-Sheriff for the duration of Ernest Cucchinello's term — something under three months.

Joe at this time was thirty-six years old, just under six feet tall, lean, leathery, durable. His hair was straight, thick and black; he had narrow eyes and a broken nose which gave him an expression of saturnine craft. He assured the supervisors that the department would function with undiminished efficiency, returned to headquarters, changed from his uniform into street clothes, moved into the office where for twenty years Ernest Cucchinello had lounged, napped, smoked cigars, drunk whiskey, watched ball games on TV, entertained his cronies and occasionally signed his name to the documents placed before him by Mrs. Rostvolt, clerk, matron, office manager and power behind the throne.

As Joe started to clean out Ernest Cucchinello's desk, Mrs. Rostvolt appeared in the doorway. She was a blank-faced woman of forty, plump and well-corseted, with a careful coiffure of tight auburn curls, a mouth like a cocktail cherry. Here it came, thought Joe — the first test of mettle. Mrs. Rostvolt said brightly, "I suppose you still want to take your regular patrol?"

"Heavens no," said Joe. "You know better than that, Mrs. Rostvolt."

Mrs. Rostvolt pursed her lips. "We're going to be awfully tight. I've got the schedule all worked out, and I can easily look after the office. I don't imagine the board wants to hire another man just for two or three months." Mrs. Rostvolt here referred to the coming election, and to the general conviction that Lee Gervase, a vigorous and progressive young lawyer, formerly of San Francisco, would sweep unopposed into office.

"There's nothing sacred about the schedule," said Joe. "Bring it in here and I'll change it around."

"It just makes work and confusion," declared Mrs. Rostvolt. "It seems to me that just for the two months —"

"We'll do it my way," said Joe. It was important to take a firm line with Mrs. Rostvolt, who had had matters pretty much her own way during Ernest Cucchinello's regime.

Mrs. Rostvolt sniffed. "I'll have to rearrange everything. I suppose I can take Bill Phipps off mornings, but on Tuesday mornings there won't be anyone in at all, because Wardell is off and the relief man is off too."

"I'll fix up a new schedule," said Joe. "For now, just let the old one ride. I want to get this office cleaned out first thing, so I can have a place to sit down."

Mrs. Rostvolt's mouth took on a sour droop. "After the election it'll have to be done all over again anyway. Seems like you'd just want to let things be." She marched back across the hall into the front office. Mrs. Rostvolt was really put out, thought Joe. Well, she'd have to get used to change, because if Lee Gervase were elected, and there was nothing in his way, changes would come in all directions. Lee Gervase, an ambitious man, would wield a new broom. It was not at all certain that Joe's own job was safe. He leaned back in Cucchinello's leather chair. Sheriff's salary was twelve thousand a year, which he'd be drawing from now till election. What he could do with twelve thousand a year steady!... A startling new idea entered Joe's mind. He reflected for ten minutes,

THE FOX VALLEY MURDERS

alternately excited and dubious. Finally he jumped to his feet, left the office, walked around to the county clerk's office on the mezzanine of the courthouse.

Henry Rose, the county clerk, was a wizened little man with a furious puff of yellow-white hair. Joe put his question; Henry Rose responded incisively. "It will cost you two percent of twelve thousand. That's the filing fee: two hundred and forty dollars."

"I get it back if I win the election?"

"No-sir-ee. That's money spent. You just kiss that money goodby."

Joe made an impulsive decision. "I'm game." He started to write a check, but Henry Rose stopped him and fumbling in a cabinet brought forth a printed form. "Fill out the blanks. Have at least twenty-five but not more than thirty people sign in these spaces. They're your sponsors."

"Right." Joe folded the form, tucked it into his pocket, while Henry Rose inspected him with candid curiosity. "You figure you can beat out Lee Gervase?"

"I won't know unless I try."

"He's a good candidate. He'll draw votes. I don't think old Cooch could have beaten him. Not this time."

"Maybe not." Joe was momentarily depressed. Lee Gervase would be a strong opponent. He was articulate, forceful, handsome, dedicated to progress. Two hundred and forty dollars might well be money pushed down a rat-hole. Still, nothing ventured, nothing gained.

Joe took the filing application and returned to headquarters, where he resumed his job with new thoughtfulness. Out went Cucchinello's massive leather-padded chair, printed with his weight, stained with the juices of his body, breathing the odor of his cigars; in came a swivel-chair. Out went the massive walnut desk with its assorted implements, calendars, mottoes, tokens, trinkets, and ornaments; in came a simple gray metal desk. Out went Cucchinello's prized photographs: Sheriff Cucchinello embracing the Lettuce Queen, Sheriff Cucchinello riding a white horse in a July 4th parade, Sheriff Cucchinello and a prize fish on the wharf at Monterey, Sheriff Cucchinello at banquet after banquet. All these and other trophies, souvenirs and keepsakes Joe Bain sent out to Cucchinello's widow.

The office looked bare. Joe Bain had nothing to put in the place of twenty years' accumulation except his diploma from the Chapman Institute of Criminology. He unrolled it, pinned it to the wall, but it looked ridiculous. He took it down and brought in a large-scale map of the county from the hall. This looked better — in fact, looked very well indeed.

He fell to examining the map. San Rodrigo County was rectangular, with the long axis tilted from southwest to northeast. The watershed of the Coast Range delineated the western boundary, which at one point approached to within twenty miles of the Pacific. To the northeast were sloughs and tule swamps, to the southeast, dry hills rolled off down the great central valley. The nearest city of any size was San Jose to the north, with San Francisco another fifty miles beyond. Pleasant Grove, the county seat, had a population of 13,000 and was second in size to Aurora with 15,000; San Rodrigo was third, with 8,000. Tourists occasionally visited mouldering old Mission San Rodrigo de Luz, attended Aurora's Lettuce Festival, stopped at Hicks' Hot Springs Resort, fished for catfish in Genesee Slough, but the great north and south arteries between San Francisco and Los Angeles, Highways 99 and 101, passed to either side. Joe located Castle Mountain at the southwest of the county. He ran his finger up Mitre Canyon Road, traced the little track which led twenty devious miles over the mountain to Fell Valley. Halfway along this track, in the very shadow of Castle Mountain, Joe Bain had been born and spent his childhood...

Deputy Frank Hubbard stuck his head through the door. "Hey, Joe, one of the prisoners wants to talk to you: old Scanlon."

Joe went down the concrete block passage to the cell block. He looked in at Scanlon, a short fat gray-haired man of fifty-five, serving ten months on a bad check conviction.

"What's the trouble, Scanlon?"

"I hear you're running things now."

"That's right."

Scanlon held up the lunch tray provided by the Bluebird Café at a cost of seventy-five cents. "Look at this slop, Sheriff. Smell that meat."

Joe Bain inspected the unsavory mess. "Looks like dog-vomit."

Scanlon held the tray even closer. "Well, then, I ask you now, do you consider that fit to eat?"

"I don't know. I never ate much dog-vomit."

"Even a prisoner has rights," declared Scanlon. "I kicked to Cooch and he told me I wasn't here on a rest cure. Well, I don't expect no big steak for lunch, but I ain't done nothing to deserve starving to death."

"I can't be worrying about special diets for all you chow-hounds," said Joe Bain. "I'll send in Mrs. Rostvolt; you can talk it over with her."

"Forget it," said Scanlon. "I'll starve in peace and quiet."

Joe returned to his office. He stood a moment thinking, then crossed the hall to the outer office. He might as well perform the dirty work as he came to it.

Behind the front counter sat Mrs. Rostvolt. Eighteen years ago she had come to the office: a soft-spoken young woman with an ample bosom and an arch trick of widening her eyes when spoken to. Time had not treated her kindly. The voluptuous curves had become ordinary fat; instead of coyly widening her eyes to get her way, she now popped them in a furious glare. Joe said politely, "Mrs. Rostvolt, the first change I want made is the Bluebird Café. I wouldn't feed a hyena the slop those belly-robbers have been sending in."

Mrs. Rostvolt looked out the window. "Food prices are way up. For seventy-five cents they can't put out a very good meal."

"Why don't they just send over their merchant's lunch? That's only seventy-five cents."

"I'm sure I don't know."

"Well, after this, order the meals from Rupe's."

Mrs. Rostvolt wordlessly reached for the telephone. Joe returned to his office. Mrs. Rostvolt's cut was probably five bucks a week, thought Joe. Even the prisoners knew it. Mrs. Renee Adams owned the Bluebird; Rupert and Mary Rampold ran Rupe's. He'd lose Mrs. Adams' vote for sure, so he'd better make certain that Rupert and Mary knew how the land lay.

He left the office, crossed Montalvo Square, went into Rupe's Café, seated himself in a booth. Rupe himself came from the kitchen. "Congratulations, Joe, on the new job. Hope it works out for you."

"News sure travels fast," said Joe. "I only got the word myself two hours ago. By the way, did Mrs. Rostvolt call you yet?"

"No," Rupe said cautiously. "What's the problem?"

"I'm making a change in catering. The Bluebird's been getting real sloppy. I want you and Mary to take over."

"Well, well," said Rupe, even more cautiously. "That sure is nice. Naturally we'll do our best to give satisfaction."

"It's simple. Fifty cents for breakfast, seventy-five cents for lunch, seventy-five cents for dinner. I want you to make your profit and put everything else into the grub. Understand? No little presents, no favors. Just fair value for a fair price."

"That's what I like to hear, Sheriff. I'm sure we can do you a good job."

"Fine. If anybody hits you up, let me know. I'm running for office in November and I want to start off right."

"I'll sure spread the word, Joe."

When Joe returned to his office he found Charley Blankenship waiting to see him.

Chapter II

Charley Blankenship never seemed to change. He was a tall, pale, horse-faced old man with long arms and legs, soft gray hair, watery blue eyes, a pendulous pink mouth. He lived the life of a gentleman farmer, with a forty-acre cherry orchard and a white two-story house on Destin Road, south of Marblestone. Joe Bain had known him for as long as he could remember. During May, a favorite recreation among the local young people was stealing Blankenship cherries. Joe retained a vivid recollection of Charley Blankenship's pallid face peering down the rows. He often carried a shotgun loaded with rock salt, and on one occasion had shot his nephew Walt Hobius. Opinion was divided on whether Charley had recognized Walt. Walt thought that he had, though Charley denied it to Walt's mother, Dora. For the last ten years Charley leased the forty acres to a Japanese family, who during cherry season maintained a patrol even more vigilant than Charley's had been.

Today he wore dark brown corduroy trousers, big round-toed black shoes, a blue denim jacket.

"Hello, Mr. Blankenship," said Joe. "What can I do for you?"

Charley Blankenship peered at him with peevish suspicion. "I came to see the sheriff."

"Sheriff Cucchinello? He died two days ago. I'm acting-sheriff for the rest of his term. I hope to make it for real at the elections."

"I see. Well —"

Joe laughed. "You don't remember me. I'm Joe Bain. You run me out of your orchard quite a few times."

Charley Blankenship seemed unflatteringly astounded. "You're Joe Bain?"

"I sure am."

"The way you used to act I figured you'd wind up inside of jail. It's a funny world."

"Sit down, Mr. Blankenship. Things are still in disorder; don't mind the mess. What can I do for you?"

Charley Blankenship eased his old bones into a chair. "I suppose you remember Ausley Wyett."

"How could I forget?"

"Well, a week or so ago he got out on parole. Did you know that?"

"Sheriff Cucchinello mentioned something about it."

"I don't know how things like that are arranged, but there it is. He's living back in the old house, bold as brass." Charley Blankenship shook his head in disapprobation. "After what happened, I don't see how he has the indecent gall to show his face."

"I guess it's his privilege, so long as he behaves himself."

"I won't say yes or no to that. Although it makes us next door neighbors, and many times my wife is alone in the house." Charley Blankenship laboriously reached in his pocket, brought forth an envelope. "This is what I've come about."

Joe Bain withdrew the enclosure, a sheet of cheap white bond. The message was typewritten, signed in a spidery hand, with a flamboyant flourish below:

> Dear Sir:
>   I am now out of jail, where I have served sixteen long years. I could write a long book on the dreadful experiences I have witnessed. How do you plan to make this up to me? I await your response with great interest.
>   Very truly yours,
>   *Ausley L. Wyett*

Joe Bain pursed his lips; Blankenship watched him in expectant indignation, and finally blurted, "Can't something be done to stop tricks like this? Threats, extortion?"

Joe said slowly, "He hasn't made any threats; he's signed his name. Maybe he doesn't show good sense, but there's no law against his writing you a letter."

Blankenship stared in peevish outrage. "The man's out on parole! The first thing he does is write a letter like this!"

"I understand your feelings, Mr. Blankenship. So far as I can see he's done nothing illegal. He asks you a question: how do you plan to make his years in jail up to him? I don't suppose you have any such plans?"

"I certainly do not!"

"If you so chose you could write him stating as much, and that would be an end to it."

Charley Blankenship squirmed in impatience and disgust. "Now what a thing to suggest. I came here hoping the sheriff would take steps in the matter."

Joe wondered how Ernest Cucchinello would have acted. Probably outdo Charley Blankenship in indignation, promise the moon, and as soon as Charley Blankenship had departed, forget the whole matter. Nine times out of ten such a situation required nothing more. Which meant, at worst, nine votes for Ernest Cucchinello to one for the opposing candidate. Joe ruefully realized that he lacked certain of Ernest Cucchinello's talents. He rubbed his chin. "I forget the case. Why should Ausley Wyett write you?"

"I was a witness against him."

"I'm sure you told the truth." Joe looked inquiringly at Charley Blankenship.

"I certainly did. I swore to tell the truth, the whole truth and nothing but the truth, so help me God, and I did exactly that, no more and no less."

"Hmm. Have you seen Ausley?"

"Just from a distance. He's been working around the old house. Ever since Jake Wyett passed away there's been tenants in and the place is badly run down."

"It never was any particular showplace, as I recall. Who else was a witness at the trial? Wasn't Cole Destin involved?"

"Yes. Cole and Bus Hacker, and — let me think — Oliver Viera and a man named Willis Neff, up Mitre Canyon Road."

"Has anyone else had letters?"

"That I don't know."

Joe Bain took up the telephone, dialed the number of Oliver Viera,

Real Estate and Insurance, at Marblestone. A voice responded: "Fox Valley Realty."

"Hello, Oliver. This is Joe Bain, at the sheriff's office."

"Joe!" Oliver Viera's voice was professionally hearty. "Good to hear from you. What's the good word?"

"Well, you know about Cucchinello?"

"I heard he died. It was in the paper. Too bad. Pretty popular old boy. Never did much except glad-hand the public, but I guess they liked it. Who's in charge now?"

"I am."

"You!"

Joe suppressed a faint sense of irritation. "Just temporary, until the election. And after that, who knows?"

"You thinking of taking it on?"

"I've been debating. I can handle the job. I just don't know about the glad-handing. But I called on a confidential matter."

"Shoot. I got nothing to hide."

"You know Ausley Wyett's out."

Oliver's tone became guarded. "Yep."

"I wonder if you've had any communication from him."

Oliver hesitated. "Well — nothing to speak of."

"Such as?"

Oliver hesitated again. "Ausley's out on parole. I wouldn't want to hurt his chances. In spite of everything."

"This is just an unofficial question for my own information."

"Well — the truth of the matter is that I got a little note from Ausley. I didn't mention it, not even to Connie, because — well, you know Ausley. Always been peculiar. I never did feel he meant harm."

"The girl was awful dead."

"Yeah. Poor little Tissie... The note said something like, I been in jail sixteen years, it was real tough, how do you figure to make this up to me? I couldn't make head nor tail of it. I just figured it for another of Ausley's goofy tricks and forgot about it."

"You never answered it?"

"No. But yesterday I drove up to the old Wyett place, thinking maybe Ausley would consider selling. He wouldn't hear of it. Remember how he used to hold his head to the side and blink? He still does it. Goofy as ever. I asked him, joking-like, what he meant by that letter. He laughed and said for me to do what I thought was right. I said, that's what I'd done sixteen years ago. Ausley said, it took him sixteen years to recover from my good intentions. I just let the matter drop."

"Okay, Oliver, thanks a lot." Joe Bain hung up. Charley Blankenship leaned forward; Joe moved back to avoid the rheumy breath. "He got a letter, eh?"

Joe Bain nodded. He thought a moment. "I have to drive up Marble-stone way this afternoon; I might have a chance to talk to Ausley." He rose to his feet, but Charley Blankenship only looked at him with mulish stupidity. Joe sat down again. Another problem he'd never faced as deputy: how to eject a constituent without losing a vote. Cucchinello never worried. He was willing to talk by the hour with all comers; maybe this was what it took to get elected.

"It's been sixteen years since that trial," Blankenship reminisced. "It seems like it was just yesterday. My, how time goes by!"

"You mentioned Bus Hacker. Is he still driving the school bus?"

"He's got a heart condition and they made him stop." Charley Blankenship gave his head a shake of grudging admiration. "Otherwise he'd be going yet. Bus is a downright obstinate man."

"He always was. You, Bus Hacker, Cole Destin, Oliver Viera, and — who else?"

"Neff. Then there was Tommy Hobius, who got killed overseas. He was little Tissie's sweetheart. And May Destin — she was May McAllister then — she came to be a witness, but I don't remember her being called to testify."

Joe leaned back in his chair, looked back across the years. "I haven't seen May since I left Marblestone. She was sure a pretty girl. She and Tissie both."

"We should have strung him up," said Blankenship. "We shoot mad dogs, and that's what ought to be done to a man like that. Now he's back, bold as brass." Blankenship glowered, lower lip pendulous. "It don't seem right. And on top of all, writing me that letter."

"I'll sure look into it, Mr. Blankenship. That's what I'm here for. But I wouldn't worry. I don't think there's anything to get excited about."

Charley Blankenship turned him a look of more yellow malevolence than Joe would have thought possible from so rheumy and dew-lapped a face. There goes a vote, he thought in alarm. He jumped to his feet. "I'll sure look into it, Mr. Blankenship. I believe in striking the iron before it gets hot. That way nobody gets burned."

Blankenship heaved himself to his feet. He said petulantly, "I figure if I can't come to the sheriff with my problems, who can I come to?"

"You're right, Mr. Blankenship, absolutely right. I'll sure do my best for you, now and after the election, if I make the grade."

Charley Blankenship smiled frostily. "Who will be running against you?"

Joe made a sound of indulgent amusement. "Every unemployed lawyer and ex-floorwalker in the county is thinking about it."

"We could use a good man in the office, that's sure," said Charley Blankenship with heavy emphasis. He glanced meaningfully at Joe and departed.

Joe went into the outer office. "Mrs. Rostvolt, I'll be out for a while, probably the rest of the afternoon."

Mrs. Rostvolt nodded. Still sore, thought Joe. Well, no matter. If the old crock didn't like having him for a boss she could quit. Except who'd run the office? Mrs. Rostvolt undeniably had her uses.

Behind a plate-glass window at the rear of the main office was the despatcher's room, where one or another of the deputies sat at the radio transceiver. During the night the job was handled by Ralph Stillman, the night jailer. At the moment Deputy Fay Insley was on duty. Joe looked through the door. "I'm taking a run over toward Marblestone."

"Right, Sheriff."

Joe went out to the parking lot, pondering the semi-facetious use of the title 'Sheriff'. No one took him seriously, he thought sadly. He guessed he didn't have that look of natural authority... Automatically he had approached Car #4, in which he usually made his patrols. He drew back his hand, as if the door handle were hot. What was he thinking of? He'd never make sheriff unless he started thinking like the sheriff. Purposefully he strode to Car #1, a glossy late-model sedan, with a gold medallion on the side reading *Sheriff*.

"I better live it up while I have the chance," Joe told himself.

"Because if I run for Sheriff and lose, the new man will fire me out of the department."

He drove out of town by State Highway 32, through flat farmlands to the little town of Tevis, where he turned west. By an old timber bridge he crossed Genesee Creek, now, at summer's end, no more than a frog-infested trickle, the banks choked with burdock, nettles, alder, and willow. Flowing east, by invisible degrees it would become Genesee Slough, part of the intricate system of sloughs, swamps, ponds and cuts linking the San Joaquin River to the Sacramento River and eventually San Francisco Bay.

The countryside changed. Massive round oaks stood in hayfields; to the left, tawny hills rolled down to the south and over the horizon. Ahead, obscured by haze, rose the Coast Range and there, a dim gray loom, was Castle Mountain.

The hills closed in; Joe turned up Candelara Creek Road. Along the ridges grew stunted firs and twisted pines, which presently became darker and taller. The road wound around a fir-clad bluff into Fox Valley, and after another half-mile entered Marblestone.

At the outskirts of town he came to a rather dingy service station. He turned in, drove up to the lube rack. A dark eagle-faced man about his own age sat in the office reading a newspaper. This was Walt Hobius, Charley Blankenship's nephew-by-marriage. Walt was an inch shorter than Joe, equally dark and lean, but more nervous and intense in his manner. He had black crisp curly hair which somehow made Joe think of Napoleon. His face was wide at the cheek-bones, the cheeks hollow, as if sucked in. The eyes were round, dark brown and always puckered as if Walt were concentrating furiously. His nose was a rapacious hook, his mouth small and tender, in paradoxical contrast to the nose and sharp chin.

The two conversed, with Walt pointing out Bus Hacker's old Plymouth, into which Ausley Wyett, so Walt alleged, had spitefully poured water. Joe finally departed, drove into Marblestone, parked in front of Fritz Hunsacker's general store.

CHAPTER III

SHERIFF JOE BAIN STOOD under the oak tree, looking off up Destin Road. The wind blew the tops of the poplar trees down by Hacker's place back and forth as it had always done. Beyond, at the end of Destin Lane, rose a black screen of Italian cypresses, concealing all but a glimpse of the Destin house... A GM pickup drove up behind him; two women, evidently mother and daughter, alighted and went into the store. The mother was thin, sinewy, brisk, about forty-five. Her gray-blonde hair hung in sparse curls; she wore a neat blue and white cotton dress. The daughter was twenty-three or twenty-four, something over average height, supple and graceful. Her face was quiet and golden-pale; her eyes as she glanced sidelong toward Joe were ocean blue. Her hair, thicker and richer than her mother's, was cut without artifice: short in front, rather longer to the side and at the back. She wore a white blouse, a dark blue denim skirt, blue sneakers. Good Lord, thought Joe, there's a real beautiful girl. Who in the world can it be? Joe followed them into the store. The mother turned him a brief incurious stare. The daughter looked at him from the sides of her clear blue eyes.

Fritz waved his hand. He was short-legged, fat, round-faced, with a bald head and an exuberant fringe of gray hair. "Hey Joe! I hear old Cucchinello died. Who's the new boss?"

"I'm it," said Joe. "They inflicted that honor on me."

"Well, I'll be switched." He spoke to the women, who were loading groceries into a cart. "What do you think of that? The worst young hellion in town, and here he is: sheriff. How do you figure a thing like that?"

"Not sheriff yet," said Joe. "Just acting-sheriff. Do you care to introduce me?"

"Sure. This is Mrs. Neff—"

"Mrs. Willis Neff?" inquired Joe.

"That's right. Mrs. Willis Neff. And this is Miss Ellie Neff, prettiest girl for miles around. And this is Mr. Joe Bain, from Castle Mountain, now Sheriff of San Rodrigo County."

"In November my name will be on the ballot," said Joe, "and I'll sure appreciate your votes."

Mrs. Neff smiled doubtfully, and turned her attention back to the shelves. Ellie gave him a long slow look, whose purport Joe could not fathom.

Fritz became busy with another customer. Joe went to the refrigerator, took out a bottle of root-beer, which he opened and drank in a leisurely fashion.

The Neff women rolled their cart to the counter. Fritz checked out the groceries, packed them in a cardboard box. A hand-lettered sign on the counter read:

MAMMOTH BAZAAR

POTLUCK-SUPPER

AUSPICES:
METHODIST CHURCH—BAPTIST CHURCH

Prizes – BINGO – Prizes
Free coffee
Admission 25 cents

– Come one, come all –

SATURDAY, SEPTEMBER 8
8 O'CLOCK, FOX VALLEY COMMUNITY CENTER

Fritz nodded to the sign and said, "You ladies planning to turn out?"

"Oh yes," said Mrs. Neff. "We wouldn't miss the church social. Ellie has a booth."

"Guess I'd better drop in," said Fritz. "How about you, Joe?"

"I might just be able to make it," said Joe. He stepped forward as Ellie reached for the box of groceries. "Here, let me carry that. Looks pretty heavy."

Ellie stood back, and Joe carried the box out to the pickup. Then he gallantly opened the door for Mrs. Neff, who hopped in with the agility of a sparrow. Ellie slid into the driver's seat, started the engine. Joe started to close the door, then asked, "Is your husband at home, Mrs. Neff? I'd like to speak to him a minute or two if he is."

"Yes, he's home."

"Maybe I'll drive out after a while, then."

He closed the door. Ellie shifted; the pickup swung out into the road.

Joe went back into the store. "Strange people," he said to Fritz. "The woman acts like she's afraid of her shadow." He tossed a dime to the counter. "One root-beer."

Fritz rang up the dime. "She never has much to say. They don't mix very much."

"That's sure a pretty girl. Is she engaged, or anything of the sort?"

"Nope. Her father runs everybody off. It's the best way to get your ass in a sling: go courting Ellie. Bob Richards tried it. Neff told him to clear out. Bob tried to date her at church. Neff stopped him on the road, told him to lay off. Bob laid off. Walt Hobius tried it: called at the house twice. Neff hemmed and hawed and finally told him he didn't want anybody bothering his daughter unless their intentions were serious. Walt said he didn't know whether they were serious or not until he got to know her. One word led to another, and Neff gave Walt a good cuffing. A college kid working for the telephone company tried to make out. Neff made a believer out of him. Let's see, who else? Herman Jacobs, from up Fell Valley, gave Neff some lip. Neff knocked him clear across Main Street."

"So this poor girl never gets out."

"Just church, and like you see today. Neff is a real old-time fire-breathing Baptist."

"Sure some funny people in the world."

"How right you are." Fritz went to the refrigerator, brought out two cans of beer, opened them, passed one to Joe. "Here's to the old days. They weren't any better, but we were a lot younger."

"Sometimes I feel a hundred years old," said Joe. He drank from the can. "What's new around town?"

"Oh, this and that. Millie Hacker passed away last fall, but I guess you knew that."

"No. First I heard. Old Bus is by himself?"

Fritz nodded. "He doesn't get around much. Bad heart, or something similar. I don't know what he lives on. Veteran's pension, I suppose. Cole Destin doesn't charge him rent, and gives him all the milk he needs."

"Cole can afford it. How many head does he run now?"

"Seven, eight hundred, I suppose. Maybe more. He's bought up a lot of bottom land along Mission Road the last few years, but he leases it all to the Japs."

"They'll do better than any white man."

"They're hard workers, that's a fact."

Joe finished his beer. "I hear Ausley Wyett's back in town."

"Yep, big as life. He's been in the store two or three times, just like nothing whatever happened."

"He's got more nerve than I've got," said Joe. "Well, I better be on my way. Where do I go to find Willis Neff?"

"Up Mitre Canyon Road four or five miles. You'll see his mailbox."

Joe drove south along Destin Road, turned west on Mitre Canyon Road. The hills rose steep; under stands of redwood and fir the shade was dark and damp.

Four miles along, Joe came to a neat white house surrounded by a garden bright with hollyhocks. Beyond and to the right were a white-washed barn, a long low milk-shed, a separator room with a dock for the loading of milk cans, a chicken-house. Joe turned into the driveway. A man he knew to be Neff stood working beside the loading dock. Neff looked up, then returned to his work. Joe alighted, and a black and white dog came forward barking. Neff spoke to the dog, gave Joe a quick, cool inspection from the palest of blue eyes.

"Mr. Neff?" asked Joe politely.

Neff nodded.

"I'm Sheriff Joe Bain. Acting-Sheriff, I should say, until the election."

"How d'you do. I won't shake hands — I'm full of grease." Neff was working on an electric motor, installing new brushes. "Bain, eh? There used to be some Bains up Castle Mountain. Blacky Bain, the man's name was. Got knifed in a Mexican pool hall, or so they say."

Joe nodded. "That was my father."

"Well, think of that." Neff put down his screwdriver, wiped his hands with a rag. "What brings you this way, Sheriff?"

"I came on two accounts. I'll mention the personal reason first. I'm running for office in November and I'd certainly appreciate your vote. I think I can do a good job. I know the county backward and forward, and I plan to run a clean efficient department."

"I'll certainly bear in mind what you say."

"Second is something strictly unofficial — information I don't have any right to ask for."

Neff's eyes seemed to become an even icier blue. "What kind of information?"

"You know that Ausley Wyett is out on parole?"

"I know that."

"My question is, have you had a communication from him?"

Neff nodded. "Yes. Don't ask me what it said. I'm going to have a private word with Wyett about that letter." He bent back over the motor.

Joe watched him. A cold man; a harsh passionate man. "Well, it's your private business," said Joe presently. "But for my own unofficial information, tell me, did the letter go something like this: 'Dear Mr. Neff: Sixteen years is a long time to spend in prison; how do you intend to make it up to me?'"

Neff said nothing.

Joe shrugged. "Well, it's your business, Mr. Neff. But just so that you won't make any rash moves, let me say that others besides yourself have received the same letter."

In a mild voice Neff said, "Seems to me these letters violate his parole. Seems to me he could be hustled back to jail."

Joe laughed. "Come now, Mr. Neff. What's he done? The letters aren't threatening. They're not even anonymous."

"I'm not worried. Just one wrong move from Ausley Wyett..." Neff clamped his big jaw shut and returned to the motor.

"Well, Mr. Neff, I wouldn't let my temper get the best of me, if I were you. It's just not —"

Neff slowly raised his head, fixed Joe with the stare of a basilisk. "When I want advice, Sheriff, I'll sure ask for it."

Joe refused to be abashed. He turned, looking around the yard. "Nice place you have here."

"As good as any hereabouts," said Neff flatly. "Excuse me, I got to get this motor back in the separator before milking time."

Joe returned down Mitre Canyon Road. Of the witnesses against Ausley Wyett there remained to be interviewed Bus Hacker and Cole Destin.

Approaching the intersection of Mitre Canyon Road and Destin Lane, Joe noticed a man stumping south along the road with a dogged angry step. He crossed the intersection, and Joe recognized Bus Hacker.

Joe made the turn into Destin Lane, stopped beside the high white paling-fence. Bus Hacker had already pushed through the gate and was crossing the flagstone path toward the steps leading up to his front porch.

Joe called, "Mr. Hacker!" Bus swung truculently about. He was a chunky little bulldog of a man, with pouches under his eyes and wattles beside his chin. He wore soiled gray trousers, a maroon flannel shirt, a dark blue baseball cap, under which untidy wisps of gray hair protruded. His face was mottled; he looked old and angry and tired.

Joe pushed open the gate, stepped into the bedraggled garden which once had been Millie Hacker's pride. "Hi there, Mr. Hacker. Remember me? I'm Joe Bain."

Bus Hacker peered suspiciously. "Joe Bain, eh? What do you want?" His voice was fretful and peevish. Then he glared. "Did you send word to meet you in town?"

"No," said Joe. "I certainly did not."

"Well, it's pretty darn queer. Playing jokes on a sick old man. Twice now. I call it a damned outrage. Somebody poured water in my gas tank and I run down my battery trying to start up. What do you think of that?" He glared challengingly at Joe.

"It's certainly a mean trick," said Joe. "Do you have any idea who did it?"

"No, I do not. I'd have sent him to jail. And that no-good Walt Hobius stalling me and putting me off, and so I walk all the way to town and back for nothing. Who'd want to do a trick like that?"

"I certainly can't imagine, Mr. Hacker."

"I tell you, it makes me pretty hot. I got enough to think about, trying to get well."

"Just what happened?"

"Somebody called me on the phone, said there was an important government letter for me at the post office that I had to sign for. Well, they never heard of any such letter. What do you think of that?"

"A pretty mean trick, that's what I'd say."

"That's what I say too. Did you want something special? I'm tired and I've got to have my rest."

"I'll make it short. I've been wondering if you've talked to Ausley Wyett since he's got back."

"I have not. I don't intend to." Bus Hacker's lips trembled indignantly. "A man like that…"

"By any chance did you get a letter from him?"

"From Ausley Wyett? I don't know. I haven't opened my mail yet. Nothing but bills and advertisements anyway. Last week they tried to sell me dancing lessons."

"I wonder if you'd look through your mail now."

"Ausley Wyett's got nothing to write me about. I don't want nothing to do with him. If he knew what was good for him he'd have stayed in jail."

Joe frowned. "What do you mean by that?"

"Never mind what I mean. How come you're so interested? Who'd you say you were?"

"I'm the sheriff."

"I thought you said you were Joe Bain."

"I'm Acting-Sheriff Joe Bain."

Bus Hacker gave his head a shake of bitter disparagement. "There's something bad happening around these parts. Somebody pretty doggone mean is trying to make me sick and I want it stopped."

"I'll sure do my best, Mr. Hacker. What about that letter?"

Bus Hacker grunted, turned, looked up the steps as if they represented a challenge. "Well, I'll go back. Maybe I did get a letter."

He scraped his feet on a steel scraper with the air of long habit — Millie Hacker had been a famous housekeeper in her day — then laboriously began to mount the steps. On the porch, panting for breath, he wiped his shoes again on a steel-mesh mat. Reaching in his pocket he withdrew an enormous bunch of keys. As he sorted through them he spoke. "These steps get longer and higher every day. Soon as I get my health back I'm gonna fix things up. Put in a nice terrace and barbecue. Don't care what it costs." He opened the screen door, reached to fit the key in the lock, and slumped forward. He gave a convulsive jerk, toppled; Joe sprang to catch him, but too late: Bus Hacker rolled down the steps, landing on the back of his neck, so that his baseball cap jarred off. He lay wheezing and gasping, his face an alarming watermelon-pink. He flapped up one hand, coughed; his lips moved. Joe bent forward.

"O Lord," whispered Bus Hacker. "I beg forgiveness...Lord Almighty..." Joe bent close. Bus Hacker's tongue clattered and clacked. "...Years and years in this house...Letter in the mail...Nothing I knew for sure...Lord Almighty..." He sighed. His eyelids flickered, and under them shone slits of yellowish-white.

CHAPTER IV

Sheriff Joe Bain knelt in the warm afternoon sunlight. He felt
for a pulse, but found none. The sun beat down into the garden; bees
droned among the hollyhocks; little goat-flies hung and twitched
through the air.

Joe went to the gate, looked up and down the road. There was no
one in sight. He returned across the flagstone path, stepped over the
corpse, climbed to the porch. Keys dangled from the lock. Joe opened
the screen door, turned the key, eased open the front door, peered into
the living room. The shades were drawn, and glowed luminous yellow
in the sunlight. The air was stuffy and hot; there was an unpleasant
odor of dust and dirty clothes and rancid food. Joe went to the phone,
summoned Dr. Hesketh, the County Coroner. Then, standing in the
middle of the room, he looked about. Knick-knacks were everywhere,
uniformly coated with a film of dust. In a corner stood Bus Hacker's safe,
a heavy steel box about two feet high. There was a worn red Oriental
rug on the floor; the furniture was a matched set, upholstered in bright
green. Over the sofa was draped a vivid Mexican *serape*. On the mantle
Joe found the letter, which had been opened. The contents read:

> Dear Sir:
>   I am now out of jail, where I have served sixteen long
> years...

Joe tucked the letter into his pocket and went back out on the porch.
The body lay as before, a grotesque heap. The sight made Joe uncomfortable. There was malice in the air, a gleeful gratified hate which Joe

had sensed but had been unable to thwart. The idea irritated him. He had been too slow, too dense, too sluggish — and someone was laughing. Joe, a proud man, began to smoulder. He, Joe Bain, was sheriff; he, Joe Bain, had committed himself and his personal dignity to the maintenance of law and order. Any breach of the peace now was like a direct and vicious personal insult.

The question remained: had there indeed been a breach of the law? This wild-goose chase Bus Hacker had been sent upon: purposeless? While Bus Hacker's heart condition was well known, a walk into town could be expected to irk him, no more. On the other hand, the water in his gas tank implied some sort of cunning premeditation…Joe frowned in dissatisfaction. The basic fact remained: the prankster could not have relied upon a walk into town to kill Bus Hacker, if indeed this had been intended. If the prankster were identified, could a manslaughter case be established? Probably not. Medical testimony must establish that the walk and Hacker's rage were proximately the cause of the heart attack, and such testimony would be hard to come by.

Joe returned within, brought out the *serape*, laid it over Bus Hacker's body. Then he seated himself on the top step and waited.

Fox Valley spread placid before his eyes. To the right, at the end of Destin Lane, sentinels of black Italian cypresses guarded the big white Destin house. Directly ahead Mitre Canyon Road led east past fields of alfalfa and the McAllister walnut grove, finally slanted up and across a saddle in the sunburned hills.

School had let out. Down the road came four small boys, hopping, swaggering. Behind were a pair of girls, flaxen-haired and very clean, dressed in crisp frocks of green and blue. They carried themselves with dignity, trying to ignore the small boys who, walking backwards, hooted and shouted raucous insults. "Prissy and Snooty Destin!" "Don't even wear no underwear!"

"We do too!" yelled the ten-year-old. "And it's not dirty like yours!"

"Prove it!" came the rejoinder. "I betcha can't prove it." And the boys yelped in delight. The girls tilted their noses, walked contemptuously past the crossroads, up Destin Lane. The boys separated, two walking east, two west along Mitre Canyon Road.

Things went along much as they always had, thought Joe.

Dr. William Hesketh, the coroner, arrived with an ambulance from the County Hospital. He made a brief examination, ordered the body into the ambulance and off to the morgue.

"I was talking to him just before he went," said Joe. "Someone sent him walking into town on a wild-goose chase. He came back pretty mad. Do you think the walk did for him?"

The coroner shrugged. "Hard to say. You could never make it stand up."

"That's what I was afraid of."

Down the road from Marblestone came a beige Chrysler hard-top. It braked to a stop beside the ambulance; Cole Destin paused to appraise the situation, then jumped out, came through the gate. He was a tall well-built man with bronzed skin, sun-bleached blond hair, a keen handsome face. He wore a blue and white plaid shirt, whipcord breeches, boots, big curved gray-green sunglasses. He noted the still form on the stretcher and turned to Joe. "What's happened? Bus finally go?"

Joe nodded gravely. "Looks like his heart went out on him."

"Poor old Bus. He hadn't much to live for after Millie went. Still it's too bad." Cole Destin's gaze roved the yard, which badly needed watering and weeding. The bridge of his nose twitched. "What a mess." He turned back to Joe. "What brings you up here?"

"I came to see Bus. In fact I was talking to him when he died."

Cole Destin gave Joe a rather careful examination. "I hear you've been appointed sheriff till the election."

Joe made a deprecating gesture. "Don't congratulate me too hard till after November."

"You'll be running?" Destin seemed surprised.

"I'll be running." Joe brought out his filing application. "Maybe I can get you down as one of my sponsors."

Destin frowned. "Well, Joe, you probably know I never supported Cucchinello. In fact, Lee Gervase has lined me up on his ticket."

"I'm not Cucchinello, and I'm planning to run things differently."

Cole Destin shook his head dubiously. "You've got two strikes against you just working under Cooch."

"That might well be." Joe replaced the application in his pocket. "But I didn't come out here on personal business." The ambulance backed around, drove north; Joe raised his hand in farewell. "This morning Charley Blankenship showed me a letter from Ausley Wyett. I wonder if you got the same kind of letter?"

Cole Destin gave him another careful scrutiny. "Is that why you came to see Bus?"

"That's right."

"What did Bus have to say?"

"I didn't get a chance to talk to him."

Cole Destin looked in the direction of the Wyett ranch. "I can't say I'm one of Ausley's admirers. I have daughters of my own —"

"I saw them go past a few minutes ago. Cute kids."

"— but I don't see any point in making things hard for him. For the moment anyway, I'm making no complaint."

"But, just unofficially, you got a letter?"

Destin nodded curtly. He walked up the steps to the porch. Joe followed, and went on into the house behind Destin.

Destin looked around, nostrils pinched. "I don't think Bus cleaned house since Millie died."

"You own this place, as I remember."

Destin nodded. "The Hackers have had it rent free for as long as I can remember — my father's wishes. Millie worked for us thirty years, and I guess the house represented a pension."

"What will you do with the place now?"

Destin shrugged. "Maybe I'll just pull it down. What rent I'd get, after taxes and maintenance, would hardly pay for the trouble. And it's an eyesore. Every time I look out of the window this little white box looks back at me." Destin walked into the bedroom, turned around, came back. "I guess I'll have to notify the relatives. I think there's cousins in Los Angeles. Millie had a sister in Iowa, but she's probably dead by now."

Joe indicated the safe. "What did Bus keep in there?"

"Lord only knows."

"I don't suppose you have the combination?"

Destin shook his head. "Bus was a secretive old codger." He walked over to the safe, tried the door without avail. "I'll have to have somebody open the thing," he said gloomily. "Do you know anyone who could do the trick?"

"Sorry, Cole. No big-time bank robbers in jail this time of year. But I wouldn't touch anything if I were you. The executor of his estate has to look things over before anyone else."

Destin grunted. "What estate?"

"Hard to say. You never know."

Destin turned away. "I suppose I better lock up." He held the door open for Joe, turned the key, rattled the knob to make sure the door was locked.

They went down the walk. Destin climbed into his beige Chrysler, and with a brief flip of his hand drove down Destin Lane toward his home. Joe went back into the yard. He considered a moment or two, then climbed the steps, pulled back the screen door, tried the doorknob. It was locked securely. He examined the hinges, the lock, the floor of the porch, moved the steel mesh to examine a hole in the gray-painted tongue-and-groove. He descended to the yard, walked around the house. A short flight of concrete steps led down to a door giving into the cellar. Joe peered through the glass pane. Shelves bore jar after jar of preserved fruits and jellies: supplies Millie Hacker had put by for the rainy day which never came. To the left Joe glimpsed a workbench, with a vise and a few rusty tools. He tried the door, then returned to ground level and continued around the house. There were two other windows into the basement; through each of these he peered, but saw only the usual accumulation of dilapidated chairs, spare mattresses, stacks of magazines.

Joe went back to his car. At the gate he took a last look back toward the house, then drove off toward Marblestone. At the Wyett mailbox he turned into the driveway, pulled up in front of the house. This was a long low shack of unpainted boards, with a roof of green composition and a stone fireplace at the far end. To the rear stood a dank-looking tank-house surrounded by a thicket of bamboo, with a windmill on top. Fifty yards to the right stood the fateful barn, concealing the now disused pigstyes. An old gray Willys station wagon was parked to the side. There was a sudden ferocious barking, a singing metallic whine. At either end of the house, tethered to overhead wires by sliding chains, two black police dogs bellowed and lunged furiously.

A shadow appeared behind the screen door, for a moment stood watching. Then the door opened and Ausley Wyett swung down the rickety wooden steps. He spoke to the dogs; the barking subsided; they backed growling under the house.

Ausley Wyett came forward, head tilted to the side. "Looks like Joe Bain," he said. "Haven't seen you for — oh, seventeen, eighteen years, I guess. You haven't changed much, Joe."

"You haven't changed too much either, Ausley." Ausley Wyett's belly was rounder, his skin showed a gray undertone, his lank brown hair was thin at the scalp, but it still seemed the same tall big-nosed awkward ridiculous Ausley Wyett. "No, Ausley," said Joe, "it don't look as if you've changed hardly at all."

Ausley shook his head sadly. "Up there at San Quentin you can't help but change. Things happen like you never imagined. You're in with the meanest, baddest people there are."

"That's why they're there," said Joe.

Ausley's mouth moved in a wry grin. "I'll tell you one thing: I'm glad to be out. I worked hard on that good-conduct rating."

"I guess you aren't fixing to go back, eh Ausley?"

"No, sir. Not if I can help it."

"You might not have heard, but I'm sheriff of the county now."

"Well, I'll be switched," said Ausley admiringly. "That's as wild as me being in jail!"

Joe made no effort to analyze the remark. Ausley Wyett's thinking had always been considered erratic. "Acting-sheriff, I should say. I'm filling out Sheriff Cucchinello's term. He died just a day or so ago."

"That's too bad. Old Cooch wasn't such a bad guy. Treated me decent, when I had that little trouble."

Joe looked around the yard. "What are you planning to do with yourself?"

"I hardly know, Joe. The place was leased all the time I was gone. I wasn't in a position to spend very much, so I've got a good bit of change stowed away. I'll probably run a few head of cattle." He fished a package of cigarettes from his pocket. "Smoke?"

"No thanks," said Joe. "That's one vice I never took to."

"Smart boy." Ausley tucked the cigarette into the exact center of his mouth, struck a match, lit up, waved out the match with an expansive flourish. "I haven't had too much of a reception around here. You're the first — no, the second — caller I've had. Oliver Viera was here just yesterday."

"Then you know why I'm here. What's the idea sending out all those letters?"

Ausley rubbed his chin. "That's what Oliver asked me. Everybody gets all excited about a little mail."

"Seems to me you've been pretty busy. Charley Blankenship, Cole Destin, Neff, Ollie Viera and old Bus Hacker."

"You've seen these letters?"

"Two of them. By a funny coincidence all these people were witnesses against you at the trial."

"And they've all complained about these letters?"

"They're all put out. Charley Blankenship thinks you should be put back in jail. Willis Neff plans to whip you. Bus Hacker wants me to arrest you on two counts: the letter, and for making him walk into town."

Ausley's foxy eyebrows arched in surprise. "Arrest me for what? Making Bus Hacker walk into town? How'd I do this?"

"You didn't do it then?"

"Did he say I did?"

"That's neither here nor there."

Ausley Wyett laughed. "Now Joe, you know better than that. I did a lot of thinking up there in the pen. The last thing I want is to get in any more jack-pots. What I want to know is, did Bus Hacker accuse me? If he did, I want him to sign a complaint and I want you to arrest me, so I can hire a lawyer, I mean a *good* lawyer."

"That kind of attitude won't get you anywhere, Ausley."

"'Attitude'? I don't have any attitude. I just asked you if Bus Hacker accused me of something."

"No," said Joe. "He didn't have a chance. He got so tired and mad that he had a heart attack and died."

Ausley stared at Joe in astonishment, then looked across the field at the line of poplar trees which concealed the Hacker house. "So that was what the commotion was about. I thought I seen an ambulance go by."

"Bus Hacker was riding in it when it came back through. If you had anything to do with that wild-goose chase, you better feel pretty bad about it."

Ausley thoughtfully sucked on his cigarette. "I seen him on his way to town day before yesterday. He walked pretty spry for a man who's ready to go."

"Well, he walked in today and it was the death of him. I know for a fact because I was right there."

"Thank the Lord it wasn't me."

"Another matter." But Joe decided not to mention the water in Bus Hacker's gas tank. He said instead, "I'm on the ballot for sheriff in the election. I don't think you're allowed to vote just yet, but if you're talking among your friends, I'd like to have you pass the word along."

Ausley puffed on his cigarette. "Do you think my recommendation would help?"

"I'll take all the help I can get." Joe climbed into his car, but paused before starting the engine. Ausley watched him placidly. "I don't know what you got in mind," said Joe, "and you don't seem to want to tell me. But my advice is to lay off bothering people. You're out on parole, and it's up to you to behave yourself."

"Look at it my way, Joe. Suppose you were put away for sixteen years. When you got out, you'd want to get even with whoever put you there, now wouldn't you?"

"Are you saying you didn't attack Tissie McAllister?"

"The jury found me guilty," said Ausley. "They went by what the witnesses told them, and the witnesses were all against me. Naturally I don't feel kindly about it."

Joe said, "I advise you not to go looking for trouble, Ausley. You might find yourself right back in the old cell block."

Ausley shook his head, threw down his cigarette, stamped it out in the dirt. "You won't catch me at anything like that, Joe. No sir."

CHAPTER V

Joe Bain drove east down Candelara Creek Road with the sun at his back. The hills fell away; to right and left the great light-drenched valley opened before him. A few minutes before five he arrived at Pleasant Grove. Swinging around Montalvo Square he parked in front of the courthouse, currently the subject of heated controversy. A group of local businessmen considered the structure not only hideous but a monument to the county's lack of a progressive spirit. An editorial in the Pleasant Grove *Messenger* presented their case in this fashion:

> The time has come — in fact, is long overdue — to make some improvements hereabouts. One of our first tasks should be to rid Pleasant Grove of that monumental eyesore, that dingy rat-ridden monstrosity, that infamous architectural freak known as the County Courthouse. We are ridiculed around the world; the noted architect Werner Neubarth, in his book *Toward a New Century*, has selected this structure as the ultimate definition of what he calls 'Fish-market Gothic'. This kind of publicity we can do without.
>
> It is well known in industrial circles that an efficient plant makes for efficient operation. So look at us. We have this dreary, creaking old bat-shelter of a courthouse and likewise we have notorious laxities of administration.
>
> Remedies are not wanting. We can exercise our franchise and vote as progressive citizens of Greater San Rodrigo County, for Greater San Rodrigo County, in the November elections. There will be a slate of attractive and vigorous candidates. There will

be a proposal to tear down this disreputable old relic and erect a modern efficient plant in its place...

The editorial had been published a month before; the "notorious laxities" referred to were those of Sheriff Ernest Cucchinello. As for the courthouse, Joe had never understood what the fuss was all about. Personally, he rather liked the old building. It had character. It stood five stories tall and each story apparently had been designed by a different architect. The first story was a square of liver-colored sandstone, trimmed with pilasters of the Ionic order upholding a cast-iron frieze, and an iron railing. The windows were tall narrow embrasures and displayed crumpled yellow shades, drawn to various levels. The second story, a slightly smaller block of buff sandstone, was set five feet behind the railing, which enclosed a promenade invaluable for the reviewing of parades and delivering of speeches. Next were three stories of frame construction painted mouse-gray, each with bay windows, balconies, columns, arches, fascia carved to represent basket-weaving. At the summit, guarded by fairy-castle crenellations, rose a green copper dome and a flagstaff. Over the front entrance a bronze plaque read:

SAN RODRIGO COUNTY COURTHOUSE
Erected 1872
TRUTH : JUSTICE : HONOR

The proposed new courthouse, as depicted in sketches submitted by the San Francisco firm Moderna Associates, would be a simple block of stainless steel and glass, eight stories high, functional in every detail. It would be a symbol of progress. Not everyone liked the design. A barber in Panoche thought it looked like a portable air-conditioner turned on its side. The magnitude of the proposed bond issue had also aroused opposition, much to the impatience of the progressive businessmen of Pleasant Grove.

Behind the courthouse, a concrete-block annex housed the sheriff's office and the county jail. When Joe entered, he was surprised to find Mrs. Rostvolt still sitting at her desk. "Mr. Griselda called," she told him in a monotone. "He wants you to call him back."

"Griselda, eh?" Howard Griselda owned and edited the Pleasant Grove *Messenger*, and so must be reckoned one of the county's most influential citizens. "Put him on." Joe went into his office, took up the receiver. Griselda presently spoke: "Griselda here."

"This is Joe Bain, Mr. Griselda. I understand you called."

"Yes, so I did. Do you have a few minutes to spare?"

"I certainly do."

"I'll drop right over. I won't keep you long; it's late in the day, I know."

Five minutes later Griselda stepped into Joe's office. He was a short powerful-looking man of forty-five, with a square blocky face, crisp iron-gray hair, a sallow rather soft complexion. He had sparkling black eyes, an expression of unquenchable energy and determination; he walked with a brisk swing, a slight forward stoop.

Joe rose, shook hands, indicated a chair. Griselda looked around the office. "I see you've cleared out all Cooch's little treasures. Place doesn't look the same."

"The place isn't the same. I'm running a different kind of office."

"Long overdue." He sat back, loaded a pipe, fixed Joe with a penetrating stare. Pipe and stare were well-known Griselda mannerisms. Joe waited.

Griselda lit his pipe and said through the smoke, "I understand you have a story for me."

Joe looked at him nonplussed. "Story? I can't think of anything offhand. Man the other side of Mulberry trapped a chicken thief two nights back and brought him in. Young Mexican. Had a hit-and-run last night on Rose Avenue. Sergeant Miggs is looking into it, and I think we've got a line. Out in Marblestone a man named Bus Hacker died — heart attack. Things are quiet otherwise." He sat back in his chair. "Where'd you get this information?"

"A tip came into the office — man's voice, wouldn't leave his name."

Joe shook his head. "I can't think of anything really hot. You can print a piece to the effect that I'm planning to run for the office of Sheriff. In fact, Mr. Griselda, I'm hoping I have your support."

Griselda puffed his pipe. "You're definitely in the race?"

"I certainly am. I think I'm the best man available. I know the business, I know the county, and I know the mistakes to avoid."

Griselda said briskly, "I'll be completely candid, Sheriff. I think the department needs a shake-up. Look at the rate of growth of other counties nearby. Phenomenal. Look at the rate of growth of San Rodrigo County. Nothing. We're falling behind, Bain — falling way back!"

"Well," said Joe in a reasonable voice, "some folks like peace and quiet. Maybe it's a good thing."

Griselda shook his head stubbornly. "We can't evade progress. I think Lee Gervase represents progress. He's a young man, keen, energetic. He's a real ball of fire. He's had a sound legal and criminological background at the university, and I think he's a man to bring modern methods to the department."

Joe made a sound to indicate complete disagreement. "Mr. Griselda, be reasonable. What good is progress? Does it catch any more chicken thieves? Or there's a brawl down at Diego's Place. What good is progress to the man making the pinch? Mr. Griselda, you're all wrong. I hate to say this, because I want your support — but you're like a cat chewing a piece of dandelion fluff; you're getting all lathered up over nothing."

Griselda raised his eyebrows, puffed his pipe.

"Now this Lee Gervase," Joe went on. "I hear he's a real hot dog. But where's his experience? Did he ever get biffed in the nose by a drunk? Did he ever pull a sick cow out of Genesee Slough, like I did three weeks back? Did he ever —"

"All this is beside the point," interrupted Howard Griselda. "A sheriff doesn't need to get 'biffed' in the nose, or rescue sick cows. That's why we hire a staff of deputies. The sheriff should be a manager, a leader, a symbol."

"Maybe so. But I don't care how much a symbol the sheriff is, when he runs into trouble he's got to know how to handle it. Trouble. That's what the sheriff's business is. I know every bad actor in the county. I know every gambling joint, every whore, every Mexican cock-pit —"

Howard Griselda jerked upright in the chair. Joe saw that in his earnestness he had blundered.

"It's hardly to your credit," said Griselda coldly. "These activities are illegal. If you know so much, why don't you stop it all?"

Joe heaved a deep breath. "In principle I agree. But I think there's a limit to how far you should push a law that maybe is a little unrealistic. I used to find out about something illegal, and I'd report to Cucchinello. He'd say, 'They hurting anybody? Anybody kicking?' Like as not, the answer was no. Cooch would say, 'Just keep things under control. Don't let anybody get obnoxious, but if somebody wants to blow off some steam over at Slough-house, and nobody gets hurt — why, what's the damage?' I think he was right. Understand, Mr. Griselda, I'm talking to you man-to-man. I don't want you to print a story about Sheriff Joe Bain being soft on vice. That's not the case. There won't be a cent of easy money coming my way. I don't want it. What Cooch did, or might have done, is one thing. I'm not built that way. I don't want favors from anybody."

Griselda said in a terse voice, "I don't endorse this philosophy. You can't be half-good. It's a case of all clean or all dirty. I think Lee Gervase will run a department that's all clean."

Joe sat in defeated silence.

Griselda said in a milder voice, "I didn't come here to hector you, Joe. You say there's nothing to this tip about something big in Marble-stone?"

Joe became alert. "You didn't say that the tip mentioned Marble-stone."

"Well, it did."

"I wish I knew who called in that tip."

"Why?"

Joe said slowly, "Just between you and me, Mr. Griselda — and this is absolutely, definitely, not for publication, not even a hint — there's something strange going on."

"Such as what?"

"I don't like to say — mainly because I don't know. Things just don't feel right."

Griselda tapped out his pipe, rose to his feet. "You'll let me know when you find out?"

"I will. And if you get any more tips — try to get a line on who's tipping."

"I'll do my best, Sheriff."

Griselda departed. Joe crossed the hall to the outer office. Mrs. Rostvolt was only just now shoving cigarettes and lighter into her big leather handbag, preparatory to departing. She wanted to hear what Griselda had to say, thought Joe gloomily. Her curiosity was no more than natural. Mrs. Rostvolt had a stake in the election too. If Lee Gervase won and brought in a new staff, she'd be out of a job with everyone else.

Mrs. Rostvolt said, "Some letters for you to sign. I've put them in your basket."

"Thanks. I'll take care of them." Joe returned to his office, addressed himself to his paper-work, which meant signing his name to four letters Mrs. Rostvolt had composed. There was a reassuring statement to a lady who had seen a tramp. A farmer had demanded investigation of a load of tin cans and rubbish which had been dumped into his pasture: Mrs. Rostvolt promised that a criminological expert would presently arrive to study the evidence. The Sanchez Elementary School had sent the sheriff a pair of complimentary tickets to the annual school play. Mrs. Rostvolt had declined on Joe's behalf with great regret. An irate taxpayer complained of deer jumping the fence into his vegetable garden; why did not the sheriff keep the deer population within bounds? The sheriff was studying the problem, wrote Mrs. Rostvolt, and as a stop-gap measure suggested a watch-dog. Or little sacks of blood-meal hung around the property were said to repel the deer.

Joe signed the letters gratefully. For all her disagreeable personality Mrs. Rostvolt was the next thing to indispensable. Who else could have composed such suave responses? A less adroit woman would have involved him in three futile investigations and a school play; or worse, have cost him a dozen votes...Joe decided to go home. He made a final round of the department. The night shift of deputies had checked in, as well as the night radio operator. The prisoners were at their dinner. Joe looked into Duke Scanlon's cell. "Well? Any kicks about the grub?"

"Coffee ain't too fresh."

"Tomorrow I'll have an expresso machine brought in for you," said Joe.

He left the office, drove out Green Street to the house he shared with his mother and his daughter. Miranda was now 16 and a junior at Pleasant Grove High School. She was a pretty, vivacious girl, and generally the house was cheerful with the sound of music and chattering teenagers. Tonight no one was home. His mother was attending a church function; Miranda was spending the night with a friend. A platter of cold chicken and a bowl of potato salad had been left for his supper. Joe opened a can of beer, brought out bread and butter, propped the evening paper in front of him and began to eat. A boxed story in a conspicuous spot at the bottom of the first page attracted his attention:

LEE GERVASE ADDRESSES ROTARY CLUB
ON NEED FOR ENERGETIC PROGRAM

Joe stopped eating and read the story. Lee Gervase, like Howard Griselda, felt that San Rodrigo County was standing still while the rest of California forged ahead.

The final paragraph mentioned that Lee Gervase would be a candidate for sheriff in the forthcoming elections.

Joe scowled, turned to the sports section, and finished his supper. Then he went outside, stood in the twilight. He felt restless, uneasy, lonesome. The image of a face came to his mind: a quiet sober face, with blue eyes and rich blonde hair. Joe frowned. Ellie Neff? That's who it looked like. Well, well, well. He went back into the house, turned on the TV, turned it off again. With no one home the house was unnaturally quiet. He opened another can of beer, and thought about Bus Hacker. Someone had it in for the old man, what with water in his gas tank and the misleading telephone call. He finished his beer, and decided to make a quick check around town before turning in. He went out to his car, made contact with the night radio operator, drove toward the center of town. He circled Montalvo Square, turned north on Highway 32, drove out into the countryside. The night was warm and quiet; the air smelled of ripe alfalfa and irrigated earth. To right and left glimmered the lights of snug homesteads. "Progress," snorted Joe. "What do they want around here, steel mills?"

Twenty minutes later he approached the hamburger stands, motels and filling stations which signaled the outskirts of Aurora. Aurora was a trifle larger, a few years newer, a shade more wide-awake than Pleasant Grove. Whenever carnivals or circuses came to the county, they tended to set up at Aurora. The County Fair, of course, was firmly and definitely the property of Pleasant Grove. Aurora, however, had a roller-skating rink and a public swimming pool, and the young folk were reputed rather wilder and faster than the youth of Pleasant Grove.

Joe cruised slowly up and down the main thoroughfare, circled through the back streets, then leaving town turned east on the county road, drove off through the night. Low hills rolled up ahead, gleaming like satin in the moonlight. The road wound, dipped, slanted down into the drab little village of Coyote, consisting of railway station, garage, restaurant, grocery store and a dozen houses in a tall grove of eucalyptus trees.

Joe turned south toward Mulberry, home of the Moeblin Bee Farm, which packed and shipped clover honey across the nation. But instead of continuing to Mulberry Joe turned left toward the sloughs. The country changed. The ground became dank, the air cooler. For a mile or two the road ran beside a drainage canal choked with tules. The air now carried a bosky, aromatic bouquet, and the sound of crickets was punctuated by the croak of frogs. A levee loomed ahead; the road swerved up and over an old timber bridge, which creaked and rumbled as Joe crossed Railroad Slough. The road struck off again, toward a far faint constellation of lights. After three miles the road mounted another levee, followed Genesee Slough toward the lights, which now were seen to festoon a big old-fashioned three-story building with a verandah overlooking the water. This was Slough-house, an institution at its heyday during Prohibition, when it acquired a reputation for picturesque vice which it never quite outlived. Slough-house was now relatively respectable. True, there were rooms to be rented on a casual basis; complaisant ladies could generally be found at the bar. On summer Saturday nights there was dancing at an open-air pavilion beside the slough. Some of the most fragrant memories of Joe's youth were connected with these Saturday night dances. The orchestra played romantic old tunes like *I'll See You in My Dreams, Whispering, Three O'Clock in the Morning;* the weeping willows changed color as the floodlights shifted through red, blue, green, and gold. After one such dance occurred the incident which culminated in Joe's marriage... Joe heaved a sigh for his lost youth. A dozen cars were parked in front of the bar. Luminous medallions advertising beer winked a cheerful invitation, but Joe drove past. It might not be too good an idea to be seen here. Not till after election, anyway.

The road followed the levee all the way to Genesee, beside moonlit water, willows and cottonwoods, occasional boat harbors. At Genesee Joe parked in front of the River Inn, a respectable counterpart of Slough-house, went into the café for a cup of coffee. Of the eight or ten customers, no one recognized him, or heeded the Sheriff's emblem on the car. Joe became depressed. Cucchinello, now, would have swaggered back and forth, exchanging banter with all, friend and stranger alike. Even while they recognized him for a Falstaffian old incompetent, they'd give him their votes. Joe shook his head mournfully. He didn't have Cooch's touch. The word "Incumbent" on the ballot would bring him a few votes and repel as many more. Joe wondered whether his position entitled him to the designation "Incumbent". Something he'd have to check with the County Clerk.

He returned to his car, drove west through a dry wasteland inhabited by owls, jack-rabbits and coyotes. After half an hour the land swelled, subsided, and the road swooped up over moonlit hills. For a mile it plunged through a bower of enormous eucalyptus trees, and a mile later entered Panoche. This was a sizable, bustling, ugly town, with four packing sheds, a cannery, a high school, a traffic light at the central intersection. Joe could turn left, drive out to Sanchez and return to Pleasant Grove via Tevis, or he could drive directly back to Pleasant Grove via Highway 11. He pulled to the curb, reached for the microphone, called into the office. "This is Joe Bain, calling from Panoche. Where's everybody?"

"Bill's at Verdalia, Ben's nailing a D and D in San Rodrigo, Gonzales is here on standby. Quiet night."

"Okay. I'm coming in."

The hour was close to midnight when he finally eased to a stop in front of his house. He had driven close to a hundred miles. What had he accomplished? Which of the sleeping farmers along the route knew that Sheriff Joe Bain had passed, alert for wrong-doing?

The moon had sunk low over the hills, and shone at him through the branches of the trees across the street. In the cool stillness Joe called into headquarters, checked himself out. He alighted, walked across the lawn. His mother had already retired; Joe switched off the porch light she had left burning. It was a comfortable old cottage, distinguished principally by its cheap rent. If Joe were elected he might have to move to a more stylish house just to keep up appearances. Ernest Cucchinello had lived in a big ranch-style house on McClellan Avenue near the country club...

At nine o'clock the following morning he arrived at the office. Mrs. Rostvolt gave him a formal good-morning, to which he made a civil reply. He went into his office; almost at once the telephone jingled. Arthur van Horn, Chief of the Marblestone Volunteer Fire Department, spoke briefly and to the point. "Last night the Hacker house burnt down. To the ground. Seeing as Bus just died I thought you should be notified."

"I'll be right out," said Joe. "Don't let anybody touch anything."

CHAPTER VI

Joe parked in Destin Lane, a hundred feet from the destroyed Hacker house. Half a dozen other cars were parked in the road; a tow-truck had backed into the yard with Walt Hobius standing at the winch. A dozen men and boys milled through the garden watching proceedings. Taking a firm grip on his temper Joe stalked back toward the ruins.

Arthur van Horn, the fish-eyed proprietor of the Marblestone Hotel and Restaurant, walked nervously back and forth. Noting Joe's approach he came to a halt, letting his arms swing hopelessly out to the side. "I told them what you told me, Joe. They wouldn't pay no attention. I just couldn't control them."

Joe nodded curtly, went into the front yard. The white bungalow of yesterday had become a rectangle of steaming and reeking ashes. A few pipes stood bent and plaintively tall, one of them terminating in a shower head. A vaguely delineated hole represented the basement. In this hole, knee-deep in ashes, embers, broken bottles of Millie Hacker's jams and preserves, stood Cole Destin, sweating and streaked with soot. With vicious tugs and jerks, he sought to force the cable from Walt Hobius' tow-truck under a bulky cubical object. Looking more closely Joe saw this object to be Bus Hacker's safe. He moved back a trifle, and around to the side.

Cole finally worked the cable beneath the safe, engaged the standing part of the line with the hook. He jerked up his hand. "Try her now. Slow and easy."

Walt engaged the winch. The cable snapped taut; the safe lurched, began to move, plowing a deep trench through the refuse. At the base of the wall it rose, hung swinging, and here Walt held it. He came to the edge of the hole, looked down. "She won't come that way, Cole. She'll raise as far as the edge and hang up."

"Go ahead, take her up."

"You need a ramp, something like that. Something to ease her over the edge of the concrete."

"Go ahead," said Cole. "Try it the way we got her."

"Okay." Shaking his head dubiously toward the spectators, Walt eased in the clutch. The safe rose until it came to the lip of the hole, where now the tension acted only to pull the safe into the foundation. Walt released the clutch, held the tension by means of a ratchet. "That's it, Cole."

"Give it a jerk, it'll break loose."

"More likely break my line. She's hung up."

"If you break the line, I'll make it good. Don't worry about that. Give it a jerk, snap her right up and out."

Walt motioned the spectators back. "Look out now. If that cable snaps she'll fly any which way." He manipulated the controls, but the clutch slipped and the safe fell back into the hole. Cole cursed. Joe winced. If the contents of the safe had been at all charred, they would now be shaken into illegible fragments.

Cole waded through the filth, adjusted the cable. "Take her up."

Once more the safe rose to the lip of the hole and halted. Cole seized a four-foot stub of 2x4, pried at the safe, standing perilously close. "Okay, now, goose her!"

Walt engaged the clutch, the safe bumped up and over, jounced across the ground toward the truck.

Joe stepped forward. "Cut off that winch!"

Walt looked at him startled, threw out the clutch. Cole scrambled from the hole, sweating and begrimed with filth. He gave Joe a curt nod, and spoke to Walt, "Just lift it easy now, and take it up to my place. I'll follow in my car."

"Just a minute," said Joe. "I wanted things left alone around here. I'm not kicking too much because you saved me the trouble of dragging that safe up. I'm taking over now."

Cole faced Joe squarely. "You're not going to take that safe, Joe."

"I'm going to get first look into it."

Cole stared at him. Joe turned to the onlookers who had pressed forward, the better to witness the altercation. "I'd like you people to get back to the road. This may be arson, and I don't want to have the place tramped under."

Cole said, "On what grounds do you claim this safe, Joe?"

"I'm investigating what looks like a crime."

"What crime?"

"First of all, arson."

"What if it was? I'm not making any complaint."

"Was the house insured?"

"Naturally."

"Are you planning to make a claim?"

Cole hesitated. Before he could respond, Joe asked, "Just to get matters straight, did you burn the place yourself, or get somebody to burn it?"

"I certainly did not."

Joe turned, went to the safe, nodded with satisfaction. "I thought that's what I saw. Somebody tried to bust into the safe. Look at the lock. It's smashed completely off."

Cole looked glumly down at the safe.

"This is one of the Kirby Triplex locks," said Joe, drawing on the lore he had assimilated at the Chapman Institute of Criminology. "Some of the old locks you can knock off with a sledge hammer, then punch out the lock, and the door flies open. A Kirby just jams. Somebody had to find out the hard way."

Cole set his jaw, and seemed to be casting about for something to say — preferably a good reason why Joe should not take the safe.

Joe asked mildly, "Why all the sweat about this safe? Old Bus never had anything special of value, did he?"

"Somebody thought he did," growled Cole, jerking his head at the ruined lock. "I want to make sure that whatever's there stays there."

"It'll be safe with me." Joe turned to Walt. "Think you can lift that safe and lay her in the trunk of my car?"

"I guess so." Walt glanced dubiously at Cole, who said nothing. "I'll raise her, drive out into the road. You back up, and we'll manhandle it in."

"Okay, take it out into the road. But lift it slow and gentle."

Cole renewed his protest. "Look here, Joe. I'm responsible for that safe and its contents. I don't want to let it out of my sight."

Joe considered. "I can't see how you're responsible. Unless there's a will naming you either heir or executor."

"Maybe there is a will in the safe."

"It's sure taken a beating, if it's there. What with the fire and the bungling around you gave it."

Cole said doggedly, "It seems to me that someone ought to be on hand to represent Bus Hacker when that safe is opened. And since I'm about the only friend old Bus had —"

"I've no objection to that."

Walt Hobius took the truck out into the road, the safe dangling behind. Joe went to his car, radioed into headquarters. Ace Wardell, the deputy on radio duty, responded.

"Call the state lab at San Jose, Ace. I want two men: an arson investigator and somebody to open a safe."

"Right. Where do you want 'em?"

"I want the arson man out here in Marblestone, at the Hacker residence, corner of Mitre Canyon Road and Destin Lane."

"Got it."

"As soon as he arrives I'll bring the safe in, so hold the safecracker at the office."

"Right. Will do."

By dint of careful maneuvering and help from the spectators the safe was eased into the trunk of Joe's car. Cole Destin stood to the side, shoulders hunched, hands in pockets. He asked, "When do you propose to open the safe?"

"As soon as I get back to the office."

"I'm going home to clean up," said Cole and departed.

Joe looked around for Arthur van Horn and found him leaning dourly against the fence. Joe asked him, "What time was the alarm turned in?"

"About two-thirty."

"Who turned it in?"

"Ausley Wyett rang the bell."

"Ausley Wyett, eh? Well, that figures. He's the closest neighbor."

Van Horn nodded in reluctant consent. "By the time we got here it was just no use. The place was gone."

Joe went back to an inspection of the ruins. Firemen and spectators had trampled the grounds thoroughly: there was small hope of finding footprints or any other sort of clue. Nevertheless — if for no other reason than that it was expected of him — he walked slowly around the house, peering here and there, examining oddments and fragments.

An hour later Edgar B. Hardwick, from the state criminological laboratory at San Jose, arrived. He was a small sober man, wearing precisely creased brown slacks, a neat tan jacket. Joe introduced himself, took him to the ruins. Hardwick shook his head dubiously. "A mess as usual." He returned to his car, slipped into blue coveralls and overshoes, then went to work.

He walked around the periphery of the house, occasionally bending over to look into the ashes. Twice he picked up a fragment of wood, smelled of it.

Joe watched a moment, then said, "I'll be heading back to town. You can give me a call when you're finished."

"Don't expect too much," said Hardwick. "So far I can tell only one thing definitely: the house burned down."

Cole Destin had returned and was grimly waiting in his car. Joe took a last look around and started back to Pleasant Grove, with Cole following.

He drove around to the rear of the courthouse, parked near the garage. With the help of Deputy Wardell and the lock expert, the safe was eased to the ground on a pair of planks.

The lock expert inspected the safe and, like Hardwick the arson expert, seemed discouraged. "The lock's so buggered up I'll have to cut it out with the torch."

"Just so long as you open it," said Joe.

"Oh, I'll open it, don't worry about that."

Joe nodded toward the lock. "Did the man know what he was doing?"

"I'd say not. Amateur job, strictly. He knew enough to bring a hammer and a set of punches and that's about all." He brought his panel truck up around, unreeled hoses from the oxygen and hydrogen tanks, connected his torch, donned a mask, and set to work. Sparks coruscated, white-hot metal puddled and dripped. He took up a heavy long-handled chisel, pecked, chipped, pounded, then burnt a few minutes longer. Presently he lifted his mask, looked up at Joe. "Something I better tell you. Once in a while after a real good fire the insulation holds the heat in. Then when the door opens the air hits and everything bursts into flame."

Joe eyed the safe dubiously. "Do you think that's about to happen here?"

"I wouldn't think so. Not enough insulation in a little can like this."

"Which means that everything inside is burnt to hell."

"More than likely…Well, here it comes." He pried with his bar; the door sagged and fell open. There was no burst of flame; the interior was hardly warm. The safecracker replaced his equipment, accepted Joe's compliments and departed.

Joe turned to find Cole Destin peering into the safe. Joe quickly stepped forward. "Give me a little room, Cole. This has to be done careful-like."

Cole moved aside. With a pair of tongs Joe reached into the bottom compartment, brought forth a large ledger. The canvas binding was charred, the covers were soft and almost crumbling to the touch, but the pages seemed relatively undamaged. Joe laid the ledger aside, returned to the safe. From a side niche he extracted a brittle packet of letters, charred on all the outside surfaces. Another niche yielded a brittle black envelope, originally manila paper, which Joe laid carefully upon the ledger. There was a warped metal drawer which Joe opened with difficulty. Within were black flakes of charred paper shaken and jarred into fragments. Joe shook his head in dissatisfaction. "You guys ought to have your heads examined, roughing up the safe the way you did."

Cole said nothing. He reached for the charred manila envelope. Joe said gently, "Better let me give things the once-over first, Cole."

"I'd like to find out if there's a will."

"If there's a will, you'll know first thing."

Cole grunted and a moment or two later departed.

Joe carried the contents of the safe into his office.

He settled himself at his desk, slit open the manila envelope. The contents were of no great interest: birth and marriage certificates, discharge papers from the army, automobile ownership certificate, a bank-book indicating savings to the amount of four hundred and ninety-two dollars. There was nothing in the nature of a will, and Joe wondered if the charred bits of paper represented such a document. If so, Bus Hacker's wishes in regard to the disposal of his estate would never be implemented.

Joe turned to the bundle of letters. He separated them, selected the least scorched. It was postmarked Marblestone, September 4, 1919, and addressed in round feminine handwriting to Corporal Clarence Hacker, Barracks 42-19, Fort Saugus, North Carolina. Joe extracted the letter and gingerly unfolded it; as he expected, it was signed "Millie", and seemed an ordinary enough letter, full of inconsequential gossip. At the time, Millie apparently had been employed at the Destin house as a servant; there were respectful references to "Mr. Destin" and "Mrs. Destin".

Joe scanned several more of the letters; in tone and content they were similar to the first. It appeared that immediately after young Clarence Hacker's demobilization, he and Millie were to be married.

Joe turned his attention to the ledger, which proved to be a record of the expenditures across the past ten years. Every cent spent by the Hackers seemed to have been meticulously noted under thirteen headings:

Food
Clothing
Health and Medicine
Tobacco
Liquor
Electricity
Tools and Equipment
Furnishing of House
Recreation
Church
Insurance
Tax
Savings

The Hackers had lived modestly, on what total income Joe could not instantly estimate. A simple enough calculation, of course. Savings averaged about ten dollars a month, occasionally going as high as twenty-five dollars.

In October of the previous year, entered under *Health and Medicine*, was the melancholy item *Funeral expenses* — *$785*, the money presumably deducted from *Savings*. There were some rather unusual gaps among the headings. Rent, for instance — which Bus Hacker had free from the Destins. Automobile expenses, for another, which possibly were listed under a different category. Bus in any case could have had very little automobile expense. Until someone had sabotaged his car by pouring water in his gas tank. Who could that someone be? An automobile salesman, hoping to sell Bus a new car? Walt Hobius, in the effort to build up his repair business? Joe wouldn't have put it past Walt... Someone had played another trick on old Bus, luring him away from home on the pretext of an important notice from the government. The two tricks almost certainly were related, constituting a scheme to get Bus out of his house for an hour or two. Why? Joe remembered the words Bus had muttered just before his death. "... Letter in the mail... Nothing I knew for sure..."

Speculations formed in Joe's mind. Suppose, after tricking Bus Hacker, someone had used the occasion to search for the "letter", but had been foiled by the safe. Suppose that after Bus Hacker's death this person had tried to crack the safe and, failing, had set fire to the house in order to destroy the "letter".

Joe considered the half-charred bundle of envelopes. Could the critical "letter" be among these? A large and highly delicate job to go through the entire lot — although Joe had learned the appropriate techniques at the Chapman Institute. There was one method, as he recalled, involving immersion in a solution of chloral hydrate; another involving a 5% silver-nitrate solution... Joe shook his head. Better let the state lab handle the job, at least the worst of the lot; it was sure to be a headache... The telephone rang; Joe answered.

"Somebody named Hardwick on the line," said Mrs. Rostvolt.

"Put him on," said Joe. He heard a click. "Sheriff Joe Bain speaking."

"This is Hardwick, Sheriff — arson investigator. On the Hacker house, I can't give you anything definite. In my own mind it's arson, or accident connected with the illegal entry, but don't ask me to prove it. Premises are just too thoroughly burned. I'd guess the fire started in the kitchen, or in the basement under the kitchen where it might just conceivably be spontaneous combustion."

"That's about what I expected," said Joe. "Excuse me just half a minute." He went to the door, crossed the hall, looked into the outer office. Mrs. Rostvolt had the receiver propped to her ear.

Joe returned to his office. "Sorry to have kept you, Mr. Hardwick. I guess that's all you can do for me. Thanks very much."

Joe rose to his feet, stood indecisively a moment, then walked into the outer office.

Mrs. Rostvolt was busy typing and did not look up.

In his most courteous voice Joe said, "I'm expecting some highly confidential calls in the next few days, Mrs. Rostvolt, so from now on I'd prefer that you hang up after you put a call through to me."

Mrs. Rostvolt raised her eyebrows so that her eyes became round and surprised. "Why, certainly, just as you like. I've just been following Sheriff Cucchinello's instructions; he often had calls he wanted someone to be a witness to, in case of controversy —"

Joe nodded sagely. "If a situation like that arises I'll let you know. Until then I want my private calls private."

Mrs. Rostvolt returned to the typewriter and Joe went back into his office. He cocked his feet up on the desk, sat back in his chair, gazed across at the map of San Rodrigo County.

Sergeant Lew Gonzales came into the office. "Taking some hard-earned rest, Joe?"

"Rest, hell," said Joe. "I'm thinking." He sat up, took the day-shift report which Gonzales had brought in. He glanced down the columns: nothing unusual. A stolen power-boat recovered in the tules, probably the work of boys. A stabbing in a Burnett bar. Complaints of indecent behavior from a housewife in Aurora, which turned out to be a photographer with a nude model. A hardware-store robbery in San Rodrigo, loot consisting of guns and ammunition. Almost certainly the burglars were teen-age boys and would shortly be apprehended.

Joe tossed the report to the side, returned to the bundle of charred letters. There were thirty, half of which could be read without difficulty. The rest he would send to the police laboratory at San Jose. He arranged the legible letters in chronological order, and began to read.

An hour later Joe sat back, not much wiser than when he had begun. Millie Landruff had been an unsuspicious young woman who accepted life precisely as it presented itself to her. Mr. Destin, seen through Millie's eyes, had been the very essence of gentleman rancher, with Mrs. Destin a domineering virago. There were hints that Mr. Destin regarded himself a gallant, and that Mrs. Destin, recognizing his proclivities, allowed him small scope. As for little Cole, he was "nice as a little boy could be, though very impatient when anybody tries to control him, then he becomes a regular little devil. A shame his older brother Harry had to die, it would be so good for Cole to know a hand stronger than his mother's."

There was much Marblestone gossip, concerning folk more or less familiar to Joe, even a disapproving comment: "Blacky Bain was at the dance with a girl from San Rodrigo, much too nice for him. He had a big bottle in his back pocket, everybody could see it. I feel sorry for the girl that marries him." The girl at the dance probably had been his mother. Millie's fears had been abundantly fulfilled; Blacky Bain had given Marian Sweet a life of difficulty and disappointment.

A figure appeared in the open doorway; Joe looked up and rose quickly to his feet. "Hi, Lee." He shook hands, rather formally. "Have a seat."

Lee Gervase seated himself, hitching at the creases in his charcoal-gray suit. He was a handsome man, with crew-cut black hair, a candid straightforward gaze. He looked swiftly around the office, gave a faint nod, as if some private expectation had been corroborated. "I hear that you're planning to run against me, Joe."

"You heard right."

"That's your privilege, of course. In your shoes I'd make the same move." He squared himself in his chair, faced Joe with an air of engaging frankness. "I feel I'd better explain myself, so there won't be any hard feelings after the election. I'm naturally running against Cucchinello. I've been planning my campaign on this basis; I'll have to follow through. It's tough for you to be saddled with Cooch and his record, but that's the way it goes. A lot of people are counting on me and I can't let them down."

Joe fiddled with his pencil. "I appreciate your dropping in, Lee. Personally I'm not worried about the hard feelings bit, since I plan to run an honorable campaign, whether you run against me or run against Cooch."

Gervase laughed politely. "I'm running to win, Joe. I'll seize on every issue I can. But I want you to understand that I don't regard the fight as anything personal between you and me. It's something bigger — between two ways of life. We're still in the tin-lizzie era, here in San Rodrigo County; it's time we began to catch up with the rest of California."

"That may be," said Joe. "But I don't have much say about things like that — either as Sheriff Bain or as plain Joe Bain. If changes come, they come."

Lee Gervase shook his handsome dark head with a trace of condescension. "It's not so simple as that. The sheriff is an important man in the county. He's a symbol of government. Cucchinello and the old courthouse — both tin-lizzie stuff. My sponsors and I want to modernize, get in line with the times. We're tired of this Mack Sennett atmosphere. It may mean jolting a few people out of their ruts, but all over the world the same thing's going on. It's either run hard or lose the race."

Joe nodded thoughtfully. "If that's going to be your pitch you'll get some votes. But I'll get some votes too. I'm going to run on the basis of law enforcement and a clean office. Cooch maybe accepted little favors once in a while. Not me. I've already made a few changes around here."

Lee Gervase chuckled. "So I understand. I gather you're running into, let us say, entrenched opposition."

Joe cocked his head sideways, looked at Gervase with a questioning frown. It seemed as if Mrs. Rostvolt didn't care whom she complained to.

"I'm probably talking out of turn," said Gervase, grinning at Joe's obvious irritation.

"It makes no difference," said Joe. "When you step on people's toes, they're bound to start screaming. After the election — no matter who wins — I imagine there'll be a few changes."

Lee Gervase nodded. "So far as you're concerned, there doesn't need to be."

"Eh? What do you mean?"

"I'll call a spade a spade. If you oppose me, I think I'll beat you. It stands to reason you'd have to leave the department — lose your job. If you took your name off the ballot, referred to yourself as, say, Captain Bain, instead of Sheriff Bain, after the election you could keep the title. With maybe an increase in pay, if I could swing it. I'm sure you know your job. You'd be an asset to the department."

"I got an even better idea. You take your name off the ballot, and I'll put you on as night jailer."

Gervase shrugged. "Suit yourself. I've warned you, I'm in this for keeps. I don't plan to let either myself, my backers or San Rodrigo County down. There's going to be a clean new deal around here. I'm going to run you and everything you stand for out of office."

"That's why you want me as captain of the department? Seems to me you talk both ways at once."

Lee Gervase smiled and nodded. "Just so long as we understand each other." He went to the door.

"I understand you all right." Joe rose to his feet, escorted Lee Gervase out into the hall. "I understand that you're not quite so virtuous and civic-minded as you'd like people to think."

Lee Gervase chuckled — a sound unpleasantly at odds with his appearance. "I never planned to be Joan of Arc. But I figure what's good for me will also be good for the county."

They stood on the concrete slab in front of the building. Joe said thoughtfully, "I don't get it, Lee. You're not the kind of man to be satisfied with the job of Sheriff, even at a thousand bucks a month."

Lee Gervase shot Joe a quick side glance. "Are you?"

"Yep. I'm not interested in the money. I like the job."

Lee Gervase smiled quietly. "Only one of us can get it."

"May the best man win," said Joe.

Gervase departed. Joe watched him walk away, brisk and assured. It surely wasn't the sheriff's job Lee Gervase wanted, Joe told himself. Not the job or the money. Lee Gervase had his sights set on Sacramento. Sacramento — or Washington. Rudolf Wark, the district's representative in the Congress, was becoming ever more rigid and doc-trinaire. He was ripe to be knocked over by an energetic young man who had proved himself as a vote-getter. Joe had wondered once or twice why Lee Gervase, a suave urban type, had settled in Pleasant Grove. It could very well be that Lee Gervase had carefully analyzed the situation in every county in California, and had chosen San Rodrigo County as the most promising. Sheriff Ernest Cucchinello was vulnerable to an imaginative and vigorous campaign. Cooch's death had probably made the job look even easier.

Joe went back to his office, took a drink of Ernest Cucchinello's whiskey to soothe his nerves and worked out a patrol schedule. This was a complicated business involving a whole manifold of subtle considerations. First, officers must be available and ready for action in the event of emergencies, crimes, or disorderly conduct. Second, it was desirable that each section of the county be visited at least once a day, with the exception of certain remote mountain settlements which might see a patrol car once or twice a week. Third, there were subpoenas to be served, court orders to be executed. To achieve these ends Joe had at his disposal seven deputies, each working five days a week — in effect, five deputies on each working day. The radio must at all times be manned, which left three men for outside duty, plus himself...Joe carefully worked out a set of staggered shifts: ten to six-thirty, four to midnight, seven to two in the morning. He rearranged days off in order to concentrate extra men on Friday and Saturday nights. Sunday and Monday could more or less take care of themselves.

The deputies must be carefully fitted into the schedule. Not just any arrangement would do. Each man had his peculiarities, his strengths and weaknesses. Casey Miggs was good with kids, uncertain in hard-nose situations. Big Ben Boso was tactless, forthright, rough and tough — the most effective man of the crew on the late shift, in spite of his tendency to drink on duty. He had a quick temper, he was harsh with obstreperous prisoners, he disliked Mexicans.

Lew Gonzales, in direct antithesis, liked Mexicans, being one himself. He was punctilious, even-tempered, soft-hearted. He hated to make a pinch and was easily taken advantage of. He and Boso were not unfriendly; Boso called him "Dago", he called Boso "Polack".

So with the other men. Frank Hubbard liked radio duty, Bill Phipps hated it. Fay Insley, a devout Fundamentalist, could not bring himself to work on Sunday. Ace Wardell was a ladies' man, and was thought to be trigger-happy. Gonzales, Insley and Miggs were scrupulously honest, Hubbard, Phipps, Boso probably less so. Joe was dubious about Ace Wardell. If he were elected he would put Wardell on permanent radio duty and hire two more men.

When he had finished, he took the schedule in to Mrs. Rostvolt. "Make about ten copies — one for every man, one for me, and one for the bulletin board."

Mrs. Rostvolt looked at the schedule with a petulant frown. "I've already worked out a new schedule. I've got it all ready to type up."

"Throw it away," said Joe. "This is the way I want things to go."

Mrs. Rostvolt shrugged coldly. "Just as you say."

Joe stood thinking a moment. He looked at his watch. The time was four-thirty. He told Mrs. Rostvolt, "If anyone wants me I'm on my way over to Marblestone."

"Very well, Mr. Bain."

Joe looked at his watch again. If he drove out to Marblestone he wouldn't be home for dinner. He went into his office, telephoned home. Miranda answered. "Hello?"

"It's me."

"Hi, Dad."

"I won't be home for dinner."

"Oh, Daddy! Granny's got spareribs and everything. Sweet potatoes!"

"Sorry, kid. I got some business to attend to."

"When will you be home?"

"Hard to say. Don't wait dinner."

"Okay."

A few minutes after five, with the sunlight slanting across Castle Mountain, Joe arrived at Marblestone. He continued along Destin Road to the Wyett ranch, turned up into the driveway, and the police dogs came racing out on their cables. Ausley's old station wagon was not to be seen. No one was home.

Chapter VII

Joe drove south along Destin Road to the ruins of the Hacker house. The fence smothered in red roses still stood. Joe leaned on the gate and considered the black rubble beyond.

The sun was gone; twilight blurred the mountain slopes, lights began to sparkle up and down the valley. Joe listened. Silence except for the warm wind in the poplars. A bat flew twittering past. The ashes of the Hacker house seemed more melancholy than ever. Joe thought of Millie's letters to Bus, written long ago when the world was young. He looked down into the rubble where the exploded glass of Millie's jams and preserves still reflected a few sullen lights from the sky. Life was a funny thing, thought Joe. You just reached the stage where you could appreciate it when you had to start worrying about how it would end... He walked back to his car, drove into Marblestone.

Lights burned bright in the Fox Valley Community Center; doings were in progress: the Mammoth Church Bazaar. Parked in front of the Town Club was a gray GM pickup, which Joe identified as the property of Willis Neff. He parked beside it, alighted, pushed through the old-fashioned swinging doors at the corner of the building.

The interior of the Town Club was illuminated by colored lights from a juke box, a shaded light over the pool table to the rear, various blinking and swirling beer-advertising devices at the back of the bar. A half-dozen men sat on stools with bottles and glasses in front of them.

Joe took the seat beside Neff, who acknowledged his presence with a stare and a nod, then continued his conversation with the man to his left.

Joe ordered a beer. Neff was talking about trout-fishing, in a measured dogmatic voice. "— of course if it weren't for the Forest Service, there wouldn't be fish. They'd be exterminated in a year. I give them credit for that. But you'll never tell me that these hatchery fish grow as big or as tasty as the natural-born fish. Stands to reason, the natural fish come of better stock, bound to."

"They're the same fish," said his companion dubiously.

"They sure as hell aren't, and I know this for a fact. I've fished every stream in these hills. There's a few that don't get stocked, and I don't think anyone fishes them except me, because they're hard to get to. The fish I take out of these unstocked streams can't be beat."

"I just don't fish that careful. Where are these streams you're talking about?"

"That I won't say. Took me better part of ten years searching them out. I might be going out for a few days next week."

"Nice weather for it."

Someone settled into the seat beside Joe: Walt Hobius. "Hi, Walt," said Joe. "What's on your mind?"

"Nothing much. Hey, Shorty. Draw me a bottle of Bud." He turned back to Joe. "What did you find in Bus Hacker's safe?"

"Odds and ends. Nothing much."

"About what I expected. Bus never had anything. I don't know what he thought he needed a safe for."

"Old folk get funny notions sometimes."

"That's for sure. Bus was no exception. Cranky old fart."

"Where did he get his gas? From you?"

"Not very often. I don't know where he dealt. San Rodrigo I suppose." Walt drank his beer. "Whenever he did buy five gallons of gas he wanted a receipt." Walt drank more beer, looked sourly past Joe toward Willis Neff. "There's another one, gets it all back," he muttered.

"What do you mean?"

"You was brought up on a ranch. I don't know if you had a tractor, and burnt tax-free gas or not. Tax-free gas works just as good as any other kind."

Joe nodded. "Pretty hard to do anything about. Especially if you use a pickup on your own land, hauling things back and forth."

Walt's hollow-cheeked face became dour. He cocked his head to

Neff's conversation. "Listen to him now," he said to Joe. "All about how good he is at fishing." He drained his glass, signaled Shorty Olson, the bartender. "Two more of the same."

Joe held up his hand. "Not for me. I got to watch it, because I'm going over to the church social and meet my constituents. I don't want to go crawling in on my hands and knees."

Walt gave him a glance of amazement. "Two beers? Is this the Joe Bain I knew of yore? Two beers were just a little appetizer."

"Well — all right. Just one more."

"That's more like it. You might get the church vote by staying sober, but you lose the confidence of the drunks."

"You have a point," said Joe. "I guess I can't please everybody."

"Here's to a long life." Walt raised his glass, drank.

"Unless you lay off the cancer sticks you'll never make it," said Joe, raising his glass.

Walt looked at him in surprise. "I've been cutting down." He glanced at his stained fingers. "Hell, that ain't nicotine. That's iodine, or ink or something." He blinked, shot Joe a sharp look. "How come you're so interested in my health all of a sudden?"

"I need your vote, for one thing. And if you can't tell the difference between ink and iodine, you're either going to have blood poisoning or a ruined fountain pen."

Walt chuckled, started to speak, but now Neff, alighting from his stool, turned to Joe. "Who burnt down the Hacker house, Sheriff?"

"I don't know. Not yet."

"Think you'll ever find out?"

Joe thought he detected an undertone of mockery. "I'll find out. I don't let things like that go by."

"You want a tip, Sheriff?"

"Sure. I'm not proud."

"You know what they say about firebugs? That generally they're the ones that turn in the alarm?"

"I've heard that," said Joe. "Sometimes people who want the fire put out also turn in the alarm. It's hard for the law enforcement officer. He can't pinch everybody who turns in an alarm, and he can't pinch everybody who doesn't."

Neff stared at him without comprehension. "I thought I might be able to help you out."

"Thanks, Mr. Neff. I'll consider what you've said."

Neff departed.

Walt Hobius finished his beer, slipped off the stool. "I got to run along myself. If you're going over to the Center maybe I'll see you later on."

Walt departed, and Joe presently followed. He stood outside on the sidewalk. Twilight had given way to night; across the park the Community Center bustled with cheerful activity. Every window glowed; a festoon of colored lights hung across the front.

Joe sauntered across the park. As he crossed the street he noticed Ausley Wyett's Willys station wagon in the line of parked cars. Joe gave a snort of amusement. Ausley was evidently trying to make it back into the social swim. At a church bazaar no one could very well tell him to clear out. No matter what you thought about Ausley Wyett, you couldn't fault him for guts. Or sheer gall, depending on how you looked at it.

Joe entered the Community Center behind a farm family. The man wore a lumpy blue suit, his wife a flowered dress. There were two boys glistening with hair oil, two girls who rustled as they walked. Joe became conscious of his own clothes: whipcord trousers, light gray wind-breaker, a white shirt. His mother and Miranda both wanted him to dress more formally, but Joe was reluctant to blossom out so soon after his promotion. Something like that a man eased into gradually, so that no one noticed. Cucchinello, of course, had always dressed to the nines, in fine gabardines, expensive sport shirts, Western-style string ties and a cowboy tie clip. Lee Gervase dressed well, but like a successful young businessman. Joe dismissed the matter from his mind. His clothes were good enough for a church social. Maybe people would consider him tireless and hard-working to see him dressed like this on a Saturday night.

Joe paid his twenty-five cents, entered the building. The outer lobby or reception room was set up with a line of card tables supporting bowls, trays and casseroles. To the left, an archway opened into the main hall, where the bazaar was in progress. There were displays of quilts, hooked rugs, homemade candy, old books and magazines. A special booth displayed the contribution of Bart North, the local rockhound: book-ends, lamp-bases, jewellery of agate, petrified wood, jasper.

Supper apparently had just been announced: a line of people had formed and was moving in front of the food. Joe went into the hall, from which a gradual exodus was taking place toward the supper. Charley Blankenship stood nearby, with his taffy-colored little wife Metty, sister to Dora, Walt's mother. Charley wore a loose double-breasted blue suit, with a splendid red and blue tie and his usual knob-toed black shoes. He saw Joe and signaled. Joe walked over to him. "Hello, Charley. Good evening, Mrs. Blankenship. Seems to be a nice party."

"It's lovely," said Metty. "We never expected such a crowd. I'm just hoping we have enough to eat."

Charley peered truculently toward the inner room. "Might be a good idea to get in line before it's all gone."

"You go ahead," said his wife. "I'm not eating: everything is too rich for me." She told Joe, "The doctor says it's gall bladder. He won't let me touch fats and I'm to go easy on sweet things, I'm starving all the time."

"That's too bad, Mrs. Blankenship."

Charley grasped Joe's arm with his long, limp fingers, pointed. "There. Look at that. Somehow I think that's a lot of nerve."

Joe followed the direction of Charley Blankenship's quivering finger. Halfway along the wall, behind a display of homemade candy, stood Ellie Neff. She wore a sleeveless blue cotton frock, a blue ribbon in her blonde hair. Joe thought that she looked wonderfully charming. There was about her a slow, unstudied grace, an artless desire to please, quite different from coquetry. In front of the booth stood Ausley Wyett, making a careful selection among the various dainties. He wore an obviously new suit which fit him not too well, the coat riding high on his buttocks, his wrists protruding from the sleeves. Ausley had groomed himself carefully. His fox-colored hair was slicked down; his shoes were glossy; he wore a sporty red tie clasped with a silver A on an ivory horse's head. He asked Ellie a question, and at her response made some sort of droll remark. Ellie smiled, blushed faintly, and smiled again.

"The nerve of the man," hissed Metty Blankenship. "You'd think he'd be ashamed to show his face."

Charley tightened his grip on Joe's arm, gave it a tug. "Can't you do something about it? Here he is offending everybody in the place, but because it's a church function no one wants to ask him to leave."

"You've put your finger on the difficulty," said Joe. "Ausley's behaving himself, so I guess nobody has any right to interfere with him."

Charley Blankenship's pendulous mouth quivered, he peered angrily through his glasses, then turned away, shaking his head. Metty darted Joe an angry glance, then taking Charley's arm marched into the next room. "Two votes shot to hell," Joe told himself sadly.

Ausley completed his selection, and counted out his money. He paused, said something more to Ellie. She frowned, looked at him carefully, then nodded slowly. Willis Neff came into the room. Ellie's glance veered to the candy; she busied herself arranging it.

Ausley saw Joe, ambled across the room. Joe said, "Looks like you're developing a sweet tooth, Ausley."

Ausley grinned. "I always did like candy. Here, want some fudge?"

"No thanks."

Ausley devoured a piece of candy, looked back across the room. "That's sure a nice girl. Awful pretty too."

"She's got an awful mean father who hates your guts. Better watch your step, Ausley, for your own good."

Ausley made a sour grimace. "I don't care any more, Joe. I can't seem to act right no matter what, so I might just as well do what I feel like."

"How do you mean, you can't seem to act right?"

"If I stay home out of sight, people say, that wicked Ausley Wyett, he knows he's no good, he's ashamed to show his face. If I try to act like other folks, they say, there's that wicked Ausley Wyett, parading back and forth like he owns the world. I can't win."

"So what? You're not surprised, are you?"

"No," said Ausley. "I'm not surprised. But some people are nicer than others."

"Such as who? Ellie?"

"Yep. I told her not to believe all she heard about me. She said all right, she wouldn't. What could be nicer than that?"

"Nothing," said Joe with complete honesty. "It's a shame she's cooped away up there in the hills."

"Being cooped away isn't much fun," said Ausley. "I had sixteen years of it. I'd be there yet if the jails weren't so full. They got to turn people loose to make room for the new ones."

"Let's go get something to eat," said Joe. "Before it's all gone."

"Better go by yourself," said Ausley. "You'll lose votes to be seen with me."

"At least people will notice me. They say every knock is a boost."

Ausley shrugged. "If you can stand it, I can."

They went out into the next room, stood in line. After paying a dollar they were handed big plates and silverware. In spite of Mrs. Blankenship's fears there seemed plenty to eat: fried chicken, baked beans, spaghetti, ham and potato *au gratin*, potato salad, green salad, rolls, muffins, and finally cake, pie and coffee.

Joe and Ausley went to sit in a corner. "I been meaning to ask you about that fire," said Joe. "Art van Horn says you turned in the alarm."

"Perfectly correct," said Ausley.

"What time did you first see the fire?"

"Oh — along about midnight, maybe sometime later. Right after I turned off the TV I went outside to stretch my legs. Soon as I saw the red in the sky I knew what was what."

"That's all you know about it?"

"What else could I know?"

"You didn't go watch the fire?"

"Give me credit for some sense, at least."

"Who do you think is responsible?"

Ausley pursed his big ropy mouth. "That's a good question. I got my ideas, of course."

"Let's hear them."

Ausley shook his head. "My opinions don't mean a thing. I hold a grudge against too many people around here."

"Seems foolish to me, Ausley. How do you figure you got a right to hold any grudges?"

"I don't like to talk about it," said Ausley primly. "The tale will probably come out some day. Right now the time isn't ripe."

"And when will the time be ripe?"

Ausley shook his head. "Hard to say. Bus Hacker dying like that — a terrible thing. Accident, I suppose."

"Do you have any other ideas?"

Ausley guffawed, drank from his coffee cup. "Do you know what I call it, Joe? Chickens coming home to roost."

Joe ate in disapproving silence. As Charley Blankenship had pointed out, Ausley showed no shame.

From the main hall came a clatter of card tables being set up in preparation for Bingo. Ausley rose to his feet. "Guess I'll see how my luck is running."

Joe watched him amble away. Shaking his head in dissatisfaction, he went to the coffee urn, drew another cup of coffee, and went to stand just inside the archway. Up on the stage Mrs. Koshlund, the wife of the Methodist minister, and Mrs. Bluett arranged the Bingo apparatus: a small rotating barrel containing numbered balls, a large checkerboard numbered from one to one hundred, to serve as a memorandum of the numbers drawn. Joe looked around the room. About a third of the people he recognized. Some had been schoolmates; others were faces barely recollected. The Destins were not in evidence, nor did he expect them to be. The Destins, with a few other families, were the elite of the region, and on their nights out drove to Monterey or San Jose, or even as far as San Francisco.

The Blankenships had taken a table close up to the stage; sitting with them were Mr. and Mrs. Al Gruber, who operated the local barber shop and beauty salon. Willis Neff and Mrs. Neff sat to the far side of the room, Neff wearing a long-suffering expression. As Joe watched, an elderly couple took the other two seats at their table. Joe sought around the room for Ellie, to see her turning over the funds from her booth to a stout woman in a lavender dress.

Joe wandered across the room; when the stout woman moved on, Joe said, "Hello, Ellie. How's everything going?"

Ellie smiled politely. "Very nicely."

"Are you going to play Bingo?"

"I guess so." Ellie looked across the room to where her parents sat.

"Maybe I will too. Let's sit over there."

Ellie looked doubtfully at the booth, but no one seemed interested in buying candy. "All right."

Joe led her to an empty table. "I should have asked if you'd eaten."

Ellie nodded. "I did, ten or fifteen minutes ago." Joe held the chair for her; Ellie laughed self-consciously, slipped into it. Joe sat down to her right. "I haven't been to an affair like this in twenty years," said Joe. "Not since I used to live back up in the hills."

"Whereabouts did you live?" Ellie asked without overmuch curiosity.

"Just under Castle Mountain. About two miles past your house there's a little road that takes off to the south. You follow that road about ten miles, up, down, winding, looping, and finally you come out on a meadow with a beat-up old house back by a spring. That's home. I wish I owned the place now."

"Who does?"

"I don't know. After my father died my mother sold to a fellow named A. N. Charr, and I don't know what happened after that."

"Charr. That's a queer name."

"I think they were Welsh. Or Basques. Or Finns. Some outlandish troop, anyway."

Ellie said nothing. She put her hands on the table: firm, slender, strong hands which in a few more years would be work-worn. Ellie noticed his gaze, put her hands back in her lap.

"I don't want to get personal on such short acquaintance," said Joe, "but doesn't it get pretty lonesome sometimes?"

Ellie smiled uncomfortably. "I try to keep pretty busy."

"Maybe this is a little fast, but could I pick you up some evening? I'm not much at dancing, but we could have dinner and go to a show or something."

Ellie's mouth drooped. She shook her head. "I don't think so, Mr. Bain."

"Oh come now, Ellie — call me Joe, by the way — surely you can take an evening off without the sky falling in."

Ellie paused, then said simply, "In the first place I don't have any clothes."

"What's wrong with what you got on? You look beautiful."

Ellie smiled and shook her head again. "There's other things too. About five years ago my sister Gertrude ran away from home, and, well, she came to grief. So now my father worries. I guess I'm still his little girl."

Somebody came to stand beside the table. Joe looked up to see Ausley Wyett grinning nervously, then trying to look composed and sedate, then grinning again. "Is these seats taken?" asked Ausley.

"No," said Joe shortly. "Help yourself."

Ausley seated himself, hitched up his trouser legs with elaborate punctilio. At this moment the Reverend Dunkwiler appeared on the stage.

"Friends, I won't take but a moment before the games, but the Reverend Koshlund has asked me to express our mutual thanks for your help, material and otherwise, and for the grand turn-out this evening. It's one of the difficult and thankless jobs..."

Joe muttered to Ellie. "This gives me an idea." He rose to his feet, made for the side door leading to the stage.

"...returns aren't all in yet, but I'm sure the maintenance funds of both churches will be enormously invigorated. Now I see the girls and boys ready to distribute the cards, so without further ado —" Joe Bain appeared on the stage, spoke a quiet word to the Reverend Dunkwiler, who smiled and nodded graciously. "Friends, Sheriff Joe Bain has a word to say to you."

Joe stepped forward, looked out over the sea of blank white faces. "I won't take much of your time. I want to say hello to all my old friends and neighbors, and to remind you that in the coming election I'm running for the office of Sheriff, and I'll sure appreciate your votes. I don't have any platform except to say that I'm for honest, efficient law enforcement without fear or favoritism. Thank you very much. Thank you, Reverend." Joe bowed stiffly, marched off the stage. There were a few desultory hand claps, but now a group of teen-age boys and girls were circulating through the hall selling Bingo cards. The Reverend Dunkwiler once more stepped forward. "I've been asked to announce that Bingo cards sell for a dollar apiece and are good for the whole evening. All prizes are donated, and we'll announce the prize and the name of the donor before each game."

Joe returned to the hall, looked sourly toward the table where Ellie and Ausley were now buying cards. Ellie took one card, but Ausley with a grandiose gesture extended a bill and was given five cards. Ellie made some marveling comment; Ausley replied in a fashion to make her laugh openly, unaffectedly. Joe frowned, went into the outer room, drew himself another cup of coffee from the untended urn.

Two elderly women came up to him. One asked in a bantering tone, "Can you be Joe Bain, the young rapscallion who was the shame of the neighborhood?"

Joe grinned. "I guess that's me. And you're Mrs. Mathews, my old third-grade teacher."

"So you remember me after all these years!"

"How could I forget?"

The other lady said archly, "I don't imagine you remember *me*!"

"I certainly do," said Joe. "You're Mrs. Beasley, at the post office. When I was ten years old I kissed your daughter. You caught me and whacked me good."

"Think of it," Mrs. Beasley marveled to Mrs. Mathews. "Ten years old he was, and kissing Arla bold as you please. Ten years old! And Arla pretending it was just an everyday occurrence. Oh, the little rascals. I hate to think what went on when my back was turned."

"It goes to show that you never can tell. Arla's married with four children, and Joe's sheriff of the county." Mrs. Mathews beamed roguishly at Joe. "How we used to pity your poor mother, coping with a pair like your father and you!"

"I imagine she felt sorry for herself at times," said Joe.

The ladies asked about Joe's mother. Joe responded courteously. Two sure votes, if they took the trouble to bestir themselves election day, plus possibly the votes of husbands, children, and friends. It was worth the effort. Mrs. Beasley reached forward, touched his arm. "There's something I'm dying to ask you —" she glanced sidewise at Mrs. Mathews, who watched her attentively. Mrs. Beasley gave a little shake of her head. "But I guess it wouldn't be proper. Not professional conduct. So I'll restrain myself."

It was not clear whether Mrs. Beasley's qualms were on her own account or Joe's, but in any event he did not pursue the matter.

From the next room the voice of Mrs. Bluett could be heard calling numbers. Mrs. Mathews looked at Mrs. Beasley. "Well, Mary, are we gambling tonight — as the church doesn't like to call it?"

"I'm always ripe for a little excitement. You know that."

"We'd better get started then, before all the prizes are gone. Are you coming, Joe? Or I suppose we should say, Sheriff?"

"I'll take a card for a round or two."

Joe escorted the ladies to a table at the rear. They were provided with cards and beans.

"Eighty-four," called Mrs. Bluett.

The barrel rolled. A little girl of eight or nine, with long dark pigtails, reached in and extracted a ball which she handed to Mrs. Bluett.

"Twelve," was the call. Ausley Wyett jumped to his feet. "Here! Bingo!"

Mrs. Bluett nodded with compressed lips. A floor monitor read off the winning numbers on Ausley's card.

"All correct," declared Mrs. Bluett. "The prize is a steam iron, donated by Olin's Drug Store."

A subdued titter, quickly hushed, greeted the news. Ausley, smiling sheepishly, sat down once more, the box containing the steam iron on the table in front of him.

A new game started. "Sixty-five," called Mrs. Bluett. Joe put a bean on his '65', then looked across the room to where Willis Neff sat. Neff was directing toward Ausley Wyett a look of ophidian menace. Joe frowned. Ausley Wyett might be pushing his debut into society a little too hard.

Mrs. Bluett called number after number. "Bingo!" "Bingo!" "Bingo!" "The prize, donated by Mr. and Mrs. Mendoza, is this lovely garden statuette." "—a meal ticket, value fifteen dollars, at the Marblestone Hotel, donated by Mr. Arthur van Horn."

Finally: "That's all, friends. Thank you and goodnight."

Ausley and Ellie rose to their feet. Ellie had won nothing, but Ausley had pressed the steam iron upon her. She held it reluctantly, obviously distressed. Then she shrugged, said goodnight to Ausley, threaded the crowd toward her mother. Joe watched her go. Graceful, charming, generous — and pretty. "I've got to do something about that," said Joe. "Unless Ausley cuts me out."

He watched as Ellie showed the steam iron to her mother. Both looked toward Ausley, but he had left the hall. Joe sought Willis Neff, but he was nowhere to be seen. Possibly he had gone to the Men's Room, thought Joe.

Mrs. Neff inspected the box askance, shook her head. Ellie made a mild remark; Mrs. Neff appeared more dubious than ever. She and Ellie looked around the room. Mrs. Neff said something with a bleak expression; Ellie's face became soft and astounded.

Joe turned, made for the door. He went to the sidewalk, looked up and down. There was Ausley's station wagon, somnolent under the street lamp. In the street beyond stood a group of men.

Joe approached quickly. Willis Neff confronted Ausley Wyett beside the station wagon, where Ausley apparently had been in the act of inserting the key in the door lock.

Neff was speaking in a guttural voice. "— what I'm going to do, but before I do it, I want to tell you, don't you ever, don't you even look sidewise at my daughter again."

"Now take it easy, Mr. Neff," said Ausley in a high-pitched voice. "I don't think I did anything wrong, and so far as I know —"

"You got a hell of a nerve showing your face; you got a hell of a nerve just being alive."

"Now, look here, Mr. Neff. I don't want no trouble with you. Please stand aside so I can get into my car."

Neff swung his fist. Ausley moved aside and Neff missed. The circle of men groaned, cheered. "Give it to the son of a bitch, Willis. Kill the bastard!"

Joe stood watching. So far Neff had committed no battery, having missed the first blow. Neff laughed now, pulled his elbow to his side, danced a ridiculous little hop-step, sprang forward. Somewhere Joe had heard that Neff had been a boxing champion in the Navy… Ausley surprised Neff. Ausley had long arms with big lumps of fist at the ends. He knew nothing of boxing, he merely stood clubbing wildly at Neff. His first blow caught Neff on the ear, then Neff charged close and was pounding Ausley's chest. Ausley jack-knifed, loped away, out into the street. Neff danced his hop-step, came forward. Ausley flailed at him, necktie flapping. The big awkward fist caught Neff on the neck, Neff stumbled, fell to his knees, more surprised than hurt. But most of all infuriated. He lunged forward, running first on hands and knees, then on bent legs. Roundhouse right, roundhouse left: Ausley's head jerked, his ruff of hair waved and flopped. Ausley gave a thin call of fear and pain, and clubbed with his great fists, catching Neff on the mouth. Neff spurted blood. He hissed, hopped, struck out, Ausley fell to the ground. Neff exhaled a deep grunt of content, stepped forward, drew back his foot to kick. Joe reached forward, pulled him back, off-balance. Neff spun around.

"All right, all right," barked Joe. "What's going on here? Break it up."

"I'll kill the son of a bitch."

"What's he done?"

"You ought to know. Tonight he was talking to my daughter."

"She's not kicking, is she?"

"What if she ain't?"

"She's over twenty-one."

Ausley painfully climbed to his feet. Neff pushed at Joe. "Get the hell out of my way."

Joe said, "You do that again, you'll go to jail. For about sixty days. When I say break it up, that's what I mean."

Neff seemed ready to challenge him, but the onlookers held him off. "That's enough, Willis, don't do no more." "— only get in trouble, boy." "Easy does it, easy does it."

Joe turned to Ausley. "You want to prefer charges against this man?"

Ausley said, "No, I guess not. He's pretty excitable and probably didn't realize what he was doing."

Neff smiled. "Next time I'll really fix you!"

"You better be careful, Neff," said Joe.

"You sticking up for him? And you expect people of Marblestone to vote for you?"

"I'm doing my duty, and I hope they see it that way."

"Here's one that don't."

"Sorry, Mr. Neff. I'd sure like to have your vote."

Neff turned, walked swiftly away. Joe looked around the group of men. "Fine bunch you are. Acting like a bunch of juvenile delinquents." They muttered, moved uneasily away, looking backward over their shoulders, faces yellow-gray in the illumination of the lonesome street light.

Ausley tucked his necktie into his coat-pocket with trembling fingers, rubbed his chest.

Joe said, "You ought to know better, Ausley. People have long memories in these parts, and it don't do to go pushing people too hard."

Ausley said, "I might agree with you, Sheriff, if I'd been guilty of what they think I did. Sixteen years in jail is a long time for doing nothing."

Joe stared at him sternly. "You mean to stand there and tell me that you weren't guilty?"

"I pleaded innocent at the trial, Joe. Nobody believed me."

"Who did it then?"

"I don't know. Not for sure." Ausley drew himself up to his full height. "I'll tell you something, Joe. If you think I came back to Marblestone just to raise cattle and forgive people — you're wrong. Sixteen years takes a lot out of a man's life. I'm gonna get something back for it. If anybody gets hurt — too bad."

Joe grunted. "Now you're talking wild. You better go home, and go to bed."

Down the street came the Neffs: Willis Neff, Mrs. Neff, Ellie. Ellie carried the steam iron. Frozen-faced she crossed the sidewalk, laid it on the fender of Ausley's car, walked on.

Ausley watched her go. He heaved a vast sigh, reached for the box, started to throw it out into the park. Joe said hurriedly, "Here, here. What're you doing?"

"I don't want the damn thing. I don't iron nothing."

"Give it to me, then. I'll take it home to my daughter. She's been yelling for one of the things."

"Take it. It's yours."

"Thanks. Now, my advice to you, Ausley, is go home and lie low for a while. I don't want to get a call from Marblestone to the effect that your body has been found swinging from a tree."

"You know what I told you."

"Yes, I heard you. I don't say I believe you. But any time you want to talk about the case, come see me at my office."

Ausley got into his car, started the engine, backed out into the street and drove away.

CHAPTER VIII

MONDAY MORNING WAS WARM, bright and quiet — a summer morning when the stillness of the air induced somnolence. Joe sat in his office, looking through the Venetian blinds across Montalvo Square.

From the front office came the rattle of Mrs. Rostvolt's typewriter, from time to time a muffled murmur of conversation, or a ring of the telephone. Down the corridor from the jail section came the sound of the six prisoners talking through the bars of their cells: banter and bragging, carefully weighed analyses of the world's ills. Joe listened with a half-grin. Occasionally there was some contemptuous reference to the circumstances which had brought them to their current plight. Joe shook his head. To hear 'em talk, you'd think they'd all been corporation presidents on a vacation when this miserable stroke of bad luck overtook them.

His phone buzzed; he reached languidly to the desk, answered. Mrs. Rostvolt said, "There's a man here who wants to see you — Mr. Leary."

Joe started to say, "Send him in," but an almost imperceptible nuance in Mrs. Rostvolt's tone — a blandness, an overcareful precision — caused him to ask, "What's he want?"

"Something about an art course for your daughter."

"If it's a salesman, tell him I'm busy."

Joe hung up, frowning. Mrs. Rostvolt should have better sense than to trouble him with something like that. What in the world was she thinking of? For all her competence Mrs. Rostvolt was a pain in the neck. Joe day-dreamed of someone with Mrs. Rostvolt's efficiency and know-how, but with, say, Ellie Neff's appearance and agreeable attributes.

The thought of Ellie Neff took his mind to Marblestone. He felt uneasy. A definitely unpleasant situation — but what in the world could he do? Impossible for him to supervise Ausley Wyett's every move. Impossible to change Willis Neff into a cooing dove…There was also the death of Bus Hacker. No matter what he suspected or inferred, there was no purchase, no toe-hold in the case. Cole Destin might or might not try to claim insurance from the burning of the house. If he did, then it was up to the insurance company to decide whether or not to pay him.

He reached in his desk drawer, brought forth the state lab's transcript of Millie Hacker's letters. They told him nothing more than he already knew. Old Mr. Destin on one occasion had gone so far as to pat Millie Landruff on the cheek, so Millie coyly reported. It all seemed innocent enough. If there were skeletons in the Destin closet, Millie had revealed none of them to Corporal Clarence Hacker.

Joe tossed the transcript back into the drawer, leaned back in the chair. He had nothing to do. The deputies were off on patrol; Mrs. Rostvolt took care of front-office routine. For twenty years Ernest Cucchinello had sat in this same office, in much the same circumstances. He had always seemed busy. The bustle and swagger of his corpulent frame could be felt in every corner of the office. Cooch had a knack for making the most of every occasion, turning every circumstance to advantage. Meanwhile, the department coasted along on its own momentum. In actuality Mrs. Rostvolt had been sheriff. Across the years, by the increment of ten thousand minor, almost inconsequential, decisions, she had completely established the routine of the office. She had arranged the patrols, managed the disbursements, to no small extent dictated salaries and promotions. Cooch was only too glad to duck the drudgery of running the department — a process he called "delegating responsibility". What was that quotation about "nature abhorring a vacuum"? Joe shrugged, reached for the Monday-morning report.

By and large it had been a quiet week-end. A few traffic violations, a few drunk and disorderlies, one attempted rape up at Vino. Joe read the particulars, which were phrased in Ben Boso's highly individual style:

Complainant: Leonora Maxwell, 14, (colored).
Accused: Eagle Jones, 24, (white, farm-
hand, arrived ten weeks ago from Texas).
Miss Maxwell states Jones hired
her to shell walnuts, then made indecent
proposals, compounded by assault.
Jones denies charge, claims
solicitation.
Witnesses: None.
Evidence: None.
Remarks: Jones guilty as hell. Miss
Maxwell seems a nice decent kid.

Joe tossed the report aside. Boso, who disliked and distrusted Mexicans, got along well with San Rodrigo County's Negro population
which was small and concentrated in Aurora, Verdalia, and Vino...
Joe frowned, sat up in his chair, reached for the report. Boso on A
patrol? Joe was sure that he had assigned Boso the C loop: Pleasant
Grove, Panoche, Genesee, Wyman in Merced County, back along 192
to Burnett, then Panoche south to Sanchez, back to Pleasant Grove
by way of Tevis. These routes were by no means inflexible; the deputy
could alter or vary it as he saw fit. But incredible that Boso could have
strayed clear across the county to Vino! Joe reached in his drawer,
brought forth the patrol schedule he had formulated with great pains.
Odd! Route A was assigned to Boso over the week-end. Joe rubbed
his chin. A mistake somewhere. An almost imperceptible blue on the
paper engaged his attention. He looked closely, then brought out a
magnifying glass and looked again. Erasure. The names of Boso and
Gonzales had been typed, then erased and switched. Boso originally
had been assigned C loop, Gonzales A loop. Then for some reason the
patrols were reversed. Now, why in the world would Mrs. Rostvolt do
a thing like that? Joe reached for the telephone — contravention of his
instructions — then paused, drew back his hand, sat thinking. A curious circumstance. It could not have been purposeless. As he thought
back, it seemed as if Ben Boso had drawn C patrol only rarely. Not
since the time he had learned of a big cock-fight on Crow Hill Ranch,
near Sanchez. Ben Boso, who disliked and distrusted Mexicans,

despised cock-fights. Appearing quietly on the scene he had removed the valves from the front tires of all the parked cars, then had radioed for reinforcements. The raid had resulted in twenty-two arrests, confiscation of many cocks and much equipment. Boso's popularity with Mexican sport-lovers descended to a new low. Since that occasion Ben Boso usually drove Patrol A, B or D.

Now, the first time Joe had assigned him Patrol C, lo and behold! an erasure and Boso was back on Patrol A.

Very odd, thought Joe. Very odd indeed. One thing was sure. If a big cock-fight had been scheduled for Saturday night, the promoters would be far happier with Lew Gonzales in the neighborhood.

Joe reached for the phone book, ascertained the number of the *Nuevos del Valley*, a small Spanish language newspaper edited and printed in Panoche. He dialed the number; a female voice responded. Joe asked for and was connected with Leo Salazar, owner and editor.

"Leo, this is Sheriff Joe Bain."

"Hello, Joe," said Salazar courteously. "How are you?"

"Fine. I want you to do me a little favor, in the line of information."

"Yes?" Salazar's voice became cautious.

"First off I want to mention that this is entirely unofficial. Hold the line just a minute." Joe went to the door, looked across into the outer office. Mrs. Rostvolt was busy typing. "I want to know, just in confidence, if there was a big cock-fight last Saturday night?"

Salazar hesitated five seconds. "Why do you want to know, Joe?"

"I can't explain over the phone. It's something unconnected with the cock-fight itself."

Salazar said uncomfortably, "I don't like to make trouble, Joe. That's not my way. I just want to run my paper and maybe make a little money, and any little gossip I hear, I keep to myself."

"There won't be any trouble," said Joe. "Not for anyone in Panoche. To be honest with you, Leo, I'm checking up on something."

"Well — I heard there was a few little bouts going on. Not in Panoche. Out toward Burnett."

"I see. Pretty big affair, eh?"

"Well — yes. But please don't let on I told you. My name would be mud."

"Don't worry about that, Leo. I've forgotten I'm talking to you right now. Who was promoting this cock-fight?"

Salazar's voice became even more uneasy. "Now, that's something I don't like to say, Joe. I don't know for sure —"

"Let me guess. Rainaldo Gomez?"

"I don't like to say, Joe."

"Don't worry, Leo. Nobody knows I'm talking to you, and I guarantee there won't be any trouble. Not this time. I'm interested in something else entirely. It was Gomez, then?"

"No," said Salazar in a despondent voice. "A guy called Tony Aguilar. Works at the Valley Bloom packing shed in Burnett. That's what I heard, but don't say nothing. I'm just telling you because I hate the dirty things myself."

"Don't worry, Leo. Nothing will rub off on you."

Joe jumped to his feet, glad for the opportunity to leave the office. He looked into the outer office. "I'll be out a couple hours," he told Mrs. Rostvolt in a carefully neutral voice.

Mrs. Rostvolt nodded. Joe spoke to the radio despatcher, then went out into the hot sunlight.

He drove east out of town by Highway 198. Alfalfa fields radiated dark green light; white-washed barns stood sharp against the dark blue summer sky. He crossed a line of tawny hills, and came down into Panoche, a town which Joe disliked. The streets were over-wide, the houses and buildings small, drab, sun-scorched. There were a great number of eucalyptus and pepper trees, a few date-palms on the grounds of Hotel Panoche. Joe drove through town, continued on into the flatlands of the valley, presently entered Burnett. This was a town about half the size of Panoche, deriving its livelihood from apricot, peach, and fig orchards. Joe found the Valley Bloom packing shed, parked, climbed up on the battered loading dock, which was stacked with lug boxes full of peaches. Inside the shed the peaches were culled, graded, packed by long lines of women. Joe spoke to one of the laborers. "Which is Tony Aguilar?"

"That's him down at the end in a blue shirt."

Tony Aguilar was a handsome young man with a crop of lustrous dark ringlets. His eyes were bright and restless; his skin olive. His blue shirt had the two top buttons stylishly open. He wore a wristwatch with a gold band, a diamond ring. Joe asked, "You're Tony Aguilar?"

"That's me." Tony Aguilar spoke with a pronounced accent. His manner was both insolent and respectful.

"I'm Sheriff Joe Bain."

"I know you. What you want with me?"

"You know what, Tony."

Tony Aguilar's eyes widened in ingenuous astonishment. "No, Sheriff, I don't know. I don't do nothing!"

"I'm talking about cock-fighting. In this county cock-fighting is against the law."

"Sure. I know that."

"Then, how come you violate the law?"

Tony Aguilar shook his head in total incomprehension.

"You know something? I could put you away for six months. Maybe a year."

"I don't know why, Sheriff. I keep my nose clean. I don't do nothing wrong."

Joe laughed. "I think you better come with me. I'm taking you to jail."

Tony Aguilar shrugged hopelessly, his mouth sagging.

Joe looked up and down the dock. "What kind of a season they having this year?"

"Oh — pretty good." Tony Aguilar's eyes were liquid; his mouth was curled in a sulky pout.

"How much you give Mrs. Rostvolt?" Joe asked casually. "Because it was money wasted."

"I don't know what you talking about."

Joe rubbed his chin, pretended to consider. "Six months in jail — you'd be out sometime after the first of next year. If you drew a year, they'd send you to San Quentin. How would you like that?"

"Not so good, Sheriff."

"Well, I don't really want to put you away, if you don't pull a stunt like Saturday night again."

Tony Aguilar licked his lips, and finally decided that silence was the safest course.

"Just between you and me," said Joe, "how much did you slip Mrs. Rostvolt? Nobody gets in trouble, but I want to find out what's going on."

"So you take the money yourself?" asked Tony Aguilar with a rush of despairing bravado.

Joe shook his head. "I don't want crooked money. In fact, this kind of deal won't happen again, because I'm going to fire Mrs. Rostvolt."

"Mrs. Rostvolt," mused Tony Aguilar, the bland innocence of his voice accentuated by his accent. "I don't know her."

"Look, Tony, let's not fool around," said Joe. "If you don't come clean I'm going to lock you up till your hair falls out. Then I'm going to tell Judge Murdock to ship you back to Chihuahua for a no-good conniving Mexican —"

"I ain't no wetback. You can't ship me nowhere."

"Maybe I can, maybe I can't. I can sure check into your family. In fact, I might just sic Ben Boso on you."

"What do you do if I tell you?"

"So far as you're concerned — nothing. Today I just want information."

"Okay. I trust you. I give her twenty bucks, I tell her keep Boso off my back. That man, he's one tough pigeon."

Joe nodded. "Twenty bucks."

"Yes, sir. Twenty bucks."

"I guess I don't need to tell you not to pull a stunt like that again. You know where bribing a law officer can take you?"

"I didn't mean nothing wrong."

"It'll take you about a hundred miles north, to a room overlooking the bay. Good old Q."

Tony Aguilar smiled a queasy sick smile.

"One more thing," said Joe. "Are you a citizen?"

"Sure I'm a citizen."

"Well, there's an election coming up. Don't forget to vote for Joe Bain. Any friends you have, tell 'em to vote for Joe Bain. That guy Lee Gervase — he wouldn't listen to reason. He'd lock you up whether you played ball or not."

"Okay, Sheriff. I pass the word."

"No more cock-fights, I'm warning you. This is going to be a cock-fightless county, if I have to put Ben Boso on permanent cock-fight detail."

"Okay, Sheriff, I hear you."

Joe drove back to Pleasant Grove. The obvious thing to do was fire Mrs. Rostvolt. And yet — he winced to think of what would happen. He'd have to break in a new clerk, which meant spending the next week in the front office. Better wait till after the election. Or at least until he could see how things were going to come out. But in the meantime...

Sitting in his office, he printed a label:

SPCA FUND

HELP THE SICK ROOSTERS
WOUNDED IN SATURDAY-NIGHT COCK FIGHTING.

He fixed the label to a jar, took it out into the front office, put it on Mrs. Rostvolt's desk. "Care to contribute, Mrs. Rostvolt?"

Mrs. Rostvolt's eyes widened, her rosebud mouth worked in and out.

"About twenty bucks should do it."

"Twenty dollars!" exclaimed Mrs. Rostvolt in an uncertain voice. "I can't afford twenty dollars!"

Joe shook his head sadly. "I thought maybe you had a spare twenty... Well, I'll leave this here, in case you feel like contributing."

He returned to his office, Mrs. Rostvolt's eyes probing his back. A few minutes later he looked across the hall, to find Mrs. Rostvolt engaged in a telephone conversation. Joe watched a moment. Mrs. Rostvolt seemed angry and tense. Joe decided he had made a mistake telling Tony Aguilar that he planned to fire Mrs. Rostvolt. There was no point tipping one's hand. But too late to worry now.

He went back to his office, picked up the Sunday edition of the Pleasant Grove *Messenger*, which he had not yet seen. On the front page of the second section a headline caught his eye.

CAMPAIGN FOR SHERIFF'S OFFICE HEATS UP
Lee Gervase Stresses Need for New Methods

There was no mystery as to whose side Howard Griselda was on, thought Joe sourly. He read the article. It seemed that on Saturday night Lee Gervase had spoken at a meeting of the Pleasant Grove Optimists'

Club. He had minced no words in attacking the "inefficient, slovenly, and corrupt" policies of Sheriff Ernest Cucchinello. "Normally I wouldn't dream of denigrating the memory of a dead man, but a man's policies don't necessarily die with the man. I want to change all this. San Rodrigo County deserves, along with the proposed new Courthouse and Administrative Center, an equally modern Sheriff's Office. I say, let's take the step from the horse-and-buggy age into the space age!" The speech was greeted with applause, noted the article. Joe flung the paper toward the wastebasket, and sat brooding. Something had to be done; counter-action must be taken.

Joe jumped to his feet, went out to his car, drove north to Aurora, parked in front of the building which housed the Aurora *Sun*. The editor, whom Joe knew slightly, was Henry Liggett, a small, sandy-haired Scot, reputedly something of a free-thinker.

Joe had astonishingly little difficulty in attaining his objective. In fact, Henry Liggett had already made up his mind to oppose Lee Gervase. Sitting back in his chair, prodding the air with the stem of his pipe, he said, "Mind you, I like things run right, and old Cucchinello was something of a crook — but I can't abide these slick young public-relations experts, with their ideas for tearing down the old and putting in the new. They want to make us another Santa Clara County, with the housing tracts everywhere you look, crowding out the orchards and fields. I like the peace and quiet, I like old things. I don't want any confounded fandangle renovations."

Joe rose to his feet. "I guess I don't need to tell you that I'm not interested in plunder. I plan to run a clean office; in fact, I've already stopped off a couple little tricks. God knows how many more I'll find."

Liggett nodded without interest. "I'm glad to hear it. You're a Marblestone man, you say?"

"That's right. Born in a shack halfway up Castle Mountain."

"You probably know this man. Died last night." Liggett pushed a galley-proof toward Joe.

Joe read, read again. "Yes," he said in a soft voice. "I knew him... Strange."

"Happens all the time. I won't touch the things myself."

Joe once more read the proof:

POISON MUSHROOMS KILL
MARBLESTONE PIONEER

Charles Blankenship, 75, a native of Marblestone, last night died in St. Luke's Hospital at Pleasant Grove after eating a meal of poisonous mushrooms. He is survived by his widow, Mrs. Metty Blankenship. There were no children.

Chapter IX

Joe found Metty Blankenship less overcome by emotion than he had expected, though her eyes were red-rimmed with weeping. She wore black and seemed more dumpy and taffy-colored than ever. She sat in a rocking chair in the front room while her sister Dora Hobius and a neighbor Clara Colmer worked in the bedroom, packing Charley's clothes into cardboard boxes. "I'm being practical," she told Joe. "The longer I wait the harder it'll be. I'm giving all his clothes to the Salvation Army. I'm selling his watch and his stick-pins — he wouldn't want them to go to Walt, which is where they'd end up. I don't know what to do with his magazines. It seems a shame to give them away. You know he had every *Reader's Digest* that was ever printed. He kept them for reference, but I don't believe he ever looked into a single one a second time."

Joe finally was able to break into the conversation. "Exactly what happened, Mrs. Blankenship?"

Metty Blankenship stared at him uncomprehendingly. "What happened when? You mean about the mushrooms?"

"Yes."

"I couldn't say. They looked to be lovely mushrooms. I guess I'm lucky with my gall bladder after all, because I can't eat anything fried in fat or butter."

"Did someone give you the mushrooms?"

"Oh my no. Charley picked them himself. They'd come up among our pansies."

"He picked them yesterday morning?"

"That's right. And fried them for his lunch. I can't understand how he could have been so careless."

"Would you show me exactly where he picked them?"

Mrs. Blankenship pointed through the window. "Just at the edge of the lawn, among those Purple Emperors."

"Were you with him when he picked them?"

"No. I looked out the window, and at first I wondered what they were. Looked like scraps of paper. Then I pointed them out to Charley and he went out to pick them; he was ever so fond of mushrooms."

"That's something I can't understand. All these years he's been picking mushrooms. You'd think he'd know a toadstool when he saw one."

Mrs. Blankenship shook her head. "It's something I don't try to understand; I don't question the ways of the Lord."

Joe put on a discreet and confidential expression. "Maybe I shouldn't ask you this — but how are you fixed financially?"

Metty Blankenship blinked her protuberant blue eyes. "I'll manage well enough. We make a nice bit from the cherries. I'll have Charley's life insurance, and we had money put by. So, thank the Lord, I'm not concerned about money."

"I'm glad to hear that."

Into the room came Dora Hobius. Joe rose to his feet. Dora was considerably younger than Metty: a woman of medium height, with fuzzy gray hair, Metty's protuberant eyes, something of the foxy concavity at the jaw and cheek which showed itself more noticeably in Walt. Joe went to the door, then paused and turned once more to the two women. "Do you still have the stem-ends and peelings from the mushrooms?"

"They'd be in the garbage." Metty gave a little moan and a shudder. "I couldn't touch them! I just couldn't."

Joe requested and secured permission to examine the garbage. He turned it out upon the ground, then replaced everything other than mushroom peelings and stems: cans, grapefruit rinds, eggshells, bones, and so secured a dozen sections of stem, cut cleanly at either end, together with a handful of peelings.

In the front garden he made a careful inspection of the pansy bed, and presently thought to find indentations in the loam. Probing underneath, he brought up four stubs. There should be more, but perhaps they had come up with the stems.

He returned inside and found Mrs. Blankenship in the kitchen drinking tea with her sister. Mrs. Colmer had departed. Joe asked, "Do you find mushrooms in the pansy bed very often?"

"I can't say as I'd noticed any before."

"Mr. Blankenship was fond of mushrooms?"

"Oh dear yes, they were one of his favorite dishes."

"Was this well known?"

Metty Blankenship looked at him inquiringly, with the beginnings of resentment. Joe said hastily, "I know my questions are a trial, but in case of sudden death it's my business to ask all kinds of questions."

"I just don't see where they're leading," said Metty.

Joe had no real notion himself. But it seemed strange that Charley Blankenship should die so soon after Bus Hacker, and by accident.

"Well?" Mrs. Blankenship's eyes were hard and sharp.

"I guess that's all, Mrs. Blankenship."

Joe drove to the hospital, where he consulted the physician who had attended the last hours of Charles Blankenship. There was no question, he was assured, but what Mr. Blankenship had died as a result of eating poison mushrooms: the *amanita phalloides*, to be precise. As for the fact that Charles Blankenship had picked, cooked and consumed mushrooms all his life — well, in a case of this sort, the first mistake was the last. The toxic principle in the Amanita was extremely powerful: a taste could kill a weak or aged man, and Charles Blankenship had been both.

"Could the effects of any other poison be mistaken for those of Amanita poisoning?"

"Certainly — but why look further?"

"If the case came to court, you could swear he died of eating an Amanita mushroom?"

"Well — the diversity of symptoms for any given poison is surprising."

Joe nodded sagely, and arranged that the contents of Charles Blankenship's stomach be reserved for analysis.

The report from the state laboratory reached him the following day. Charles Blankenship had died of Amanita poisoning. There was no trace of any other lethal principle. The stems and peelings he had sent in were from the common edible mushroom *agaricus campestris*. Stomach contents tested positive for phallin, but the actual substance of the Amanita mushroom itself could not be distinguished in the masticated pulp.

Joe sat brooding. Of the five witnesses against Ausley Wyett, two had died within the week — accidentally.

Accidentally?

The word was open to speculation.

How Bus Hacker could have been killed — purposely killed — was a puzzle. Joe had a glimmer or two of an idea — but unluckily he had no way to verify his speculations: the house had burned to the ground.

The case of Charley Blankenship seemed equally straightforward. Blankenship had picked and cooked the mushrooms himself. Suppose Metty had covertly dropped a handful of chopped Amanita into his pan of mushrooms? Possible — but extremely unlikely. Metty Blankenship did not appear overcome with grief. She evidently expected to rejoin Charley in the hereafter, and perhaps intended to enjoy the intervening Charley-less years to the fullest extent.

Joe drove out to Marblestone. Summer heat, smelling of bleached hay, pressed down upon Fox Valley. He parked in front of Fritz's General Store, where the big oak created a dark puddle of relative coolness, went inside to find Fritz leaning on the counter reading a newspaper. Joe went to the refrigerator, brought out a couple bottles of root-beer, tossed two dimes on the counter. "Have a drink on me, Fritz."

Fritz removed the caps. "Happy days."

Joe took a pull at his bottle. "Just between you and me, Fritz, what do you make of all this sudden death?"

Fritz looked blandly at the ceiling. "You mean Charley Blankenship so close to Bus Hacker?"

"Correct."

"Well — I don't have any ideas myself. Some of the town fellers think it's strange happening so soon after Ausley Wyett gets out."

Joe nodded slowly, as if Fritz had uttered a hitherto obscure truth. "Anything else?"

Fritz considered. "Nothing worth repeating. A lot of wild talk. Some want to run Ausley Wyett out of town."

"That's no great surprise. So long as they don't try it." Joe tilted the bottle of root-beer. "Where does Oliver Viera live?"

"Well — it's hard to describe. You go up Quarry Road about a mile, then there's a little side road that turns in and follows along the ravine. Oliver's got a nice new house about two hundred yards in along the side road."

"I know about where it is. Oliver must be doing pretty well."

"As well as anyone around these parts."

"I think I'll go call on him."

"Better telephone first. Here, I'll call him for you." Fritz went to the telephone, spoke, returned to Joe. "He's home, and he'll be expecting you."

Quarry Road, after passing the Community Center, slanted behind the cemetery and off across a dry meadow dotted with oaks. At the foot of the hills it crossed Candelara Creek, swung up the hillside through a copse of eucalyptus, to come out on a wide, slowly rising plateau. Across the canyon, on land belonging to Ausley Wyett, could be seen the quarry from which the road derived its name: a dull salmon-colored scar streaked with brown, gray and the black-green of wild holly and blackberry bushes. A mile beyond, Joe came to the side road Fritz had mentioned, marked by a fancy black and silver mailbox.

Oliver Viera's house was an ostentatious structure of redwood and stone and glass, poised on the edge of the ravine, the deck cantilevered out into space with a view far down into Fox Valley.

As Joe came up the flagstone path, the door opened and Oliver Viera appeared in the doorway. He raised his plump arm. "Hi Joe! Come along in."

Joe paused, looked at the house. "Quite a place you got here, Oliver."

"It's not finished yet, but it's livable. Come on in. I don't know whether you know my wife or not."

Joe stepped into the house. Connie Viera, like Oliver, was dark and plump, and there was an indeterminate number of small dark children scuttling, creeping, crawling and running back and forth across the gleaming hardwood floors.

At Oliver's behest, Joe gingerly settled into an oddly-shaped chair which proved to be not quite so uncomfortable as it looked.

"I never expected to find a place like this up Quarry Road," said Joe. "The newest house in these parts, as I remember, was Mrs. Sullivan's pink stucco house with the big window looking out on the lawn."

Oliver made a deprecatory gesture. "I drew up the plans myself, on the order of some houses I saw in one of the magazines."

"You sure did a good job."

"It's not quite finished yet. I was my own contractor, and I've still got a few details to finish. Come on outside." He pushed back the sliding doors; Joe rose from the chair, stepped out on the deck. At the far end were a drop cloth, a ladder, several buckets, where Oliver had been painting the redwood fascia along the edge of the roof. "That's what I mean," said Oliver. "I plug away, a little bit every day. About the only exercise I get nowadays." He pointed down the valley. "Look. Way off yonder. See that little speck of white? That's the Methodist church in Marblestone."

"It's a fine view."

"Anytime you feel like moving back to the old town, I'll fix you up with something just as nice. In fact there's another property just up the road, got a little house on and everything. He's asking fifteen thousand, but I could get it for less."

"Not just now." Joe looked down into the canyon, where Candelara Creek ran between round gray boulders. "You ought to throw a dam across, and you'd have a big lake right in your front yard."

"I thought of it," said Oliver, "but there's a problem." He nodded to the opposite side of the ravine, about a hundred yards distant. "I don't control the other bank."

"Who does?"

"It's part of the Wyett place."

"Why don't you talk to Ausley? He might go for the idea."

Oliver pursed his lips dubiously. "I'm not sure I care to get too chummy with Ausley. Not after the letter." He darted Joe a quick sidelong glance. "It seems strange, Bus Hacker and Charley Blankenship dying so close together."

"That's what I was thinking," said Joe. "I came up here to discuss the subject."

Oliver laughed nervously, ran his fingers through his shock of black hair. "I can't think of much to discuss — unless I get killed somehow or other. Then it'll be too late."

"Not if I can help it," said Joe. "Specifically I want you to be careful about situations where you might get hurt accidentally. For instance, there's some steep slopes on Quarry Road. Every time you go out give your brakes a quick test."

Oliver smiled tremulously. "You're kidding me."

"I'm not kidding. I'm suggesting that you be real careful of accidents until this business blows over."

Oliver stared blankly off into the sky. "I can't imagine Ausley, or anyone else, holding a grudge against me. I've never done anybody wrong in my whole life. Not even Ausley. I just told the truth."

"That might be enough."

Oliver laughed. "Come now, Joe. After all, it's been sixteen years."

"Sixteen years in jail."

"You really think that Ausley is responsible for Bus Hacker and Charley Blankenship dying?"

Joe considered. "Let's say I'm not completely satisfied that the deaths were accidental. There were funny circumstances in both cases. I'll also say this. I spoke to Ausley the other night, and he didn't act like a guilty man. But you never know."

"I tell you what I'm going to do," said Oliver decisively. "I'm going to see Ausley about building that dam. It would be good for him as well as me. We could get a government loan without any trouble, and then we'd both have a nice little lake here, for fishing, swimming, irrigation."

"What's the dam got to do with accidents?"

"I want to see how he acts. I can tell when a man is plotting against me. I run into it all the time in the real-estate business."

Joe turned away from the rail. "Well, I just wanted to warn you."

"Thanks, Joe. I'll take care. Not that I expect any trouble."

Joe returned to Marblestone, but instead of entering town he turned right along Destin Road. He passed the Blankenship cherry orchard, the ramshackle Wyett cabin, continued up Destin Lane to the Destin house.

The two Destin girls were sitting in a lawn swing at the far side of a cool lawn; both wore white shorts and white T-shirts; both looked clean and freshly laundered and watched Joe go to the front door with expressions of innocent hauteur.

Mrs. Destin, the former May McAllister, opened the door.

"Remember me?"

"*Joe!*" May Destin laughed in delight and excitement. She took two quick steps forward, threw her arms around Joe's neck, kissed him resoundingly. "I'm so surprised to see you!"

"It's been quite a while." He cautiously disengaged himself, looked her over. "You haven't changed much. A few more curves."

"Curves — hah! Fat! Be honest! Now you haven't changed at all, you still have that devilish look —"

"Come now, May. You know better than that." Joe took time to look about him. Twenty-five years before an errand had brought him into the Destin house, when he had marveled at its princely elegance. Now the house seemed less vast and palatial, but still quite definitely the product of long-established wealth. From the foyer archways opened on one hand into a vast living room with Oriental rugs and heavy old-fashioned furniture; on the other, into a walnut-paneled dining room with a chandelier hanging over a massive dining table. Joe turned back to May. "I actually came to see Cole. Where is he?"

May smiled and pouted. "He's up at the north meadow. He wants to put in a cherry orchard. The things that man thinks to keep himself distracted." She moved a half-step forward, raised her face. "Let me fix you a drink. We'll talk over old times."

Joe grinned, shook his head. "I might start wanting to revive some of those old times. That wouldn't work out."

May smiled wistfully. She looked into Joe's face and began laughing. She came another half-step closer, and put her hands on his shoulders. "You've got lipstick on your face."

Joe reached up to disengage her hands. "Maybe I better…" He became conscious of a sudden awful pressure, and looking around stared into the face of Cole Destin, who had entered through the kitchen.

"Let go of me!" yelled May Destin. "Keep your beastly hands to yourself. I'll tell my husband, he'll…Oh Cole!" May sobbed in relief. "I'm so glad you're here."

Cole stalked into the foyer. Joe foolishly brought a handkerchief out and began rubbing at his face. "Hello, Cole," he said. "Now don't get any—"

Cole Destin lashed out suddenly. Joe jumped back, but the rug slid under his feet and he fell. Cole picked him up by the back of the collar and the belt, carried him to the front door.

"Cole, listen here," said Joe. "Things aren't the way you think they are."

Cole opened the door, pitched Joe out onto the graveled path. He came out on the porch, stood looking down at Joe. From behind him came May Destin's hysterical voice. "I'm so glad you came, I've never been so scared in my life. Oh, Cole..."

Cole said in an ugly low-pitched voice, "This isn't going to end here, Bain... Sheriff Bain, I should say." He spoke with sardonic emphasis.

"Listen to me, Cole. I came here to warn you—"

"Yeah, I'll warn you. If I see you on my property again I'll shoot you. Meantime you better get yourself a good lawyer."

Joe picked himself up off the gravel, turned away. The two girls in the lawn swing watched him attentively. "What were you doing?" asked the oldest.

"Your daddy and I were playing," said Joe. He limped to his car, got in. From within the house he could hear the faint high-pitched sound of May Destin's voice. "Treacherous little slut," grated Joe. "My God, what a mess for a man to get himself into."

He drove slowly off down Destin Lane. He'd tried to put Cole Destin on the alert. If Cole wouldn't listen, it was his own fault. What was that Cole had said about a lawyer? Probably just talk. When Cole cooled off he'd surely see the folly of dragging his wife through a lot of unpleasant publicity. Joe heaved a deep rueful sigh. A man sure had to be careful, no question about that... At the intersection of Destin Lane and Mitre Canyon Road he came to a stop. There was still Willis Neff. It was his duty to talk to him, no matter how sick he was of the entire affair. He turned up Mitre Canyon Road, and presently arrived at the Neff ranch. He parked in front of the house, got out of the car, looked around the open area between barn, milk-shed, and house. There was a somnolent hush in the air. Flies buzzed in the hot dust. The pickup was gone; there was no indication that anyone was home. Joe turned to the house. It looked clean and neat; the garden bloomed with hollyhocks, roses, daisies, calendula, snapdragon…Ellie appeared behind the screen door, then came out to stand on the top step. She wore a blue and gray housedress, in which she looked completely easy and graceful. She spoke in a half-whisper. "Mother is lying down, she's not feeling well."

Joe spoke in a quiet voice. "That's too bad. But I came half to see you, and half to see your father."

Ellie looked off toward the hills. "He's off fixing a water-tank, I think." She smiled faintly. "But here I am. Would you like a cup of coffee? I only just made a fresh pot."

Joe nodded. "I sure would."

"I'll bring it out," said Ellie. "If we go in Mother will wake up. Cream? Sugar?"

"Just black."

Ellie went into the house and a moment later returned with two cups, one of which she handed to Joe, who had seated himself on the steps. She sat beside him, and turned a rather puzzled glance at his face.

Joe remembered the lipstick. He wiped his mouth on a handkerchief. "Is that better?"

"A little. Mainly you've just smeared it."

Joe sipped his coffee. "The strangest thing happened. A woman just up and flung her arms around my neck and kissed me. I didn't do a thing."

Ellie had no comment to make. Joe noticed a fishing rod leaning against the house. "Looks like your father has been fishing."

"He's getting ready to go. Every few months something comes over him and he has to go off for a few days."

"Maybe he catches a fish, maybe he comes on a deer which dies of fright and he brings that home too."

Ellie moved uncomfortably. Joe reassured her. "I can't get excited. I was raised in the back-hills. Most of the meat we ate was out-of-season venison."

Ellie said softly, "I'm always afraid the game warden will catch him."

"There's always that chance," said Joe. "When is he leaving?"

Ellie looked at him doubtfully. Joe said, "The reason I ask is that I'd like to take you to San Jose for dinner and a show, or something like that."

Ellie shook her head. "There'd be such awful trouble. You know how he is. And my mother's not feeling well."

Joe made a sympathetic sound. Then he said, "This is a personal question and maybe you won't like my asking — but does he ever mistreat you? Or your mother? Because if he does —"

Ellie shook her head quickly, and, Joe thought, with a trace of fear. "Here he comes now."

The pickup appeared from behind the barn, came to a stop. Neff jumped out, stood stock-still looking at Joe and Ellie. Then he turned on his heel, stalked into the barn.

Joe rose to his feet. "Thanks for the coffee. And don't forget: if things ever get too tough for you — let me know."

Ellie wordlessly took the cups, went inside. Joe walked over to the barn.

Neff stood at a workbench taking tools from a box, hanging them on nails. He looked around briefly as Joe came in, but continued with his work.

Joe said, "I'm here on a funny kind of errand, Mr. Neff."

"Yeah?" Neff's voice was cold.

"You remember our conversation a few days ago. Well, since then there's been two deaths. They might have both been coincidence — but I think it's my duty to warn you to be a little cautious and suspicious until I find out what's going on."

Neff turned, put his broad back against the workbench, stared at Joe with his bright blue eyes. "I'll tell you what ought to be done, and that's castrate that son of a bitch with a dull knife. If he ever talks to my women-folk again, I'll fix him so he won't talk again."

"Better be careful, Mr. Neff! It's not a good idea, making threats."

Neff warmed to his subject. "I'll tell you something else. I've heard some stories about you, and they're pretty low. I don't want you fooling around my daughter either. Might as well know it."

Joe said reasonably, "Well, I don't see how it's much concern of yours, Mr. Neff. My intentions are perfectly honorable. We're both over twenty-one."

"I don't give a damn if you're a hundred and one. You keep away from here or I'll bust your neck."

"In the first place," said Joe, "you're not man enough. In the second —"

Neff stepped forward, a grin splitting his face. He swung his big right fist, which Joe caught in the palm of his left hand. "Take it easy, Mr. Neff."

Neff, still grinning, seized him, threw him to the ground. Then he jumped forward, kicked Joe in the ribs. Joe caught the heavy boot, jerked; Neff hobbled back. Joe pulled himself to his feet. It had been a trying afternoon, with first Cole Destin ejecting him, now Neff kicking him in the ribs. Joe's resentment knew no bounds.

Neff charged forward, heavy and strong as a bull. Joe threw a pair of punches: a left to Neff's mouth, a right to his kidney. The blows seemed to hurt Neff not at all; if anything, they infuriated him even further. Once more he lurched forward, with more care. Joe chopped at him — once, twice, three times with his left, then took a terrific blow to the face which dazed him. His knees felt weak. But it wouldn't do to go down. Not out here in the barn with no onlookers to keep Neff from methodically kicking in his ribs. He backed away, keeping his left in Neff's face. Neff swung, missed. Joe put every ounce of strength into a counterpunch to Neff's jaw. Neff sat down, startled. He reached behind him, seized a pitchfork and, sitting, hurled it at Joe, who batted it aside. "Be careful, Neff!" panted Joe. "You're liable to wind up in jail for a stunt like that."

Neff bounded to his feet. He took another pitchfork, advanced slowly. Joe retreated, picked up the first pitchfork, stood on guard. Neff jabbed, Joe caught the prongs with his own fork; they strained, each trying to force aside the other's fork. Neff won, Joe's fork fell away, but instantly he brought the handle around, clouted Neff on the head, just over the ear. Blood began to spurt; Joe hit him again, harder. Neff groaned, staggered to the workbench, where he leaned back, staring at Joe.

"Want some more?" asked Joe, panting. "I'll give you all you want, you mean son of a bitch."

Neff put his hand to his head, looked dully at the blood. Joe turned away, marched to the house. Ellie peered in horror from the door. "Better go tend to your father," said Joe. "He's got a pretty sore head."

He marched to his car, drove out to the road and back down toward Fox Valley.

A mile from the Neff house he laughed harshly. "I guess I lost a couple of votes today."

He inhaled, exhaled. His ribs pained him. All in all, an unusual and trying day... He toyed with the idea of dragging Neff into jail for assault with a deadly weapon. It might be a good idea to teach Neff a lesson. Joe thought of Neff looking out from one of the cells. He grinned, then laughed. But it would make a terrible amount of work for Ellie and Mrs. Neff. Joe decided to forget the whole matter.

He continued directly on through Marblestone, and down Candelara Creek Road. The central valley opened out before him; Pleasant Grove shimmered white and gray in the afternoon sun. Joe felt calmer, as if, on leaving the mountains, he had passed into a different world.

By the time he parked behind the courthouse, his composure and dignity, sorely taxed earlier in the afternoon, had returned.

Mrs. Rostvolt looked at him with an odd expression as he entered the office: a spiteful half-smirk which irritated him immensely. Perhaps he looked disheveled. Lipstick? Surely that was gone. Mrs. Rostvolt said, "The district attorney wants you to call him."

"Put him on," said Joe. He went to his private office, slumped into his chair, picked up his phone. Presently the baritone voice of District Attorney Paul Wentzman sounded in his ear. "Sheriff?"

"Speaking."

Wentzman seemed at a loss for words. Finally he asked, "What the devil have you been up to, Joe?"

"What do you mean?"

"Cole Destin called me. He wants to press charges against you. Assault, battery, attempted rape. The works."

"I didn't think he'd go through with it," said Joe in a marveling voice. "He's pretty mad."

"There's nothing in it. The trouble is, I don't know if I can prove it."

"I'd think hard if I were you."

"The situation is this," said Joe. "His wife is a slut, and Cole probably suspects it. She made a pass at me, Cole saw it, and she began yelling blue rape. She didn't have any other choice, I'll say that much for her."

Wentzman's voice was cool. "Cole wanted to call in the state police, but I told him that wasn't necessary, that you'd be sure to appear in court."

"Certainly. Any time he wants."

"Well — I set it at ten tomorrow morning. Just a preliminary hearing, to set bail."

Joe considered a moment, then asked cautiously, "How far has this story got out?"

"I couldn't say. Griselda knows about it."

"Oh, my Lord, I better do something quick. Or my name is mud."

"I wouldn't be surprised."

Joe hung up, paced back and forth across his office. A fine how-de-do! He threw himself into his chair, reached for the phone, then changed his mind, and half-walked, half-loped the two blocks to the Pleasant Grove *Messenger*. He burst in through the door so abruptly that Amelia, the pretty young receptionist, stared at him in wonder.

"I want to see Mr. Griselda," he said. "Right now."

Amelia stepped hurriedly behind the low partition which cut off a view of the composing room. From the background came the dry clatter of a linotype machine.

Griselda himself returned. He stood in the doorway, shirt-sleeves rolled up, necktie loosened at the throat, big head thrust forward. He nodded dourly at Joe. "What can I do for you?"

"You planning to run a story about me?"

"It's going in tonight's edition."

Joe drew a deep breath. "I think we ought to talk seriously about that story. Before the damage is done."

Griselda smiled heavily. "Seems to me the damage is already done. A complaint was filed — which makes it news."

Joe said, "Can we talk in private?"

"Come into my office."

Joe followed Griselda into a room more den than office. The walls were lined with books and photographs; through the glass doors of a buffet twinkled reflections from a dozen bottles. Griselda seated himself at his desk, motioned Joe to an ancient leather chair.

Joe sat stiffly erect. "I guess we're talking about the same story."

"The head as I recall reads, *Acting Sheriff Bain Accused in Attack of Marblestone Matron.*"

"That's the story," said Joe. "I don't think it will help my prospects for election."

Griselda attempted a grim joke. "For all you know, it might get you a few votes."

"I don't want those votes," said Joe. "The situation is this. I went to the house to see Cole. He wasn't there. It so happens that May Destin was one of my old-time sweethearts and she suddenly wanted to return to the scenes of her youth. Cole came in and she put it all on me, an innocent bystander."

"It'll come out in the trial."

"Meanwhile the election has come and gone, and I'm gone too. I don't know my legal recourse, but if I were you I'd move pretty careful. Somehow I don't think there's going to be any charges made, and if the story gets printed anyway, I'll be extremely merciless."

Griselda inspected Joe under bushy eyebrows. "The complaint has been signed. That's a matter of public record."

"Whether it's true or not? You just looking for a chance to smear me, Howard?"

Griselda's heavy face went maroon. "You know me better than that. As I said before, the complaint has been signed — and it's news."

Joe said, "I want to make a phone call, and I want you to listen in. Can you do that?"

Griselda considered, then nodded with poor grace. "I don't like the idea, but I will, provided you mention the fact that there's a witness on the line."

Joe shook his head. "That wouldn't work. I want you to listen only to convince yourself the whole thing is phony."

"Very well," growled Griselda. "Make your call from that phone. I'll listen from the front office."

Joe looked in the phone book, dialled. The phone rang. Twice, three times. Joe's heart sank. Then May answered. Joe sighed. "This is Joe Bain."

May gave a little shuddery sob. "Oh, Joe. I don't know what to say."

"I don't care much what you say. What counts is, what are you going to do?"

"I don't know."

"You know that Cole came ramming into town and pulled the roof down around my ears?"

"Yes." May's voice was low and hopeless. "But what could I do? I lost my head, I suppose. But it was all I could think of. Self-preservation, I guess. I know I'm utterly silly."

" 'Silly'? That's one word for it. Anyway, you've got to get Cole to back away. I don't care how you do it, but I can't stand the publicity. I'm running for Sheriff."

May began to whimper. "You don't know Cole. He's so strait-laced it's terrible."

"It'll be worse if the case comes to court. Because I won't take it lying down."

May said simply, "I don't see what you can do. It's your word against mine."

"It'll be more than that in the courtroom. First of all, you might as well realize it'll be a juicy case. Everybody you know will be in court. I'll call up your two little girls and ask if you yelled or screamed. They'll say no, we just heard Mama laughing. In fact they might have seen the thing just as it happened. I'll call Reverend Dunkwiler, and he'll testify as to how he caught us under the church when we were supposed to be in Sunday school. I'll call Walt Hobius to testify how you wanted me to marry you, pretending you were pregnant. I'll get in some experts in lipstick smears. When a man attacks a woman, she don't generally plant a nice neat print across his mouth. Another thing: it just plain doesn't stand to reason that I'm going to make a pass at a woman when I come to see her husband, and when she can scream bloody murder to her kids. And one more thing. I'll check high and low to see what other boy-friends you got and bring them to court to testify. You see what I mean? I'm not making threats, I'm trying to show you how I'll have to defend myself."

There was silence from the other end of the line. Then a dreary voice said, "Very well. I'll make Cole stop. Somehow."

"You'd better do it fast. Because he's signed a complaint."

"I know where I can reach him. I — I think I can handle him. I'll tell him something or other. It'll be all right."

— 108 —

"I'm sorry about this, May. But it's just one of those things."

May's voice, barely a whisper, said, "You're not really a gentleman, are you, Joe?"

"I'm Sheriff first, and gentleman second. It's tough, but that's the way it goes."

May hung up.

Griselda came back into the room. He nodded heavily, not meeting Joe's eyes. "I'll kill the story...Unsavory mess."

"Nothing I brought on."

"Except maybe by the entire state of your character, your reputation, your background, and your moral nature."

"Here now, Howard. I didn't come in here for a slanging match. As far as my morals go, I'll stack them up against your man Gervase any day of the week."

"Be that as it may." Griselda made an impatient motion of his thick, hairy hand to signify that he had had enough of the interview. Joe took his leave. He walked slowly back to Montalvo Square. "That was a near thing," he told himself.

When he returned to the office, Mrs. Rostvolt eyed him speculatively. Joe told her nothing. Presently she brought him the day's correspondence for his signature. As usual she had done a masterful job. Mrs. Rostvolt, the paragon! Too bad she was such a crook. She belonged on the other side of the bars. Oh well — sufficient unto the day the evil thereof. He went home where both his mother and Miranda wondered why he seemed so irritable.

After dinner Joe's mother sat at the television and Miranda did her homework. Joe showered, then opened a can of beer and went to sit in pajamas and bathrobe on the back porch, as far from the squawk of the television as he could get.

An eventful day, in which the single agreeable element was Ellie Neff. Joe looked up into the sky where the moon, near-full, floated over the back-yard pepper tree. Thirty miles away Ellie might be looking up at the same moon...Joe slapped at a mosquito, finished his beer, and went inside. Miranda had finished her homework and was talking on the telephone. Joe opened his mouth to remonstrate, then closed it again. His mother got up to change channels. Joe went out into the kitchen, opened another can of beer, seated himself at the kitchen table. On the back of an envelope he wrote:

Unfinished Business

A. Bus Hacker.

    1. Who had watered Bus Hacker's gas tank? Why? To arrange that Hacker walk into town?

    2. Who advised Hacker of an important letter at the post office? Why? To make Hacker walk into town again?

    3. Why make Hacker walk into town?

    Possibilities:

    a. Simple prank.

    b. To cause him rage, excitement, and possible heart attack.

    c. To get at contents of safe. What in the safe was so important? Was it destroyed in fire?

Joe considered what he had written. Somebody was afraid of that safe for sure. Cole had been anxious to get into the safe. Both he and Walt Hobius had given it rough treatment. Joe could not envision any possible connection of Ausley Wyett with this business. Ausley had nothing to fear now. In spite of his tactless acts, he gave the impression of elaborate caution. And—Joe was forced to admit he had professed innocence of the original crime with great conviction.

Joe pondered the circumstances of Tissie McAllister's dreadful death. Charley Blankenship had overlooked the road to the north of the Wyett barn, Bus Hacker to the south. Blankenship testified that he had seen Tissie and later Cole Destin. Hacker testified that he had seen only Cole Destin. Cole Destin testified to seeing only Ausley and Tissie. If Ausley were innocent, he himself would have noticed any-one approaching from the hills. Either Hacker or Blankenship or both would have seen anyone crossing the fields east of the road. If Ausley was innocent, someone was lying. Joe thought it was Bus Hacker. On the morrow he would check the trial record.

He continued his notes:

B. Charley Blankenship.

    1. How could Charley Blankenship, a well-known mushroom

fancier, be induced to pick, cook and eat Amanita mushrooms? Mistake? Emphatically unlikely. No one, not even a tyro, could fail to note the Amanita's characteristic white gills.

2. *Who else would want Blankenship, as well as Hacker, dead? Ausley, perhaps. Somebody else? Why? Money? Metty Blankenship inherited on Charley Blankenship's death. The mind reeled at the idea of Metty's poisoning Charley. Where would money go if Metty had died first?*

Joe paused for a tilt of the beer can. A peculiar situation. If Ausley Wyett were responsible, Cole Destin, Willis Neff and Oliver Viera became poor insurance risks.

If Ausley were not responsible — what then? Ausley's release, the deaths of Hacker and Blankenship made a very strange coincidence in time. In connection with Viera, Cole Destin, Willis Neff, who held grudges against them?

Willis Neff had antagonized half the countryside.

Cole Destin had stepped on toes here and there. He showed no mercy when it came to extending his holdings, and tended to act like a feudal lord.

Oliver Viera had always been popular, and in all likelihood had not an enemy in the world.

Except Ausley Wyett.

Joe sat back, considered the beer can. Empty. Slowly, carefully, he opened another, and sat back, his mind roiling with a dozen speculations. Someone as clever, malicious, and mischievous as a mad ape was having the time of his life, performing murders which were not quite murders...Joe put the beer can on the table, slumped back in his chair. How, he asked himself, would I murder Bus Hacker so that he had a heart attack and Charley Blankenship so that he cooked himself some poison mushrooms? Looked at in this fashion, the situation became ridiculous...Joe pondered. Old Bus Hacker had been pretty red in the face: a symptom of electrocution. But Joe had performed the identical acts without a tingle...Joe finished his beer and went to bed, where he lay awake long hours thinking.

CHAPTER X

AT THE NORTHWEST EDGE of the county, in a region of densely wooded hills and deep valleys, was Nazareth, a religious community founded fifty years before, and maintained in as complete isolation as possible. There was no telephone service, no mail delivery, no electricity. The community educated its own children, nursed its own sick, buried its own dead, and in general lived as self-sufficient a life as possible. Needless to say, there were neither bars, theaters, bowling alleys nor soda fountains in Nazareth. The young people occasionally became restless and sought entertainment in Verdalia, to the anguish of the elders of the community.

Not far distant was the town of Vino, so named for vineyards in the surrounding hills and several famous wineries established nearby.

On Saturday evening four Nazareth lads returning home from a debauch at a Verdalia ice-cream parlor were buzzed by as many youths from Vino in a jazzed-up old car. A minor accident occurred, resulting in recriminations, threats, counter-threats and a fight. Joe got word that a full-scale rumble was brewing, since the young men of Nazareth, while meek and Christian, were also sensitive.

On Tuesday Joe drove out with Deputy Phipps, showed the official car in Vino and Nazareth, laid down the law to the first group of boys he encountered in either town. His warnings went unheeded.

Tuesday evening at dusk thirty or forty boys from Vino, ages fourteen to twenty, made a foray over the hills, and began to paint an enormous Star of David on the slope overlooking Nazareth. They were almost immediately discovered. For a few minutes indecision reigned in Nazareth; then a group of young men surged to the attack.

Joe, who had been summoned by an anxious mother in Vino, arrived about this time with three deputies, and marched dutifully up the hill. Several Negro families lived in Vino and as Joe neared the fracas, he heard the cry, "Religious boy, look out! I gonna whip yo' ass!" And the answering challenge, "Come try it, if you dare!"

Joe was struck on the back of the neck by a bunch of grapes, but even with this incentive was unable to capture any of the combatants, who fled in all directions at the sight of the police. Joe left two deputies on patrol and went home, with the certainty that the raid would undoubtedly be repeated, and perhaps become an annual event…Well, there were worse ways to let off steam. Probably did the Nazareth boys considerable good.

The next day was Wednesday. Joe, having secured twenty-five sponsors, paid the county clerk two hundred and forty dollars and made his candidacy for the office of Sheriff official. The *Messenger* made a brief mention of the Nazareth–Vino brawl, but remarked only that "the hostilities were quickly quelled." Joe sought in vain for recognition of the swift action of Sheriff Joe Bain and his deputies. On another page he noticed a story headed:

PROGRESS COUNCIL PLANS
OPEN-AIR POLITICAL RALLY

Joe learned that the San Rodrigo County Council for Progress had taken out a permit to hold a public meeting in Montalvo Square on the night of Saturday September 29. There would be musical entertainment, free doughnuts and coffee. Among the speakers would be Fred Hatch, President of the Pleasant Grove Chamber of Commerce; Henry Heilbronner, President of the County Grange; Howard Griselda, Editor and Publisher of the *Messenger*; Lee Gervase, attorney and candidate for Sheriff; Edgar H. Laumeister, Executive Secretary of the Pleasant Grove Lions Club.

Joe grimaced. "About the only celebrity not invited is the sacrificial pig, and that's me."

"What's the matter, Daddy?" asked Miranda brightly. "Indigestion?"

"I was feeling pangs of hunger," said Joe, "because it looks like hard times after the election."

"Oh now!" his mother declared. "That's probably not even nearly true!"

"I'll be out of school pretty soon," Miranda chirped. "Then we can take a trip to Mexico. Goody! I hope you get skunked, Daddy!"

"Miranda!" chided Joe's mother.

"Let her alone," said Joe gloomily. "Somebody might as well enjoy the situation."

"I'm tired of your being Sheriff anyway," said Miranda. "I want you to be a senator or a diplomat, or something real important and glamorous."

"I was a lettuce-picker once. I guess I still have the knack. We'll make out, one way or another. Miranda can go to work in the packing shed."

"Daddy! You don't mean that!"

"We got to eat."

"I'll get a job as a fashion model. Didn't you know? I'm beautiful. I've got that lean ferocious man-killing look —"

"Now, Miranda," said her grandmother. "Girls didn't talk like that in my day. They didn't even *think* things like that."

"Oh, Granny. You were just pure. Most girls weren't like you."

Joe's mother limited her response to a faint wistful smile.

Miranda hitched herself up to the table. "What's the big crime for today, Daddy?"

"Nothing very much. A drunk or two. Come to think of it, we nabbed a pick-pocket in Aurora. Old man sixty years old. Real experienced, but awful slow."

Joe's mother asked, "What in the world is going on over in Marblestone?"

Joe looked up slowly. "What did you hear? And from whom? Mrs. Henderson?"

"She visited her daughter Sunday. She says the whole town is in a turmoil over that dreadful Wyett boy."

"What did he do?" asked Miranda.

"He got sent up for murder," said Joe. "Before you were born. But I don't know. There's so much dust blowing back and forth it's hard to figure out who did what and to whom."

"Exactly what is happening?"

"Well, Ausley got out of jail, and right away the five main witnesses against him got notifications from Ausley. It's hard to figure what he had in mind. You could read the letters as threats, as requests for cooperation, as almost anything. It might have been just another one of Ausley's mad schemes. Anyway these five people weren't too happy to get these letters. They figured Ausley was putting pressure on them. Especially as right away two of them died."

Miranda's mouth made a scarlet O, while Joe's mother *t'chk-t'chk-t'chked*.

Miranda asked, "So now everyone is wondering who's next?"

"Exactly."

"And what does Ausley Wyett say?"

"He says he doesn't know what all the fuss is about."

"And who *will* be next?"

"Well," said Joe, "there's Oliver Viera, and Cole Destin, and Willis Neff. I warned them all. Willis Neff beat hell out of me, Cole Destin tried to put me in jail, Oliver Viera wanted to sell me a house. I'd say they were running neck and neck."

On Thursday morning Joe served a subpoena in Mulberry, and was late arriving at the office. He bade Mrs. Rostvolt a civil good-morning, received a nod and a smile in return. The smile disturbed him. "Now what?" he asked himself. "What can she know that I don't?"

For the remainder of the morning he was tied up in the office talking to Milo Gentry, the oldest and most tiresome of the county supervisors. Joe was on pins and needles during the entire conversation. If he eased Mr. Gentry out on the plea of urgent business, Mr. Gentry might become waspish and add his influence to the weight against him. If Joe relaxed, met Mr. Gentry and his long-winded vagaries halfway, Mr. Gentry might be just perverse enough to wonder if this were all Joe did to earn his money.

Milo Gentry finally took an amiable departure. Joe decided to eat a quick lunch and run out to Marblestone. He announced his plans to Mrs. Rostvolt, who nodded blandly. Joe set out for Marblestone in a troubled frame of mind. He disliked unsolved problems, and he had come upon a real puzzler. Mrs. Rostvolt must know that her days are numbered; still she behaved as if she owned the office…

Coming into Marblestone he noticed Oliver Viera's white Ford convertible parked under the sign *Fox Valley Realty*. Joe turned off on the road, parked beside the Ford. From the direction of town came a gray GM pickup which turned into Walt Hobius' service station. Willis Neff alighted; Walt came unsmilingly from the lube shed, and began to fill the gas tank. Neff rolled a tire from the front compartment, gave Walt curt instructions. Walt nodded glumly, his mouth an inverted V. Joe noted that Neff wore clothes different from his usual working gear: brown slacks, black shoes, a red and blue plaid shirt.

Joe sauntered across the road. Neff saw him, bent over the water fountain for a drink. Joe glanced into the bed of the pickup. The rack for the spare tire was empty. There were a sleeping bag, a Coleman stove, a cardboard box of groceries, a shovel, an axe. Joe went to look into the driver's compartment. On the seat were a creel, a sectional fishing rod, a rifle.

Neff came around the car. "Hello, Mr. Neff," said Joe. "Looks like you're going fishing."

"Might be," Neff grunted.

"Might be you were going to do some hunting likewise."

"Hard to say," answered Neff.

"Deer seem to be out of season," mused Joe. "It would certainly be a shame if the game warden caught you making a silly mistake."

"Don't worry, if you're worrying," said Neff with a savage grin. "Where I go there aren't any game wardens."

"I'm glad to hear that," said Joe, "for your family's sake."

"Leave my family out of the conversation, unless you'd like another tussle."

"Don't push your luck." Joe walked back across the street to Oliver Viera's office. The door was open, Joe walked in. Oliver looked up from a desk where he sat painfully typing a small card. "Hi, Joe. Just a second, let me finish this blasted description."

Joe went to stand by the window and watched as Walt washed Neff's windshield, checked the oil, accepted money, rendered change, all with the same surly expression: Walt had also felt the weight of Neff's fists.

Oliver rolled the card from the typewriter, swung toward Joe. "Well, Joe, what's new?"

"Nothing much," said Joe. He watched Neff get into his car, make a U-turn and drive back the way he had come.

"There goes a real hard man," said Joe.

"Yep," said Oliver. "As my grandmother used to say in Spanish, even the flies won't land on him."

"I can't figure him out," said Joe. "He's probably well off — not rich, but comfortable; he's got a nice ranch, nice wife, nice daughter; he's got his health —"

"And a nice daughter."

"— probably doesn't have to work too hard, goes fishing when he feels like it —"

"And a nice daughter."

"Oliver," said Joe. "You're a lecherous rascal, and a married man, to boot. I was wanting to ask you about Ausley. Did you see him?"

Oliver's round face creased in puzzlement. "See Ausley? Why do I want to see Ausley?"

"About that dam. You said it had to be anchored on his property."

"Oh, the dam. I forgot about that. No, I haven't seen him. But it's a good idea." On rare occasions, when Oliver was excited or forgetful or careless, a musical Mexican lilt came into his voice. "Maybe I'm scared, Joe, I don't know. Bus Hacker and Charley Blankenship had accidents — why not me too?"

"Which reminds me," said Joe thoughtfully, "something I wanted to ask you. Outside of Ausley, is there anyone around here who might have a grudge against you?"

Oliver's expressive eyebrows rose to his hair-line. He shook his head. "I don't think so. Nobody's mad at me. I never even had a fight with Neff, like everybody else in town."

"What about your business? Are you stepping on anybody's toes?"

Oliver shrugged. "You can't take money from a man without hurting his feelings. Did I tell you Cole wanted me to sound Ausley out about selling?"

"You told me Ausley wasn't selling."

"That's right. He must be worth a pretty penny, old Ausley. Sitting in jail so long."

"It's a wonder more people don't try it." Joe went to the door. "I think I'll drive up, say hello to Ausley. If you like, I'll pass the word that you want to see him."

"Okay, Joe. Tell him I'll be down here all day today, and maybe part of tonight. My sister-in-law is visiting; there's too much noise at home."

But when Joe drove out to the Wyett ranch there was no sign of Ausley's old station wagon, and Oliver's message went undelivered.

Joe cruised aimlessly up Mitre Canyon Road, until he realized that his aimless cruising was bringing him closer and closer to the Neff ranch, whereupon he turned around and drove back. When he wanted to see Ellie he didn't need to wait till Neff had taken himself off the premises.

Sometime between Wednesday evening and Thursday morning Willis Neff met his death. The world at large knew nothing of the occurrence until Saturday morning, when an old pensioner named Theodore Hill came upon Neff's body in an open glade high in the Santa Lucia Mountains of Monterey County. Neff had been shot through the head, and lay about a hundred feet from his pickup.

Theodore Hill notified Sheriff Edward Mulligan at Salinas, who sent two deputies to the scene, along with the coroner.

From the fact that the bullet had entered Neff's head but had not emerged, the investigators deduced that the shot had come from a distance. They cast about and on a nearby ridge found a new red cap, of the type worn by deer-hunters, a half-used folder of matches, bearing the advertising of the Top Hat Bar and Restaurant in San Francisco, a spent .30-30 cartridge. The deputies and the coroner were in angry agreement. Some irresponsible city-bred hunter had decided to bag an out-of-season deer, and Willis Neff was the first moving object to cross his sights: a hunting accident.

The coroner set the time of death provisionally at 2 a.m. Thursday morning plus or minus four hours. In short, so he declared, Neff might have died at any time from ten o'clock Wednesday night to six o'clock Thursday morning.

At the request of Sheriff Joe Bain of San Rodrigo County, the contents of Neff's stomach were investigated with a view to pinpointing the hour of death more exactly. It was found that Neff had ingested a meal of bacon and eggs very shortly before his death.

This fact went to suggest that Neff had been killed at dawn Thursday morning, since beside Neff's pickup a gasoline stove had been set up, on which a meal of bacon and eggs might well have been cooked.

The deer-hunter from San Francisco was ordered to step forward and reveal himself—a demand no one expected to be obeyed.

Joe Bain was happy he did not have to search for the hypothetical deer-hunter. He had problems enough of his own.

Chapter XI

On Sunday morning it became Joe's unpleasant duty to notify Mrs. Neff and Ellie of Willis Neff's death. Driving through Marblestone he noticed the cars parked along Holy Row, and it occurred to him that Ellie and Mrs. Neff might be at church. Turning up Quarry Road he saw Ausley Wyett's old station wagon near the Baptist church. "Hmmf," said Joe to himself. He parked in front of the church, walked up the steps into the vestry. From within issued the Reverend Dunkwiler's voice, and Joe was whisked twenty years into the past. Everything even smelled the same: warm varnish, stale flowers, old hymnals, dry wood, Sunday clothes. There weren't too many changes. Joe looked into the nave. Ellie and Mrs. Neff were not instantly visible, but there sat Ausley Wyett, primly erect in one of the back pews, wearing his new brown suit with a flowing blue satin tie. Joe signaled a boy in the row behind him, pointed. The boy prodded Ausley, indicated Joe. Joe beckoned. With exaggerated delicacy Ausley tiptoed out into the vestry. Joe took him outside, into the glare of sunlight.

"The Neffs in there?" Joe asked casually.

"No," said Ausley. "They didn't come."

"You're sure?"

"Certain sure."

Joe nodded heavily. "Well, Ausley, what about it?"

Ausley grinned weakly. "What about what?"

"Neff is dead."

"Neff? Willis Neff?" Ausley's demonstration of astonishment was convincing. "What happened to him?"

"You don't know?"

"I have no idea, Joe."

"Somebody shot him."

"My goodness!...Well, I don't know what to say."

"Do you have a rifle?"

"There's my father's old gun somewhere around. I don't dare touch it, being on parole. You know that, Joe."

"So you say. Well, I'll give you a tip, Ausley. If I were you, I'd stay pretty close to home for a few days. There's going to be talk around town, and I don't want to have to cut you down out of a tree."

Ausley shook his head sadly. "People want to blame me for everything. In the old days they used to burn witches, now they got Ausley Wyett instead."

"I'm telling you for your own good. There's no sense getting people excited."

"Where did all this happen?" Ausley asked mildly.

"Up in the mountains. Over the ridge, down toward Big Sur."

Ausley massaged his chin, looked thoughtfully off into the hazy western sky. "Well, well." A new thought seemed to come to him. "Yes sir!" he said in a sprightly voice. "Yes sir!" He nodded as if in approval of his idea.

"I guess Mrs. Neff and Ellie stayed home, not having the pickup," said Joe. "I better get on up there. It's my place to bring them the news."

Ausley shook his big head in sympathy. Joe went to his car, leaving Ausley standing in the road.

Ten minutes later he turned into the Neff driveway, parked in front of the house.

Ellie came to the door, looked out through the screen, then stepped out to welcome him. The sun shone on her hair; she seemed placid and sure and at peace with herself.

"Good morning, Ellie," said Joe soberly. "Where's your mother?... No, don't go get her."

"What's wrong?"

"It's some very bad news. I know you can bear up, but I'm worried about your mother."

Ellie went pale; the muscles of her face set. "Something about my father?"

"Yes. He's been in an accident. That's what it looks like. A hunting accident."

Ellie's mouth drooped. "He's hurt — badly?"

"He's dead."

Ellie nodded slowly. "I see." She turned once more, looked toward the house. "Will you come in?"

Mrs. Neff was in the living room ironing. The radio was tuned to a program of gospel songs, and she moved the iron in time to the music.

Ellie turned down the radio. Joe awkwardly broke the news. Mrs. Neff went white, gasped, sat down in a chair, stared numbly at Joe. Then she fell to her knees, rested her elbows on the chair, bent her head. Ellie watched from the side, then slowly went to her mother, patted her head.

Joe said, "I know this is a poor time to pester you with questions, but there are a few things I'd like to find out."

Ellie nodded.

"Do you know where your father was headed?"

"He said he was going up Bull-frog Creek, at the top of Ham Valley, so he wouldn't have too far to drive. He was only going to be gone two days."

"The accident happened in Monterey County, behind Big Sur. Two hours' drive, I'd put it, or maybe even more."

Ellie said, "He hasn't been down there for years."

"I guess he changed his mind at the last minute."

"Maybe." Ellie bent over her mother, helped her into the chair. Mrs. Neff's face bore a strange rapt expression. Ellie said vaguely, "It's — it's a great shock to us." Tears suddenly appeared in her eyes, and she blinked rapidly.

"Why don't you and your mother come back into Pleasant Grove and stay at my house for a day or two until you've got accustomed to things?" asked Joe.

Ellie shook her head. "We can't leave. Not for a while. There's a boy who's doing the milking, and I help him."

"Do you have any relatives who could come stay with you?"

"No. But please don't worry, Mr. Bain; we'll be all right."

From outside came the sound of an automobile.

Ellie went to the door. Joe followed.

Ausley Wyett alighted from his station wagon, came slowly to the door. Ellie went out to stand on the porch. Ausley said in an embarrassed voice, "I just heard about your father. I want to say I'm awful sorry. He was a rough man — but he probably did what he thought was right."

"Yes," said Ellie. "Although sometimes — I don't think he cared."

"Well — that may be. But what I came mainly for was to tell you not to worry about the chores — milking and such. I'll be happy to oblige."

Joe raised his eyebrows, looked at Ellie. She smiled. "Thank you, Ausley. That's very nice of you."

Joe said sourly, "I guess I'll be going. Looks like Ausley can make himself useful for once in his life."

"I'll sure try," said Ausley.

Joe returned to Marblestone. He went into the phone booth in the Town Club, telephoned Sheriff Ed Mulligan at Salinas.

"Hello, Ed. This is Joe Bain."

"Yes, Joe."

"I'm calling about Neff — the man you found shot."

"Oh yes. Neff."

"Just between you and me, there's been some funny things happening around Marblestone, and I'm wondering if anything off-color caught your deputy's eyes."

"So far he hasn't reported anything."

"As I understand it, the body was found by a man name of Theodore Hill."

"That's right. Old codger living on his pension."

"My thinking is that Neff's death might be tied in with a case I'm working on in Marblestone. I'd like to look over the situation, if you don't object too hard. I just might catch something which ties into this other business."

"Look all you like," said Ed Mulligan. "What's the background on Neff?"

"It's a long story. I'll be glad to go into it if you've got the time."

"Well — maybe later. Unless you can just give me a bare outline."

"Let's say that Neff wasn't the most popular man in town. His shooting might have been some kind of put-up job. A fake accident."

"Hmm… Such things happen. Tell you what. I've assigned Sergeant Pallard to the case. Why don't you meet him somewhere and arrange things with him?"

"Fine. One thing I'd like to know: have you fixed the time of death?"

"Doc says after so long a time he can't be too definite. Put it sometime after midnight Wednesday, give or take a few hours… Wait. Here's a note on that. 'Contents of stomach: bacon and eggs. Died half an hour after meal.' That seems to make it Thursday morning because he'd been cooking, and his sleeping bag had been slept in."

"That gives us something to go on. Where can I meet Pallard?"

"Where are you now?"

"In Marblestone."

"You'd be coming out by Bosco Ridge, I imagine. Why not at Lupin? That's on the way for both of you."

"Fine."

"It'll be about an hour or an hour and a half."

"Suits me."

"An hour and a half, then, at Lupin."

Joe hung up the phone, stepped out of the booth into the dimness of the bar. He looked at his watch. Two o'clock. Lupin was half an hour's drive; he had an hour to kill.

The men sitting at the bar had been watching him furtively. They quieted as he approached. He knew four of the five: Shorty Olson the bartender, Art van Horn, Walt Hobius, Stub Caramino. The fifth man was a stocky sandy-haired man about thirty, with a skin the color of raw potato, and lashless red-rimmed eyes.

Joe took a seat at one end of the group, ordered a bottle of Lucky.

Stub Caramino, proprietor of the shoe-repair shop two doors down First Street, started the conversational ball rolling. "Well, Joe, what's new in the world of crime?" He was a small paunchy near-bald man, with the brown heavy-lidded gaze of a camel.

"Nothing much," said Joe. "Every day it's different, every day it's the same. So many fighting drunks, so many chicken thieves, so many clouted cars. The other night we had a war going over in Nazareth. That bit in the Bible about turning the other cheek didn't even slow 'em down."

"Seems to me," said the nameless blond man, "that the more religious a man is, the more he's got preying on his mind. It stands to reason that if you lead a good life you don't need to worry."

Walt Hobius hooted. "Where does that leave old Reverend Dunkwiler? He's been espousing religion for years. Does that mean he's a villain?"

"How about Sam Overbury?" suggested Caramino. "That man, he's a religious pirate."

"And Willis Neff," suggested Walt Hobius with a side glance toward Joe. "He was a real deep-dyed Baptist."

"That's what I'm talking about," said the blond man volubly. "Overbury is — well, I don't like to talk about people, but you all know Overbury. And Neff — there's a good example."

"A dead example," murmured Walt Hobius.

"Maybe so, but even when he was alive, he was considered a hard man!"

"Speak no ill of the dead," said Shorty the bartender. "They can't talk back."

Art van Horn turned abruptly to Joe. "Let's have the inside dope, Joe. What's going on around here?"

Joe shook his head slowly. "It's possible that nothing is going on. The story from Salinas is that Neff was killed by accident."

"Come now, Joe," said Walt Hobius. "Three accidents in a row?"

"I'm not pushing the idea," said Joe mildly. "I'm merely suggesting that it's possible."

Art van Horn slapped the bar with emphasis. "I'll give you my opinion. It's common knowledge that Ausley Wyett threatened these men — together with Oliver Viera and Cole Destin — and now they're dead. Accidents? Bah!"

"Maybe you can explain how Ausley, or anyone else, made Bus Hacker have a heart attack, or Charley Blankenship fry himself a batch of poison mushrooms. Did he hypnotize them?"

The blond man snickered. "Maybe Ausley's one of them voodoo types, that sticks pins in little statues."

"It ain't a good idea to mention names," grumbled Shorty the bartender. "Sooner or later it gets back to the party concerned, and then there's bad feeling."

Art van Horn pounded the bar once more. "Certain kinds of people I want bad feeling with. Wyett should have been fixed and fixed right sixteen years ago."

"Easy now, Art," said Joe. "This ain't Russia. I'm supposed to represent the law around here, not you."

"Then represent it!" snapped van Horn. "Do something!"

The swinging doors opened; into the bar from the blazing sunlight strode Cole Destin. He stood blinking in the dimness, then came over to the bar, sat down beside Joe.

"Hello, Cole," said Shorty. "What'll it be?"

"Just give me a bottle of beer." Cole peered at the man beside him, jerked in startled indecision, then swung around, stared stonily forward.

"Hello, Cole," said Joe in an easy conversational tone. "About that business the other day, no hard feelings. On either side, I hope. An easy mistake to make."

Cole jutted his big jaw, stared straight ahead. Joe turned back to Art van Horn. "You say you want me to do something?"

"Don't ask me to tell you your business. Just do it."

Joe reflected. "I could always arrest Ausley Wyett and drag him off to jail."

Art van Horn grinned wolfishly. "I wouldn't object."

"The only thing is, I don't know what I'd charge him with."

"There's three people dead. How many do you need?"

"Maybe Ausley's responsible, maybe not."

"Check on him. Do some of this high-power detective work we're paying you for. Check his alibi."

"For Bus Hacker's heart attack? For Charley Blankenship cooking a toadstool? Come now, Art. Be reasonable."

"You could find out when poor Willis Neff was shot."

"We're working on that. Right now. Thursday morning is the best guess."

"Well then," said Art van Horn.

Joe shook his head. "It's not so easy. I ask Ausley, where were you Thursday morning? And Ausley says, I was in bed. Then what do I say?"

Art van Horn was silenced.

Walt Hobius asked, "How far off is this place where he got shot?"

"I don't know for sure. Down the coast a couple hours' drive."

"That time should be figured on too."

Joe spoke patiently. "I realize that. But the business of alibis doesn't mean hardly anything. No unmarried man can be expected to prove where he was at four or five in the morning."

Stub Caramino chuckled. "I can prove where I was four o'clock Thursday morning. I was playing poker. Unless my buddies here want to call me a liar. In which case they can give me my money back."

"You fellows are all forgetting one thing," said Joe.

"What's that?"

"We don't know for sure that any crime has been committed."

"Five men testified against Ausley Wyett," said Art van Horn. "Three of them die like flies, just as soon as Ausley gets out of jail." He looked along the bar. "You better watch yourself pretty close, Cole, or you'll be next."

"Don't worry about me."

"It's strange," said Joe. He looked at his watch, drained his glass, slipped off the bar stool. "Time for me to get in motion. Don't forget to vote the right way in the election."

Sergeant Irvin Pallard, a big round-faced young man with a thatch of blond curls, was waiting when Joe arrived at the little café, post office, grocery store and service station which on the road map bore the designation "Lupin".

Joe alighted from his car, sauntered across the wind-scoured flat. This point, on the boundary between Monterey County and San Rodrigo County, occupied a small stony meadow at the top of Bosco Pass, with the landscape ahead falling away to the Pacific. The air smelled faintly of salt; the sky was like blue gingham, dotted with bits and puffs of white clouds; the sun shone alternately warm and cool.

Sergeant Pallard got out of his car as Joe approached. Joe had met him once or twice before, and had formed a favorable opinion. Pallard would never set the law-enforcement world afire with his brilliance, but he was steady, patient, and would lose very few votes for his boss.

With Pallard driving they set off to the south along Hooper Ranch

Road, a narrow winding dirt and gravel track. "Mind telling me what this is all about?" asked Pallard. "I don't figure it's just a simple hunting accident."

"I'd like to find out for sure myself."

"We don't have even the smell of a lead. Old Ted Hill didn't even notice the pickup come in. Which is strange, because he doesn't miss much…You might as well relax and enjoy the scenery. We have quite a way to go."

The road slanted down through a forest of fir and redwood, so dense and dark that the road could hardly be seen. "There's a wet spot in here," said Pallard. "For no reason anyone can figure this valley gets twice as much rain as the rest of the county."

"It's pretty country."

Pallard agreed. "Monterey County has the scenery, no question about that."

The road returned to the ridge, where the trees were gnarled, wind-twisted cedars.

"What puzzles me," said Joe, "is why Neff decided to come so far. He's always bragged about the spots he knew close to home."

"It might mean a lot or it might mean nothing," said Pallard. "People do the damndest things for no reason at all, and the poor cop goes out of his mind trying to figure out why."

They passed a lonesome cabin, dropped down into a valley, crossed a stream by an ancient bridge, rose back to the ridge, dropped down once more to another stream. And now Pallard, stopping the car, pointed up an intersecting road, hardly more than a pair of tracks, which ran along the bank of the stream.

"Up here is where Neff was found."

Joe alighted, looked at the surface of the intersecting road. It was hard adobe, and showed no tire-tracks. Getting back in the car, he asked Pallard, "Where does this road wind up at?"

"Nowhere in particular. Thirty or forty years ago it was a logging road. Nobody uses it now but Ted and maybe a few stray hunters and fishermen."

Pallard turned off into the side road. For ten minutes they bumped over stones, ruts, an occasional fallen branch. The country was wild and beautiful. The creek ran swift and clear; at times the trees came down to the water's edge; at other times a strip of meadow intervened. After two miles they came upon a shack sitting fifty yards back from the road. It was built of rough redwood planks, nailed horizontally, each plank lapping the one below.

Pallard halted the car. "That's where Ted Hill lives. Want to talk to him?"

"If he's home."

"He's home. He goes into town once a month to cash his pension check and buy groceries."

The door to the shack opened. An old man in black trousers and a hickory shirt looked out, then came down the steps and approached the car. He was thin and not very tall; his scalp shone brown as varnished oak between two tufts of white hair; his nose was long and inquisitive. Sergeant Pallard and Joe alighted from the car, and Pallard performed the introductions. "Mr. Hill: Sheriff Joe Bain from San Rodrigo County."

"Doin' some investigatin', eh?" asked Ted Hill.

"We're looking the place over. Do you remember anything more that you can tell us?"

"Nope. Mainly there wasn't anything to remember."

Pallard turned to Joe. "Mr. Hill didn't hear the shot, and didn't see Neff drive in."

"That's a fact," said Ted Hill. "Still it ain't nothing to wonder about. Where you found the red cap the wind comes over the ridge in a gust and blows the sound clear over the canyon. As for Neff driving in, it's just possible if he came by real quiet in the middle of the night — but I won't even say that. I hear most everything that stirs. I keep pretty well alert, I'll tell you. There's been three cars on this road in the last month and I've heard them all."

Joe looked at him skeptically. "How can you be sure of that?"

"Instinct, you might call it. I don't sleep sound. And it's surprising how loud a car sounds coming through at night. A week back there was a party of campers up the road. They left early in the morning and I heard 'em go. Friday night a car drove in, turned around, drove out again. I heard him. But Wednesday night — nope. No traffic whatever."

Joe tugged at his chin with thumb and forefinger. "You're sure of that?"

"Certain sure."

"You were home all Wednesday night and Thursday morning?"

"Most of the time."

Joe took a deep breath. Impossibilities had almost been piled upon improbabilities. "When were you gone?"

"Thursday morning, real early." Ted Hill now seemed to speak reluctantly. "I had a little business up the mountain. I might have been gone an hour or two."

"What time would this be?"

"Sun wasn't up yet. Five o'clock in the morning or thereabouts."

"Pretty early, eh?"

"Yep. I go to bed early and I get up early. I don't like to buy coal-oil."

"I see. The reason I'm so particular about this…well, let's just say there's a reason. As I understand it, you say the only time Mr. Neff could have driven in was between five o'clock Thursday morning and say seven o'clock."

"That's pretty close."

"And there wasn't any other traffic on the road?"

"Not since the week before, and not until Friday night, when one car went in and out."

Pallard spoke, "Mr. Neff couldn't have come in by another route?"

"Not unless he flew. I never seen a car with wings yet."

"How far back does this road go?"

"Two miles or so. Then she just peters out."

"What about hunters?" asked Joe. "Do you see lots of those?"

"In deer season quite a few. Out of season not too many — although the deer is thick as flies and I can't keep a vegetable garden on account of them dang deer."

"Have you seen Neff before?"

"No sir. I have not."

"How's fishing in the creek? Pretty good?"

Ted shrugged. "Nothing out of the ordinary. There's better streams. This one flows through clay, and trout don't seem to like clay. Above the clay it's better, about two miles back up-stream."

"Suppose a hunter was waiting up on that ridge Thursday morning. How could he have got up there? Where would he have left his car?"

"Hard to say." Ted Hill hunched his skinny old shoulders. "If he came up from Raccoon Valley, he'd probably park somewhere along Raccoon Creek. Long walk he'd have, but that's where you'd go to look for him. Ask Mrs. Whitney in the Raccoon Valley Store. She might have seen the man."

Pallard nodded. "We'll do that." He looked at Joe. "Anything more, Sheriff?"

"Nothing just now."

"Thank you, Mr. Hill," said Pallard. "You've been a real help."

"I ain't told you nothing much," said Hill. He watched them walk away.

Pallard started the car; they bumped forward. "Independent old codger," said Pallard. "But what in the world would take him up the hill at five o'clock in the morning?"

"He might have been out to shoot himself a nice young buck. That's most likely. Anyway it tells us pretty close when Neff came through. And that's another puzzle. Because I saw him leave Marblestone myself— about five o'clock Wednesday evening, as I remember."

"He might have stopped off to see a friend."

Joe nodded. "I'll have to ask his family if he had any friends in this direction."

They entered a meadow a hundred yards across. Pallard said, "There's the pickup."

He stopped the car; the two men alighted. Forested hills rose at either hand; the ground was carpeted with wild millet and foxtail, dry and crisp after the long hot summer. Reeds grew along the creek; there was an occasional tangle of blackberry vine. At a time far in the past someone had set out an apple orchard, the relics of which were three or four crotchety trees more dead than alive. Thirty feet off the road Neff's pickup was parked on a slight hummock. The tarp, which when Joe saw it had been laced neatly across the box, hung loosely.

Pallard indicated a spot ten feet from the pickup. "He lay about there. Face down, arms out. Shot went into the side of his head, slanting down. Killed him instantly."

Joe scrutinized the dry grass. "No blood, eh?"

"A wound like that doesn't bleed much."

JACK VANCE

"Where did you find the red hat?"

Pallard pointed to the top of the ridge. "See that tall pine? Right there."

"Two hundred yards or better," muttered Joe. "The pickup was out of sight…Neff doesn't look like a deer, but these city hunters shoot first and ask later."

"We're trying to trace the cap, and we're making inquiries at the Top Hat in San Francisco, but I don't have much hope of getting a line on the guy."

"Nor I." Joe went to the pickup, looked under the tarp, found only a spare tire and a typical fisherman's camp kit. He dropped the tarp. "The sleeping bag was laid out? And the stove?"

"That's right." Pallard frowned thoughtfully. "A cot and a sleeping bag. The bag looked as if it has been slept in — it was all rumpled around. There was a pan on the stove, but it had been wiped out. No dirty dishes. He could have eaten out of the pan."

"What about garbage — eggshells and the like?"

Pallard, half on the defensive, said, "I saw nothing like that."

Joe walked back and forth, looking through the dry grass. "It's a funny situation," he said. "Another thing, do you notice something odd about the pickup?"

"No," said Pallard. "Nothing too odd."

"Look at the dust."

Pallard looked. "The rear end is a lot dirtier than the front, if that's what you mean."

"Right. The rear wheels are covered with dust, the front wheels are clean, almost as if it had been halfway into the creek."

"Why in the world should he do a trick like that?"

"I wish I knew…I'll drive the pickup back, if you like."

"Might as well," said Pallard. "It's got to be done sooner or later."

Joe got into the pickup, started it, backed around, set off up the road with Pallard behind.

They passed Hill's cabin. Ted Hill came to his door, waved a hand without too much interest.

At Lupin Pallard shook hands, departed to the west. Joe parked the pickup beside the store, lashed down the tarpaulin, locked the doors, and returned east down Bosco Ridge Road.

So Willis Neff was dead. Number Three in a group of five. Accident? Possibly. There were queer features to the affair. For instance, the business of Neff, the adept angler, fishing a mediocre stream when there were better closer to home.

If Ted Hill were to be believed, Neff had not arrived until five o'clock Thursday morning, and must have been killed almost immediately. If Neff's death had been a purposeful killing, the killer must have followed him — a tricky business on a winding mountain road with frequent switch-back, blind-turns. Neff could hardly have failed to notice. Was it possible that Neff had arranged to meet the killer at this spot? Unreasonable. Could someone have been riding with him and walked back to the road? If so, where had Neff spent Wednesday night? What of the car which had come and gone Friday night? If it had passed the meadow in the dark, the driver would not have seen Neff's body.

In any case, the most immediate matter was to find Ausley Wyett and see what he had to propose as an alibi.

CHAPTER XII

DUSK WAS FADING OVER Castle Mountain as Joe came west up Mitre Canyon Road from the direction of San Rodrigo. At the corner of Destin Road, he halted and sat indecisively. Sunday night. He should be home having his dinner. Come to think of it, he hadn't had any lunch. He looked across the field. The Wyett house was dark; apparently Ausley was not at home. Why not call it a day and head for home?

Joe started the car, but instead of turning right toward Pleasant Grove, he continued straight up Mitre Canyon Road. It was his duty to see Mrs. Neff and Ellie, to make sure they were getting along all right. After all they had no car and might need groceries. Joe smiled grimly. When a man was trying to fool himself, he might as well pile it on thick.

The road wound up the flanks of Castle Mountain; ahead appeared the lights of the Neff house. Joe turned into the driveway, and saw without overmuch surprise the Willys station wagon parked near the barn.

There were lights in the milk-shed, from which came the sound of running water. Joe walked up the slope, looked through the door. The air was warm and heavy with the scent of cow. Ausley Wyett, wearing hip-boots, stood washing down the concrete floor with a high-pressure hose.

Joe turned away, walked to the separator room. Here was Ellie, in blue jeans and a T-shirt, rinsing out the milking-machines.

"Ellie!"

She looked over her shoulder, straightened, wiped back a wisp of hair with a wet hand. "I didn't hear you drive in."

"I wanted to make sure you and your mother were all right."

"Oh yes. We're doing fine."

"I see you've got help." Joe could not completely keep the sardonic edge from his voice.

"Yes," said Ellie simply. "Ausley's been doing the milking for us."

"That's nice of him," said Joe.

Ellie gave Joe a dubious look, returned to her work. Joe watched a minute, then he said, "Here. Let me do that." He stepped forward.

"Oh no," said Ellie. "Please. You'll get all wet. I'm almost finished."

Joe stood back, feeling rather foolish and ineffectual. Ellie said, "I've been doing this every night for years."

After a moment Joe asked, "Have you and your mother talked over what you're going to do?"

"We'll probably sell the ranch. Mr. Destin has already come past, and so has Mr. Viera."

Joe rubbed his chin. "Did Cole Destin make you an offer?"

"No. He just said he might be interested."

Joe laughed. "Don't let Cole fool you. He tried the same game on old Weaver, and your father bought the place out from under his nose. I don't know what your price is, but don't let Cole talk you into selling cheap."

"That's what Mr. Viera told us. He wants us to let him handle the property."

Joe reached forward, took the stainless-steel tank she had just washed, turned it upside-down on a rack. "I guess he's as good as any. But I wouldn't give him any exclusive arrangement. List the place in Pleasant Grove. Which reminds me, I'll have one of the deputies bring your father's pickup here tomorrow, so you won't be cut off."

"We're not cut off, now that Ausley's coming out."

Joe looked toward the barn. "I guess I'll have a word with Ausley, then I'll be on my way."

"The funeral is Tuesday morning," said Ellie, "in Pleasant Grove, in case you care to come."

Joe said, "I'll be there." He reached out, took her hand, which was cold and wet. "This is all a tremendous shock now — but in a week or two the world will seem a different place."

Ellie nodded indifferently. "It does already." Gently she disengaged her hand. Joe essayed a reassuring smile and backed from the room. He went to the milk-shed, where Ausley had finished washing down and was coiling the hose over a peg.

"Hi there, Ausley," said Joe.

Ausley cocked his head sidewise, mildly surprised. "Hello, Joe."

"Keeping busy, eh?"

"I thought I might be able to help out a little. Lots of work around here."

"I was just talking to Ellie. She says she'll probably sell."

Ausley's face became a trifle glum. "I suppose it's the thing to do... It seems a shame though. There's a good living in this place."

"I wonder if Neff left much money."

Ausley shrugged. "I don't imagine he spent much. He was a pretty strict man."

"Strange that he should die like that," mused Joe.

"We all have to go sometime," said Ausley piously.

"First Bus Hacker, then Charley Blankenship, now Willis Neff. All accidents."

Ausley smiled uneasily. "You'd have to call it coincidence, I guess."

"If it isn't," said Joe, "somebody's going to the gas chamber."

"Pretty hard to imagine anybody being so wicked," suggested Ausley.

"There's people feverish enough to suspect you."

"Me?" Ausley laughed weakly. "That's really silly. You *know* I'm not going to stick my neck out. I got two strikes on me now."

"These people believe that the accidents were all faked — but faked good enough so that nobody can really be sure one way or the other."

"I guess anything is possible," said Ausley reluctantly.

"Just for the record: where were you when Willis Neff was killed?"

"Where was I?" Ausley hunched his skinny shoulders, scratched his nose. "Let's see — where was I? Come to think of it, when did Mr. Neff pass on?"

Joe was watching him intently. He said, "A good guess would be around five o'clock Thursday morning."

"Thursday morning, five o'clock?" Ausley pondered. "I was probably in bed. About six I got up and put out feed for the cattle."

"Anybody see you?"

"No. I guess not. Oliver Viera came by a little later, around seven, I'd say."

"Oliver Viera? What was he doing up so early?"

"There was a carpenter he wanted to see before the carpenter went off to work. That's what he told me, anyway. After he talked to the man, he came by to see me."

"What did Oliver have in mind?"

"He wants to build a dam where his property and mine come together. I don't see how it helps me too much, but I won't stand in his way."

"Well, if Oliver verifies this it puts you in the clear. More or less anyway."

"That would sure be nice."

Joe went back to his car, where Ellie was waiting. She asked, "Did you — do you know any more about how my father died?"

"Nothing definite."

"Was it an accident? Or —"

"It looks like an accident. And again — it doesn't." He glanced toward the barn and laughed hollowly. "If he knew that Ausley Wyett was here, washing down his barn, he'd come back to life and chase Ausley all the way to Marblestone."

Ellie's face was unreadable in the darkness. She said in a soft voice, "Ausley's never been treated fairly, by anyone."

"I'm not so sure of that," said Joe. "A lot of people once wanted to hang Ausley."

Ellie made no response. Joe started the car and drove away in an unreasonably surly mood.

A mile down the road he radioed headquarters. Bill Phipps responded: "HQ; come in."

"Joe Bain here. Telephone my house and say I'll be home in about an hour."

"You're in trouble, Joe. Your mother called twenty minutes back. Seems like you promised you'd be home at five o'clock and she put some chickens in to roast."

"Oh my Lord," groaned Joe. "Tell her I got hung up — an emergency."

"Will do."

In the distance twinkled the lights of Marblestone which by some trick of perspective suddenly seemed a toy town. And in the darkness, brooding over it, Joe thought to see a shrouded figure. Joe strained to see the spectre's face, so real was the fantasy, but the shape became once again part of the darkness. Joe hitched himself up in the seat. "I must be going nuts," he muttered peevishly. "When I start seeing spooks…"

He approached Marblestone: there was the Kipburger stand, brightly lit with blue and white lights, and across the street, the old houses with boarded windows and porches askew. Then Marblestone proper, all dark on a Sunday night. Only the Town Club remained open for business. Joe hesitated, considering his exasperated mother, hungry daughter, and chickens drying out in the oven. Then he pulled over to the curb. "Just one phone call," he told himself. "Three minutes more won't affect the chickens."

He pushed through the swinging doors, and saw himself to be alone in the bar except for Shorty Olson, who leaned on his elbows, reading a newspaper. Shorty tucked the newspaper into an unseen niche. "Glad to see you. Seems like Marblestone has suddenly become a city of abstainers. What'll it be?"

"I just want to make a phone call, Shorty."

Joe went into the phone booth, dialed Oliver Viera's number, and received the busy signal. He muttered a mild curse or two, went over to the bar. "Let's have a bottle of Lucky."

Shorty poured, and with careful casualness asked, "How's it going, Joe?"

"Well — I won't say I'm happy."

"No. That's tempting fate."

Joe took a gulp of beer, went to the phone booth, once more got the busy signal. He returned to the bar. "My family will skin me alive when I get home. But I've got to check out something or I'll be awake all night."

"When are you going to make a pinch?"

"If I knew something for sure I'd make a pinch right now."

"Some of the boys around town don't have any doubts."

Joe snorted. "There's no solid evidence that any crime has been committed."

"Funny string of coincidences. It starts taxing the imagination."

"Stranger things have happened, and innocent men have been treated pretty badly."

"Maybe so. But Ausley Wyett better watch himself."

"I'll tell you something." Joe considered his words carefully. The Town Club was the social hub of Marblestone; anything told Shorty Olson reached the ears of everyone in town. "Willis Neff was killed Thursday morning, about five o'clock, according to the evidence. Well, it so happens that Ausley Wyett puts forward an alibi for seven o'clock. If I can talk to Oliver Viera for two minutes, I'll find out for sure. And if Ausley Wyett was home at seven, he wasn't shooting Willis Neff at five. There just isn't that much time."

"That may be. Providing things are the way you say they are."

"I don't say anything, I just check what other people say." Once more Joe walked over to the phone booth. This time he made connection, and the voice of Connie Viera sounded sharply in his ear. "Hello?"

"Hello, Mrs. Viera," said Joe. Connie Viera sounded somewhat on edge. "This is Sheriff Joe Bain. May I speak to Oliver?"

Connie's voice became even more noticeably disturbed. "I'd like to talk to him myself. He should have been home an hour ago. It's our anniversary and he promised to take us out for dinner. Of course he's forgotten all about it."

"That's too bad," said Joe. "It doesn't sound like Oliver."

"He's so absent-minded, once he starts talking business with someone."

"We're all that way more or less. Maybe you can help me. You remember Oliver telling me about wanting to build a dam."

"Yes."

"Do you know if he talked to Ausley Wyett about the project?"

"I really don't know. He didn't say anything to me about it."

"It would have been Thursday morning."

"Thursday morning he got up early to go into San Rodrigo. He didn't say anything about seeing Ausley Wyett."

"Guess I'll have to talk to Oliver. You don't know where he is?"

"I've been calling everywhere I can think of. He left his sister's house about half an hour ago."

"Thanks, Mrs. Viera. Tell him I called, and that I'll talk to him tomorrow."

Joe returned to the bar, emptied the bottle of beer into his glass. He asked casually, "Do you see much of Cole in here?"

"Not too much. He doesn't associate with the peasants."

"I hear he wants to buy up the Neff place, now that Willis Neff's dead."

"He's wanted that for a long time. And maybe a couple of other things around the Neff ranch."

"Along with the rest of us."

The door opened; into the bar came Walt Hobius, eyes glittering. He was wearing slacks, a western-style sport shirt, a chamois sports jacket. "You'll never believe it," he said.

"What?"

"Well — being as Neff is dead, I thought I'd go up and see if the ladies needed anything — maybe help 'em out one way or another."

"Big-hearted Walt," said Shorty.

"I turn into the driveway, and who do you think is driving out — with Ellie and Mrs. Neff alongside of him?"

"I know for sure it wasn't Willis Neff," said Joe.

"It was Ausley Wyett, big garbage-eating grin on his face, that son of a bitch!"

"Calm down," said Joe. "You'll blow a skull-fuse."

"The nerve of the guy!"

Shorty grinned. "The nerve of the guy — running off with your girl-friend."

"I guess he figures he got dibs on her," said Joe. "Since he was the last guy Neff beat up."

"That don't cut no ice," said Walt. "Neff beat hell out of me too. What does it get me? A horse-laugh from Ausley! Right after he's bumped off her old man."

Joe stood up. "I got to get home. My ma is going to run me out of town as it is."

Joe started down Candelara Creek Road. A quarter of a mile from town he met a white Ford station wagon traveling at a high rate of speed. Joe caught the merest glimpse of car and driver, but it seemed to be Oliver Viera. Joe laughed, a tension released. "If Oliver got accidentally bit to death by a pack of wolves, or accidentally struck by lightning, I'd either have to jail Ausley or go into hiding."

He drove directly home. His mother viewed him coldly, went into the kitchen, began clattering pots and pans. Miranda said, "Daddy! How could you be so cruel? Sunday dinner and it's almost nine o'clock."

"Well," said Joe, "I was delayed."

"You can't just joke and get out of it. Where in the world have you been? You've been drinking beer, because I can smell it."

"Just in the line of duty."

"You better not let Grandma smell it. She'll be even madder than she is now."

"I'll hold my breath. My, you look pretty tonight."

Miranda raised her eyebrows skeptically. "It's flattery, but I love it."

In the morning Joe arrived at headquarters early, exchanged the coolest of greetings with Mrs. Rostvolt, went into his office.

On his desk was the Monday morning edition of the *Messenger*, folded — with malicious intent? — so that prominently displayed was a headline:

MONSTER RALLY TONIGHT
TO BOOST PROGRESS, GERVASE

Tonight in Montalvo Square, citizens for Greater San Rodrigo County will present their views to the voting public. Speakers will include Lee Gervase, candidate for Sheriff; Wilfred Mortimer, President of the San Rodrigo County Council for Progress; Cole Destin, prominent rancher; Dr. Henry Gomez; and Howard Griselda, Editor of the Pleasant Grove *Messenger*.

Free coffee and doughnuts will be served, according to Pete Rollins, chairman of the Gervase for Sheriff Committee.

"At this election we hope to get rolling," Rollins told the *Messenger* yesterday. "If we're successful, and I'm sure we will be, because we've got a great candidate in Lee Gervase, we plan to consolidate our organization and really become a force in the county. But for now, we're concentrating on the sheriff's office, long a rotten spot in the government of San Rodrigo County.

"Needless to say, we're also pulling hard for the County Courthouse Bonds…"

Joe tossed the paper aside, leaned back in his chair, gazed bleakly across the room. He was saddled with twenty years of Ernest Cucchinello, and that was all there was to it. Lee Gervase had a big-time background, a big-time personality, a big-time program. Joe Bain had Cooch.

Joe heaved a deep, bitter sigh. Why exert himself to do a job, when for all practical purposes he was working on borrowed time? If one thing was certain it was that Lee Gervase would sweep the Sheriff's Department with a new broom. There would be no place for ex-Acting-Sheriff Joe Bain…Maybe he could go to work in Monterey County, under Ed Mulligan. Something to keep in mind, at any rate. And in the meantime — Joe hauled himself wearily upright in his seat — he was collecting a salary and he'd do his job.

First on the agenda: the unsettled business of Ausley Wyett's alibi. He reached for the telephone, but just as he touched the receiver, the buzzer sounded. "Sheriff Joe Bain speaking."

Over the wire came a heavy voice. "Hello, Joe. Art van Horn here."

"Yes, Art?" Joe's heart began to pound.

"It's happened again."

"What? You don't mean —"

"Another accident."

"Good Lord! Who?"

"Oliver Viera."

"Dead?"

"As a door-nail."

"How'd it happen?"

"Fell off a ladder, broke his neck."

"An accident, you say?"

"That's what his wife says."

"I'll be right out, with the coroner."

Chapter XIII

CONNIE VIERA WAS NEAR-HYSTERICAL. She lay in a darkened bedroom, her mother sitting beside her, occasionally breaking out into wild sobs and desperate lamentations. The children had been conveyed to the house of an aunt.

Joe, the coroner and two deputies brought the body of Oliver Viera up from the gully. He had fallen almost sixty feet, counting the height of the ladder. The ladder itself had slid a few feet farther down toward the creek. Joe made a second trip down, examined it, brought it back up the steep slope. It was an ordinary aluminum ladder, twelve feet long, and, so far as Joe could see, completely innocent of structural defect: the same which Joe had noted on his previous visit.

Joe diffidently entered the bedroom where Connie Viera lay swollen with grief, her mother holding her hand. "Excuse me, Mrs. Viera, for intruding — I sure wish I didn't have to," said Joe. "Do you feel able to answer a question or two?"

"Yes," said Connie Viera in a hollow voice.

"Exactly what happened?"

"Oliver climbed the ladder. He seemed to slip, or something of the sort, because when I looked around he was falling over backward, ladder and all going with him. He fell over the side of the deck, I saw his face as he went; he gave me such a look — he knew he was going — oh…" Connie Viera gave way to racking sobs. Her mother, a gnarled, rather dark old woman, stoically patted her hand.

"There wasn't anybody else around?"

"No. Nobody. Just me."

"You were on the deck?"

"I was in the doorway, looking out. Half in, half out."

"Why did Oliver climb the ladder?"

"He wanted to take the ladder down, and there was a can of paint up there, just perched ready to fall. So he had to climb up to take down the can of paint. I told him to be careful, but he was still half-asleep. Oliver never wakes up till he's had breakfast —" and once again Connie burst into throat-wrenching sobs.

Joe went out on the deck, waited till Connie had quieted. Then he went back into the house. "I hate to trouble you, Mrs. Viera, but I have to ask a few more questions. Would you come out on the deck a minute?"

Connie drew a deep shuddering breath, heaved herself to her feet, and followed Joe out upon the deck.

"Now — just where was the ladder?"

"About there. Yes. Just about there." Connie pointed.

"And where were the feet?"

"Oh — about here."

"That's pretty close in. Sergeant, bring that ladder out here, please." Phipps went off after the ladder. Joe stood looking up to the fascia, none of which had been painted. He turned back to Connie. "Was Oliver painting up there? Seems like he'd start down at the end."

Connie looked up dully. "I don't know how the ladder got there… The kids might have been playing. Oliver wouldn't leave a gallon of paint perched like that."

Joe gave a profound nod. "Did you ask your kids if they'd been playing with the ladder?"

"No." Connie once more began to sag with grief. "No. Of course not. I couldn't think of anything but Oliver." Her mother took her back inside the house.

Phipps came with the ladder. Joe stood it against the house on the position indicated by Connie. He shook it, tested it for stability. "Stand below here and hold this thing steady," he told Bill Phipps. "I don't want to go over like Oliver."

Bill Phipps gripped the ladder; Joe climbed up, step by step, until he could look over the redwood fascia and across the tar-and-gravel roof, which spread away flat, neat, undisturbed, without a scuff-mark, without so much as a nail in evidence. Joe turned, looked gingerly around. The deck seemed alarmingly narrow. The distance to the bottom of the ravine was frightening. It was possible, thought Joe, that Oliver had become dizzy, or slipped, or lost his balance… How else could he have fallen? There had been no one else on the balcony. Joe chewed his lip, went on tiptoe back into the bedroom. "Excuse me again, Mrs. Viera. Just one more question. We can't rule out the possibility that this was something other than accident."

"You mean — somebody did it on purpose? Why should they?" Connie Viera's voice was harsh and shrill. "Everybody liked Oliver. He was the nicest guy in the world. He got along good with everybody, even that Ausley Wyett, who I wouldn't let come in my house. Who would do a thing like that?"

"I don't know. In fact, I —"

"How could they, even if they wanted to? I was right here. There wasn't anybody near. He fell of his own accord."

"Could there have been somebody on the roof who could have kicked the ladder over?"

"What would somebody be doing on our roof?"

"I don't know. I'm just asking. Would it have been possible?"

Connie Viera thought. "No. I would have seen him if he pushed Oliver. Oliver would have said something, made some kind of remark."

"He had a minute or two to look across the roof, then, before he went over?"

"Yes. There wasn't anybody up there. He just took hold of the can of paint and went over backwards, ladder and all."

Joe thought a moment or so. "You didn't see anyone else nearby? No cars or anything?"

"No. I don't see why you ask me such questions. I told you Oliver fell — right in front of my eyes!"

"I just have to look for every possibility, Mrs. Viera. I'm almost as sorry as you are about Oliver. I've known him a long time. He was a fine man."

"He was the best!" Again Mrs. Viera broke into sobs. "Whatever will I do? I'd like to die myself."

"Now, now," said Joe, "think of the children. You'll have a life with them."

"No I won't. They can't be my husband. They can't be their own father! Oh, why did it have to happen to me?"

Joe retreated once more. He went out on the deck, looked up the ravine toward the mountains, down toward the far faint bird-dropping which was Marblestone, across the ravine to Ausley Wyett's property. He leaned on the railing, stared morosely down at the spot where Oliver Viera had lost his life. "Another accident. Bus Hacker, Charley Blankenship, Willis Neff, Oliver Viera. One to go. If I was Cole Destin I'd leave town for a bit." He walked back and forth along the deck. A new thought occurred to him. Oliver's death had eliminated Ausley's alibi for the death of Willis Neff.

Joe halted. His first task would be to learn Ausley's whereabouts at the time of Oliver Viera's death. Although, since there was no hint of foul play, it made little difference whether Ausley had an alibi or not.

And yet — four deaths. Four accidental deaths, of witnesses against Ausley Wyett. Coincidence?

"Suppose I wanted to kill five people," said Joe. "How would I go about it, knowing I was sure to be suspected? Maybe I'd want to be suspected — just to show the town what I thought of it. I'd arrange these accidents. I'd give Bus Hacker a heart attack. I'd have Charley Blankenship dig some mushrooms and poison himself. I'd have Willis Neff camp where some trigger-happy hunter would shoot him. I'd have Oliver Viera fall off a ladder and break his neck. And Cole? I wonder how I'd have Cole die? Maybe I'd have his wife run over him with a lawn mower, or have Lee Gervase go mad and stab Cole while he's giving a speech tonight…"

Dr. Hesketh, the coroner, joined Joe on the deck. "Well, Sheriff — what do you think?"

"Looks like an accident."

"Yes."

"But I know it isn't."

"It doesn't seem likely. And yet —"

"Exactly. What can you say? You feel a fool saying 'accident', you feel a fool claiming foul play. So what do you do?"

"I think," said Dr. Hesketh heavily, "that for a while, we'll say nothing."

"Right. We're investigating." Joe pondered a moment. "Do you see any reason for an autopsy?"

"Under any other circumstances — no. But it might not be a bad notion."

"Is there a drug that could make a man dizzy enough to fall off a ladder?"

"Certainly. Whiskey, for one. The trick would be to get a man to climb a ladder in that condition."

"Not very likely."

"Not at all likely." The coroner clapped his hands down on the railing. "I'll take the body into town and see if I spot anything."

Joe made one last visit to the bedroom. "We'll be going for a while," he told the miserable hulk which was Connie Viera. "If you think of anything which seems peculiar, let me know, will you?"

"Yes."

Joe departed, following the ambulance down Quarry Road. In Marblestone the ambulance turned left toward Pleasant Grove; Joe turned right. Ausley Wyett's car was parked in front of his ramshackle old home. Joe drove up, parked. The police dogs dashed forth, jerking and straining at their chains.

Ausley Wyett stepped out on the porch. He wore levis and a new blue flannel shirt, and looked ungainly and lanky. "Hi Joe, what's on your mind?"

"How come you're not up milking for the Neffs?"

"They wouldn't let me. Chased me off." He smiled.

"They can't do it themselves."

"Nope. They hired a couple Mexicans."

"Then you've been home this morning."

"Correct. Shouldn't I have been?"

"Ausley," said Joe, "I hate to suspect a man just because he's obvious — but you're sure a suspicious object."

"Now what?"

"Don't you know?"

"If I did, I wouldn't be asking, would I?"

"Yes, you would. Well, I'll tell you. Oliver Viera's dead."

Ausley Wyett grimaced sadly. "What happened to Oliver?"

"Fell off a ladder. Broke his neck. An accident, looks like."

"A peculiar set of accidents."

"I'd say so. I've come to hear what you have to say about them."

"If it was an accident, why bother me?"

"Exactly," said Joe. "That's it, exactly."

Ausley sat down on the edge of the porch. "Look at it this way, Joe. Either I'm guilty or I'm not."

"That's simple enough."

"If I'm guilty, everything's clear. Except one thing. How am I expected to shoot Willis Neff when I'm talking to Oliver Viera at the same time?"

"It wasn't the same time, and Oliver Viera's dead."

"You didn't ask him?"

"I couldn't find him to ask him. I asked his wife, she knew nothing about it."

"Too bad." Ausley ran his fingers through his mop of brown hair. "Well, let's say I'm not guilty. The question arises: who is?"

"Do you have any ideas — conceding you're not guilty?"

"Naturally. You think I've spent the last sixteen years filing my fingernails? I'm an innocent man. But nobody believed me. You can't expect me to feel any deep sorrow, Joe. These people did me dirt."

"And there's one of them left."

"I'll be interested in what happens to him," said Ausley.

"That's all you got to say?"

"What else is there to say?"

"You hinted that you had some ideas."

"Ideas are cheap. I can't prove a thing. I can't even prove I didn't kill Tissie McAllister. And I didn't. Why, I loved that child. I wouldn't have harmed a hair of her head."

Joe threw his hands in the air. "Ausley, you just vex me till I can hardly see."

"Sorry, Joe. All I can say is, I plead not guilty to everything. Take it from there."

"Somebody's mighty all-fired clever," said Joe, "and the sad thing, Ausley, is that it might be you."

Ausley rose to his feet in a stately fashion. "I'm sorry you don't have more faith in me, Joe."

"I'll give you a warning. You better lie low. There's going to be some harsh talk about you in Marblestone."

Ausley shrugged. "People been talking harshly about me as long as I can remember."

Joe backed around, departed. Entering Marblestone, he parked under the big oak in front of the general store, and sat thinking.

Ausley Wyett was right. Either Ausley was guilty, or someone else was. Assuming the accidents were not accidents.

If Ausley was guilty, the only question was, *how?*

If Ausley were not guilty, there were three questions: *how? who? why?*

Joe brought out his notebook, examined the various notes he had made on each case. A glimmer of a pattern? Joe frowned, stared at his notes as if they were alive, with tiny black tongues all anxious to speak. His mind began to move, to fit fact to fact.

If I wanted to give Bus Hacker a heart attack, how *would* I do it?

If I wanted Charley Blankenship to poison himself on a toadstool, how *would* I do it?

If I wanted to shoot Willis Neff on Wednesday night or Thursday morning and give myself an alibi, how *would* I do it?

If I wanted Oliver Viera to fall off a ladder…

Joe nodded slowly. There had been a hole in Bus Hacker's front porch. Most likely another inside the front door.

In the matter of the Blankenship killing, something stuck out like a sore thumb, which he hadn't thought of to now. In a clump of field mushrooms, like that which Charley Blankenship had found in his pansy bed, it would be most unusual to find an Amanita. Unless somehow it had been disguised and put there.

Neff had died Wednesday night or Thursday morning. Old Ted Hill had heard no cars during this interval — but he had heard a car enter and leave Friday night. And the front wheels of Willis Neff's pickup were clean.

Oliver Viera? In order that he fall off a ladder, first it was necessary that he climb a ladder. What better incentive than a precariously arranged can of paint? And once he was aloft, any little tug would pull him over…

It was all clear, thought Joe in awe and amazement. Almost clear, anyway. Evidence? He pulled at his chin. There had to be some serious thinking done.

"Oh, Sheriff," said a soft feminine voice. "You seem so worried, I hardly like to interrupt you."

Joe looked up, into a soft round face surrounded by electric violet curls. "Oh, hello, Mrs. Beasley." A vote was a vote. "How are you?"

"As usual. I just thought I'd say hello. I've known you so long, from the time you were a dirty-faced little boy. There was something which always gave me a good opinion of you, no matter what other folks said. You probably won't remember, but Widdie, my poor old calico cat, was on a fence, with dogs barking at her, and some nasty little boys were pushing at her — and you made them stop."

Joe grinned. "I remember. You took me in the post office and made me a cup of hot chocolate. First time in my life I ever had any."

"After that I always had a warm spot in my heart for you. I knew you weren't really a bad boy."

"I guess I wasn't any worse than average." Joe sought for means to break off the conversation. "Excuse me, Mrs. Beasley, I have to call into headquarters."

"Oh don't let me stand in the way of official business." Mrs. Beasley started to trundle away, then returned with a bashful smile. "There's something I've been dying to know; perhaps I shouldn't ask, but in a sense I'm a government official too, so maybe it isn't too wrong to ask."

Joe blinked, unable to follow Mrs. Beasley's progression of ideas. "Ask what?"

"About the letter from Mr. Hacker. I've been ever so curious as to what was in it."

"Letter?" Joe felt a peculiar sensation in the skin of his face, a cool tingle. "What letter?"

Mrs. Beasley spoke hurriedly. "Perhaps you wouldn't remember, or perhaps you never even received it, since it was addressed to Sheriff Cucchinello."

"A letter from Bus Hacker to Sheriff Cucchinello?"

"Yes. About three years ago he brought me the letter and told me, 'Mary, if and when I die, I want you to drop this letter in the mail. And

— 150 —

not before.' It was just a letter, as I say, addressed to Sheriff Cucchinello. Every once in a while he'd remind me of it, and I'd say yes, Mr. Hacker, yes, I still have your letter safe and sound. Then he died, and I sent the letter. Postal rates had gone up. I had to put another stamp on it, which I did out of my own pocket."

Joe's mind was racing. "Sheriff Cucchinello was dead."

Mrs. Beasley nodded brightly. "I didn't know it at the time. Although I couldn't have done anything about it even if I had known."

"But you sent it off?"

"Yes."

"On the same day Bus Hacker died?"

"Yes. The very same day. Because he'd always made such a point of the letter."

"How was it addressed?"

"Just 'Ernest Cucchinello, Sheriff, Pleasant Grove, California'. I remember distinctly."

Joe nodded. "It probably was delivered to Sheriff Cucchinello's home, and Mrs. Cucchinello decided that it wasn't important."

"Oh." Mrs. Beasley's face fell. "I've been so curious."

"But I'm glad you mentioned it. I'll make inquiry of Mrs. Cucchinello, and perhaps I'll have news for you next time I see you. Meanwhile — please don't mention this letter to anyone else."

"I wouldn't think of it."

Joe started the car. "I've got to run now. It's been nice talking to you."

"Yes, I enjoyed it so much. And next time you're in Marblestone, drop by the post office and I'll fix you another nice cup of hot chocolate."

Joe forced himself to smile eagerly. "I sure will, Mrs. Beasley. Goodby, now."

Joe proceeded back down Candelara Canyon, winding around curves and turns with gravel kicking up under his wheels. Time was too short, the road too long; he could hardly contain his impatience. The letter. Perhaps it would contradict the theory forming in his mind. But he thought not. So many small discords and oddities now seemed reasonable. Bus Hacker's ledger with its strange omissions...The many curious features in the death of Willis Neff...The motive — primary or secondary? — in the murder of Charley Blankenship... And now — Bus Hacker's missing letter! Joe pressed a trifle harder on the accelerator. His speedometer needle pushed past 70. Rather odd, considering all the circumstances, that he had never received the letter...

Ernest Cucchinello's widow was a round little woman, with the smallest of hands and feet. She still lived in the big ranch-style house on McClellan Avenue near the country club. When Joe rang the bell, Mrs. Cucchinello answered the door herself. "Why, it's Mr. Bain! I should say 'Sheriff Bain'. Though it sounds strange after so many years of 'Sheriff Cucchinello'."

"It sounds strange to me too," said Joe. "I came for some information, Mrs. Cucchinello. About two weeks ago, you might have received a letter addressed to Sheriff Cucchinello, sent by a Clarence Hacker from Pleasant Grove."

"Oh yes. So I did. Of course."

"What did you do with it?"

"I opened it, naturally. It didn't seem to be personal, more like official business. As I recall, it was something about a school bus, I didn't pay a great deal of attention. I happened to be downtown shopping and left it off with Mrs. Rostvolt." Mrs. Cucchinello spoke the name with exaggerated primness. Rumors had certainly reached her ears.

"So," said Joe. "Mrs. Rostvolt received the letter."

"Yes. Didn't she pass it on to you?"

"She probably did, but it slipped my mind. I'll ask her about it when I see her. Thank you very much, Mrs. Cucchinello."

"Not at all, Sheriff Bain. Drop by again sometime."

"I surely will."

Chapter XIV

Joe drove back down McClellan Avenue even faster than he had come. Then, as thoughts began to circulate through his brain, he slowed to a near-crawl. The line of logic ran down a chain of forking alternatives. Either Mrs. Rostvolt (A) opened the letter or (B) she did not. Undoubtedly A. Either she deemed the letter unimportant, when she might have filed the letter or thrown it away; or she had considered it important, in which case she might also have filed the letter, or used it for her own purposes. Joe bared his teeth in a mirthless grin. He'd find out quick enough.

He parked in his usual spot behind the courthouse, and sat thinking. How to handle the situation? He got out of the car, went to the third-floor office of Paul Wentzman, the District Attorney.

Wentzman indicated a chair, glanced at Joe sidewise through glistening rimless glasses. He was a stocky stolid man with pale heavy cheeks, a high narrow forehead, a deceptively mild expression. He spoke in a dry, didactic voice, which might or might not — Joe had never decided — camouflage a nimble mind. "What's on your mind?"

Joe carefully set forth his problem. Paul Wentzman leaned forward, made a cage with his fingers, nodded several times in comprehension. His glasses gleamed with reflections from the overhead light. "In essence, you suspect that Mrs. Rostvolt withheld this letter for her own purposes, and you want to bring it home to her."

"Right. And I want the letter. I don't want her to say that it was unimportant, so she threw it away."

"As I understand it, you believe the letter is valuable evidence?"

Joe nodded. "There's been all these accidental deaths out in Marblestone, and it turns out they're not accidents. I'll fill you in on this, because you'll be prosecuting — a real spectacular case, by the way — but the first step is to get that letter."

Wentzman considered. "We can demonstrate that she received the letter, through the statement of Mrs. Cucchinello. If we could demonstrate that the letter contained obviously important information —"

"I can make a guess or two what was in the letter."

"You could try either a casual question — which would give her a chance to feign absent-mindedness — or a direct accusation —"

"In which case she'd feign virtuous indignation."

"Well, if she's been blackmailing someone — and that seems to be your implication — the fact will sooner or later become known."

"The man I have in mind doesn't seem the blackmail type. This letter must hem him in pretty close. Come to think of it, he burned down Bus Hacker's house trying to destroy the letter... I take back what I said about him not being the blackmail type, because that's part of the main case, which I don't want to go into now."

Wentzman hitched himself forward. "Let's ask her for the letter. It all boils down to that eventually."

Joe nodded glumly. "I suppose so." He rose to his feet. "Let's go... It's something I don't like to do. Much as I detest the woman."

They descended the terrazzo steps to the second floor, walked around the balcony overlooking the main lobby to the fine marble stairs with the ornate bronze banisters, descended to the lobby, walked back through a dark hall to the annex.

Mrs. Rostvolt looked up from her typewriter, automatically reached her hand up to her aureole of tight auburn curls, pursed her lips, returned to her work.

Joe walked slowly across the office, Wentzman loitering casually behind. Mrs. Rostvolt sensed an ominous quality to Joe's approach, looked up, her eyes round and liquid.

Joe spoke in a measured voice. "A week or so ago Mrs. Cucchinello gave you a letter from a man named Clarence Hacker, to be delivered to me. Where is it?"

Mrs. Rostvolt's lips pursed more tightly. A slow flush mounted her neck. But she said in an airy voice, "Letter? From whom?"

"Where is it?"

Mrs. Rostvolt's eyes began to give off sparks. "I don't care to have you take that tone with me, Mr. Bain." She looked past him at Paul Wentzman. "In fact I'm not going to put up with your rudeness another instant—"

"If you don't produce that letter, you're going upstairs into Cell 13."

Mrs. Rostvolt became icy. "What letter are you talking about?"

"You know what letter I'm talking about. I've already told you."

Mrs. Rostvolt squinted. "Mrs. Cucchinello brought in some odds and ends. I don't know what happened to them."

"Mr. Wentzman is a witness to everything you say. If it turns out that you've used the information in this letter for purposes of your own, you're only making matters worse for yourself."

Mrs. Rostvolt rose wearily to her feet. "You make me simply sick... I'll see if I can find it... I might have thrown it out."

Joe followed her to the filing cabinet. She looked at him over her shoulder. "Don't be so pushy. I'll get the letter."

Joe laughed grimly. "You haven't seen anything yet."

Mrs. Rostvolt glared, hesitated, then pulled open a drawer.

Joe read the label on the front of the file: "'H'. For 'Hacker'?"

"Naturally."

"All right. I'll find it." Joe pushed forward, and Mrs. Rostvolt perforce stood aside. "H... Ha... Hall... Harris... Harzat... There's no Hacker letter here."

Mrs. Rostvolt shrugged. "It probably wasn't important."

"Filed under 'U' for 'unimportant'?" suggested Joe.

"If you'd move—I might be able to find it."

Joe moved aside. Mrs. Rostvolt suddenly seemed indecisive. She pulled out first one drawer, then another. Then she stopped, turned around, faced Joe. "I'm not going to continue this. I want a lawyer."

"You must be pretty badly rattled, Mrs. Rostvolt."

"I'm not rattled!" she shouted. "I'm just sick and tired of your accusations!"

"I haven't accused you of anything, yet."

Mrs. Rostvolt looked desperately at the file cabinet. Joe said in a silky voice, "It'll only take me an hour or so to go through the entire mess."

She said sulkily, "It's probably under 'X'."

"'X', eh? For 'extraordinary'."

"That's where I file miscellaneous items."

Joe opened the "X" drawer, withdrew a manila folder. He laid it on the counter, gingerly turned over paper after paper. Toward the back he found the Hacker letter. He read it, then glanced agate-eyed at Mrs. Rostvolt. "How come you didn't show this to me?"

"It didn't seem important."

Wentzman had stepped forward, and was reading. Joe looked at him. "Do we have enough to put her on the books?"

Wentzman nodded. "Withholding of evidence, obstruction of peace officers, misconduct in a position of trust."

Joe said, "This case is going to break. Today or tonight. If that's enough to hold her, we might be able to add blackmail and being accessory to murder."

Mrs. Rostvolt quailed. She cried out, "You're absolutely insane! Why are you persecuting me? I haven't done anything of the sort!"

"That remains to be seen." Joe looked sardonically toward the back of the room. "Well, Mrs. Rostvolt, it's sure funny how things turn out. Almost twenty years you've been sitting in this office, looking after the girls in the upstairs cells. Now it's your turn. You know the way. Upstairs you go!"

"No!" Mrs. Rostvolt was defiant. "You can't arrest me for being forgetful, or negligent. I didn't do any of the things you claim, and you can't prove I did."

"This letter is highly important — obviously so. Forgetfulness, negligence — they won't pass. Do you realize that because you didn't show me that letter, two or maybe three men have been killed? This is a serious business."

"I want to see a lawyer." There was a sudden gleam in Mrs. Rostvolt's eye.

"That's your privilege. Who do you want?"

The gleam became a malicious glitter. "Lee Gervase!"

Joe was taken aback. "Lee Gervase? He won't touch this kind of case. If he's got any sense he won't."

"I want to call Lee Gervase."

"Go ahead. Call him. You know where the phone is."

"I don't want you around when I talk to him."

"You can have all the privacy you want in your cell."

Mrs. Rostvolt turned, went slowly to the telephone. She dialed a number. Joe watched her with suddenly narrowed eyes.

Mrs. Rostvolt spoke. "Mr. Gervase, please...Mr. Gervase, this is Mrs. Rostvolt, in the sheriff's office..." She listened, pulled in the corners of her mouth, spoke hurriedly. "I've been *arrested*. Yes, *me*! Arrested! This poor excuse for a sheriff—" She listened. "Something about a letter he claims I hid from him. Anyway, I want you to represent me." She listened, frowned, glanced at Joe. "He says he's going to lock me up, which is sheer —"..."Very well. I will...No. I won't...Yes, I realize that." She hung up, turned defiantly to the fascinated Joe and Paul Wentzman. "Lee Gervase is my lawyer. He says for me not to talk to you, to make no statements or admissions. So — that's all I have to say."

Joe grinned wryly. "I see. Well, Mrs. Rostvolt, as your last official act, do you care to write up the book on yourself?"

"No. I certainly do not," snapped Mrs. Rostvolt.

"You never did have a sense of humor."

"I demand a matron on the premises."

"There'll be a matron here inside of an hour. In the meantime, your virtue will be respected." Joe turned, motioned to Ace Wardell in the radio room who had been watching with interest. Wardell stepped around the partition into the main office.

"Mrs. Rostvolt is under arrest," said Joe.

Deputy Wardell's jaw dropped. "Are you kidding?"

"Nope. Book her, lock her in Cell 13. Felonious concealment of evidence."

Wardell turned to Mrs. Rostvolt. "Well, old gal, you finally got caught with jam on your face."

Joe took the manila folder into the so-called laboratory — a room to the back where a few pieces of equipment were maintained. Paul Wentzman followed. "What's the background on the case?"

Joe went to the cabinet, returned with a box containing the fingerprint development kit he had assembled while a student at Chapman Institute. "It's a long story. It starts sixteen years ago, when a young fellow named Ausley Wyett was arrested for the murder of Teresa McAllister."

"I remember the case, vaguely. It was before my time."

"It seems, from the letter, that Bus Hacker had doubts — more than doubts — as to Ausley Wyett's guilt." As Joe spoke he lifted the letter by the corner, inserted it into a rectangular glass case. Paul Wentzman watched with a quizzical frown. "Why are you doing that?"

"Simple curiosity, you might say." Joe sifted a quantity of purple-brown-black crystals into a pan, plugged a cord into a nearby outlet. "Iodine vapor," said Joe. "Watch the fingerprints pop out."

The paper became faintly brown, then with startling suddenness fingerprints appeared — everywhere. Some faint, some distinct. Joe took the letter, laid it under a copy camera, weighted it with a glass plate, switched on the lights, snapped the shutter. Then, removing the letter, he tucked it into a cellophane envelope, and with Paul Wentzman returned to his office.

"Sit down," said Joe. He went to the sideboard. "Cooch left a legacy which we might as well make use of." He brought out a pair of bottles and two glasses. "Scotch or bourbon?"

"Scotch. Just a finger. I'm not much of a drinker."

Joe poured a liberal inch into both glasses. "Sorry there's no ice. Cooch never bothered with the details."

Deputy Wardell pushed his head through the door. "Lee Gervase is here. Says he's representing Mrs. Rostvolt."

"The man is crazy," said Joe. "Send him in." He reached for another glass, polished it on his sleeve. Lee Gervase looked in through the door. His face was set in worried lines. He frowned at the sight of Paul Wentzman.

Joe said affably, "Come on in, Lee. Just the man I want to see."

Gervase came a step into the room. "I don't need to tell you how reluctantly I take on a case like this — whatever it is — just before election. Still if I don't, then I get panned for that too."

"Sit down, Lee. We can probably work something out. What are you drinking?"

"Nothing, thanks. What's the charge against my client?"

Joe poured a finger of Scotch into the glass, thrust it into Lee Gervase's reluctant fingers. "Sit down, relax, while I give you the sorry details. Maybe you'll still back away from the case, because it's not going to win you any votes."

Lee Gervase peevishly put the glass on the desk. "That's something I can't worry about. The woman is in a bind; she's asked me to represent her and that's all there is to it."

Joe shrugged. "No need to get excited. This is the situation. Ever since I took over, I've been uncovering little rackets Mrs. Rostvolt has been working. Nothing big — a few bucks here, a few bucks there. I've been jumping back and forth trying to shut off all these enterprises at once. Mrs. Rostvolt naturally resented it, and I guess she knew her days were numbered. Anyway, a letter came into the office — a very important letter — and she hid it from me. I suspect she was indulging in blackmail. It's just a suspicion so far."

"Isn't it possible she made a mistake?"

Joe shook his head. "Not very likely, considering the circumstances. I'm sure that will be her defense. Mr. Wentzman will try to prove that such a mistake was impossible, and I think he can do it."

Lee Gervase jumped to his feet, glanced at his watch. "I'd better talk to her. Exactly what are the charges?"

"Well — right now they're a little vague. I wouldn't be surprised if we could pin her with an accessory-to-murder rap. Mr. Wentzman and I will have to talk it over."

"Then you're not going to let her out of jail?"

"Not until the judge says so. I think bail might run pretty high."

"Where is she?"

"Cell 13. Go up the steps. There's nobody up there but her. Don't pass her any hacksaws or opium; it might cost you my vote."

Lee Gervase gave him a glance of contempt, departed. They heard his feet ascending the staircase.

Paul Wentzman sipped his whisky. "What's the story?"

Joe settled himself, spoke at length: of the death of Tissie McAllister, of Ausley's parole and the letters which circulated to the five witnesses; of the strange deaths of Bus Hacker, Charley Blankenship, Willis Neff and Oliver Viera.

"A juicy case," said Paul Wentzman with a grin, revealing a side to his nature Joe had never suspected.

"Juicy is right. Four men die, by accident. I know it's not accident, and the man responsible knows that I know, and laughs at me. All I can do is laugh back. Up to now. Because today I began to see the hows and whys.

"Then I fell into the letter which Bus Hacker wrote, and the whole business comes clear. More or less clear, anyway. A few points are still vague."

Lee Gervase reappeared in the doorway. "I've talked to Mrs. Rost-volt."

"You're going to act for her?"

"Yes. She states that the whole affair is a ridiculous accident, and I'm inclined to agree."

"Naturally. You're her lawyer."

"Under the circumstances, considering her long years of faithful service —"

"Don't make me laugh, Lee."

"— it seems to me that the big thing to do on your part is let her resign her position, and forget about the whole business."

"It's not as easy as that. If it weren't for the woman's greed or malice or whatever her motives, two men, or maybe three, might be alive right now. She knew the letter was important evidence, and she deliberately kept it from me. I plan to push this as far as it'll go."

Lee Gervase shrugged. "You can't *prove* this greed or malice. You can't prove that she wasn't merely absent-minded, or incompetent."

"That'll be for the jury to decide."

Lee Gervase gave a terse nod. "In that case I'll draw up a writ and have her out of jail."

"That's your duty to your client," said Joe.

Lee Gervase departed, and so presently did Paul Wentzman.

An hour later Lee Gervase returned. Joe was in the laboratory; Ace Wardell called him into the front office, where Lee Gervase silently presented him with a document.

Joe shook his head. "It's no good, Lee."

"No good? Why on earth not?"

"I've got new evidence. I'm now charging her definitely with being an accessory *post facto* to murder. This writ is too low-power. You'll have to get a new one."

Lee Gervase said coldly, "I think you could have told me this before."

"As I say—new evidence has turned up. No inconvenience intended."

"That's a serious charge. Unless you've got very good grounds, you're laying yourself open to big trouble. Namely, a suit for false arrest."

"I'm not worried."

Lee Gervase departed. Joe shook his head sadly, turned away.

Ace Wardell called to him: "Telephone call for you. Art van Horn, from Marblestone."

Joe froze, and his throat felt tight. "Good Lord. Another?" He took the phone. "Sheriff Bain speaking."

"Joe, this is Art van Horn. You better get out here right away. Looks like there's going to be trouble."

"What kind of trouble?"

"Ausley Wyett tried to kill Cole Destin. Some of the folks are ready to let him have it."

"How do you mean, tried to kill Cole?"

"Ran him off the road. Another 'accident'. Only Cole kept control of his car."

"Where's Ausley now?"

"He's home. But he may not be long, because the bar is full of guys getting drunker and meaner by the minute. That's where I'm calling from."

"Who's the drunkest and meanest of the lot?"

"That's hard to say. Stub Caramino is the drunkest. For meanness it's a tie between two or three guys. Cole is acting pretty mean himself."

"Well—talk to each of these guys separately. Try to make them see reason, until I get there—which will be half an hour."

Chapter XV

Joe parked in front of the Town Club, jumped out of the car, along with Sergeant Miggs and Sergeant Boso. Art van Horn met him at the door to the bar, raised his hand in limp relief. "I'm glad to see you. I don't know whether these guys are just shooting their mouths off, letting off steam, or whether they're working themselves up into a real rage."

"Most likely they're just talking. Lynching isn't so stylish nowadays."

"There aren't too many guys like Ausley Wyett around, that's the only reason."

"Maybe so."

They turned toward the bar when a Willys station wagon pulled sedately in to park against the curb. While Joe, Art van Horn and the two deputies watched in astonishment, Ausley Wyett alighted. "Hi fellas."

Art van Horn strode forward. "What in blazes are you doing in town?"

"I came in to get me a glass of beer," said Ausley in an aggrieved voice. "Anything wrong with that?"

"You set foot inside that bar and there'll be a dozen guys taking you apart."

"That's kinda narrow-minded." Ausley turned to Joe. "What about it, Joe?"

Joe said in a neutral voice, "Cole Destin claims you tried to run him off the road."

Ausley's eyes popped in disbelief. "Cole says that? He's crazy."

"What happened?"

"I was out to the Neff place, and Cole came out — wanted to talk to Ellie about selling. She asked me what I thought and I told her to hang on to the place. Well, a few words passed and Cole told me to clear out. So, rather than cause trouble, I left. I don't know what happened — I guess Ellie run him off — but a few minutes later Cole comes up behind me, going like blazes.

"I moved over to let him pass, and just then a big oil truck comes around the curve. The way things was Cole didn't have a chance. I jammed on my brakes to let him pass, but he had the same idea, he jammed on his brakes, we were still filling the road, and there was the truck. All he could do was run himself into the ditch. He was lucky, because just a little way back the road ran through a cut, without any ditch, and fifty yards ahead there was a drop-off. I stopped, the truck stopped. Cole was raving. I could see he wasn't hurt, so I came on in."

"He's saying you tried to kill him."

"I wouldn't try such a trick. You know me better than that, Joe."

"There's Ausley Wyett now!" said a voice, rapt in amazement.

Cole Destin came out of the bar, followed by a half dozen others. Cole marched forward. "Joe — you're acting as sheriff till the election. This man tried to kill me not two hours ago, headed me into a big truck. I want you to arrest him."

Joe said, "Just a minute now, Cole. The way he tells it you were passing him on a blind curve."

"My story is that he deliberately tried to head me into the way of a big gas truck."

Joe shrugged. "If you want to sign a complaint, I'll sure as hell see that he shows up in court. But you'll have your hands full proving your accusation. And if you can't he might have a civil case against you."

"Why? Ausley Wyett?" Cole Destin laughed harshly. "He's a disgrace to the human race. And he has the gall to hang around a nice girl like Ellie Neff."

Joe heard Ausley take a deep slow breath, then relax. Joe said, "You people don't seem to realize that Ausley Wyett isn't guilty of anything — unless you can prove it."

"No?" jeered Walt Hobius. "What about Tissie McAllister?"

"That's in the past. He's out of jail now, and until something else is proved on him, he's got the same rights as anybody else."

"We got rights too," shouted Stub Caramino hoarsely. "Four men dead since he got out of jail. Today he almost made it five. Aren't you going to do something about it?"

"Yes," said Joe. "I sure am."

"When? That's what I want to know, when?"

Joe considered. "There's one or two details to be cleared up — but I promise you action inside a day or two."

"I want action now," said Cole. "I'm charging Wyett with attempted murder, and I've got the truck driver for a witness."

"You're going to sign a complaint?"

"Yes. I am."

Joe turned to Ausley. "In that case, you might as well come into town with me. Save me the trouble of coming after you, once I make out a warrant."

Ausley took a step back. "I don't aim to make things easy for anybody. Why should I?"

"That's up to you, Ausley. However, there's a big political rally in town tonight. Everybody's out for my scalp, and your pal Cole Destin is going to speak."

"You're damn right I'm going to speak. I'm going to speak up one side of you and down the other."

"There isn't any law against heckling the speaker, so far as I know. In fact, maybe I'll do a little heckling myself."

Ausley rubbed his chin. "What's that got to do with me?"

"You'll be out on bail, and you can watch the fun."

"Well — all right … if that's the case."

Art van Horn guffawed. "If that's the case, I'll be there too."

"Sure, why not?" said Joe. "The more the merrier. Everybody come. Don't forget, I'm the hometown boy, and it's me they're planning to jump on tonight."

"You don't seem too worried, Joe," Walt Hobius observed with a dour grin.

"I've been jumped on before. I'm still in one piece." He turned to Ausley Wyett. "Let's go and get this business over with. Are you coming in right away, Cole? Because that's the only reason I'm taking in Ausley."

"As soon as I go home and change clothes."

"Good enough. I'll wait for you at headquarters. Come along, Ausley."

Four o'clock came, and five, but Cole did not appear. Ausley sat in a chair in Joe's office reading a magazine. Finally the telephone rang. Cole Destin spoke in a subdued voice. "I've been talking to Paul Wentzman, and he tells me he won't prosecute. Says there's not enough evidence."

"What about the truck driver?" Joe asked ironically.

"I talked to him. He says all he saw was me trying to pass Ausley, then running into the ditch. In fact —" Cole hesitated.

"In fact," said Joe, "he figures you deserved to be killed, passing on a blind curve."

Cole spoke with vast dignity. "So far as I'm concerned, I'm not pressing any charges."

"What about Ausley? Are you going to apologize, or what?"

"Are you crazy? He tried to kill me, man! I just can't prove it."

"I guess it's up to him," said Joe. "He may want to take action against you and he may not."

"Look here, Joe. You're just filling that job on a interim basis and don't forget it. In fact, I've had enough of your sanctimony. Tonight the curtain is going up, and if you get hurt, so much the worse for you."

"It's a chance I have to take. I'll be there."

"You might as well be. It won't do you any good to stay away."

The sun sank into a brassy summer sky; after-glow gave way to dusk. Tonight Montalvo Square presented a festive appearance. A dais near the fountain had been decorated with red, white and blue crepe paper, festoons of red, white and blue lights. A pair of searchlights, rented from a company in San Jose, began to explore the sky; the PA system broadcast military marches. At a booth near Main Street a group of women made coffee in four big percolators, while others arranged doughnuts on trays. They were well-fed, well-dressed wives of local businessmen, and chattered gaily together.

A floodlight illuminated the dais, a man in black slacks and a white shirt adjusted a set of microphones: "Testing: one — two — three — four. Testing —"

People began to trickle into the square, taking seats on the benches alongside the walks, and on the balustrade around the fountain. Up on the dais climbed a group of men with musical instruments: an accordion, a guitar, a string bass and a banjo. They tuned up and began to play and sing old-fashioned songs, western tunes, camp-fire ditties.

The crowd grew in the square, encouraged by the warmth of the evening and the full moon. At the base of the dais the dignitaries of the evening began to collect, and presently a group of them mounted the dais and seated themselves on chairs provided for the purpose.

At eight o'clock Fred Hatch, president of the Pleasant Grove Chamber of Commerce, stepped up to the microphone, waited with a smile of indulgent courtesy for the musicians to finish *Red River Valley*. Montalvo Square was now half-full of people, with others arriving.

The musicians ended their tune, bowed with artistic modesty; Fred Hatch clapped politely; the audience offered a spatter of applause.

Fred Hatch tapped the microphone, nodded in satisfaction at the answering sputter of sound, began to speak.

Joe Bain telephoned his mother, who, after exclamations of astonishment at Mrs. Rostvolt's incarceration, agreed to serve as matron until a replacement could be found.

Joe swung around, faced Ausley Wyett, who sat reading a year-old copy of *Hunters Afield*. Ausley carefully put the magazine down. "What's the situation?"

Joe reflected. "So far as the law is concerned, you're a free man. If I were you, I'd play it cool and figure on spending the night in town."

Ausley shuffled his feet. "Maybe so. I'm a bit worried about my dogs. Somebody might figure to toss in some poison bait."

"My guess would be that they're safe," said Joe, "so long as people figure you're in trouble with the law. Of course, I may be wrong."

"I can't understand it," said Ausley Wyett. "The way people always want to believe the worst of a man."

Joe gave a dismal chuckle. "Most times they got good reason."

Ausley gave him an injured look.

Joe went on: "You do as you like. I'm going to look in on the rally.

These big-shots are fixing to run me out of my job. I might have something to say about that."

"I'll come along too," said Ausley. "I don't have anything else to do."

"Just keep away from the Marblestone bunch. I don't want any more fights than absolutely necessary."

"I won't start any fights," said Ausley somberly.

"You go on ahead. I've got to arrange things with the deputies. I'm putting five men into the square, just in case of trouble."

"Why should there be trouble?"

"You never know," said Joe. He ushered Ausley to the door. "I'll see you, in the square."

Ausley departed; Joe went to the back room, where he told Deputies Boso, Miggs, Gonzales, Taylor and Phipps what he expected of them.

Then he himself went out into the square. He arrived just as Fred Hatch uttered his first words into the microphone: "Good evening, ladies and gentlemen! I'm sure glad to see you here in such respectable numbers; looks like we're going to have a real enthusiastic rally. Well, I won't take up much of your time. There's people here who came prepared to speak, to tell you their ideas of what's good for the county and what's good for you, and respectfully urge for your votes. Then after the talks, we'll have a musical program, featuring the famous Traveling Hoosiers, with lovely little June Perkins. And don't forget, free refreshments in the booth to the north of the square.

"Now I want to introduce our guests who have so generously contributed their time and ideas for the benefit of the county.

"First: one of our leading citizens, and candidate for the office of Sheriff: Mr. Lee Gervase!"

Lee Gervase arose, bowed, smiled with a clenched jaw. In a dark blue suit, he contrived to look a man indifferent to careful grooming, yet nevertheless well-dressed. Joe saw a number of women commenting to each other. He smiled dourly.

"Next," said Fred Hatch, "is the distinguished editor of the county's leading newspaper: Howard Griselda of the Pleasant Grove *Messenger*!"

Griselda rose, frowned, nodded his heavy head, sat down.

"Next, the respected President of the San Rodrigo County Council for Progress: Wilfred Mortimer!"

Wilfred Mortimer, a tall white-haired man with a crisp white mustache and drooping eyelids, gave the crowd a careful salutation.

"Then, a spokesman for our Latin American citizens — Dr. Henry Gomez!"

Dr. Gomez, plump as an olive, eye-glasses glittering with red, white and blue reflections, bobbed quickly up and down.

Fred Hatch looked dubiously at the fifth seat, then leaned forward, nodded across the crowd. "And last but not least — I see him coming now — a man from one of the oldest families in the county, a man who knows ranching and cattle like few others, just now arriving — he'll be here in a jiffy — Cole Destin!"

Cole Destin, formidable in mouse-gray gabardine, climbed up to the dais, nodded briefly to the crowd, took his seat.

Fred Hatch said, "Before I introduce the first speaker, I want to define the purposes of our organization. We believe in a bigger, better, thriving San Rodrigo County. We are for progress, we are for sound efficient administration; we are against stagnation and bureaucratic inefficiency and corruption. We are for a new county courthouse to replace this ancient joke —" Fred Hatch made a gesture toward the old courthouse "— and we are for a complete revamping of our county offices, starting, in this coming election, with the Sheriff's Office. So — without further ado — I give you a man qualified by his education, his training, his unique capability, and his will to serve — I give you our next sheriff — Lee Gervase!"

To a burst of polite applause, Lee Gervase approached the microphone.

Joe took a deep breath, and with a curious loose sensation in his knees climbed the steps to the dais. Fred Hatch saw him, frowned, walked casually over to speak to him. Joe said a few words to him. Fred Hatch's mouth fell open. Lee Gervase watched over his shoulder with a frown. Joe crossed the platform, took the microphone. Lee Gervase made as if to grab it back, then shrugged, smiled, held out his hands to the crowd as if to apologize for the interruption. The crowd, aware that here was a situation by no means on the schedule, became still. Joe said, "What I'm doing is extraordinary, and maybe not in very good taste. What it amounts to, is that I'm horning in on a big program put on and sponsored by people who oppose me in next week's election. Under normal circumstances I wouldn't dare act like this — because — well, it's just not the thing to do.

"However, there's a peculiar situation which, when I explain it, I believe will cause you to overlook my rudeness.

"Lee Gervase is standing here beside me. He was primed to tell you of the corruption in Sheriff Ernest Cucchinello's department —"

Lee Gervase grinned broadly, pushed himself in front of the mike. "Mr. Bain, what you say about yourself and your rudeness and your gross lack of good taste is absolutely accurate. But if you want to argue about the corruption and inefficiency of Sheriff Cucchinello's system, I'm more than willing."

"No, Lee. Nothing like that. Old Cooch is dead. I'm running a different department. That's not what I'm here for."

"Well — why are you here?"

"To make it clear to the people of the county why you won't be their choice for sheriff."

Lee Gervase's smile was deadly. "Don't you think this is a matter which should be left to the voters?"

"It's impossible, Lee. Since you'll be in jail. You're under arrest."

The crowd gasped, muttered. Lee Gervase jerked, stared, then laughed. Howard Griselda bounded forward, took Joe's arm, led him away from the microphone. Cole Destin sat back with a frozen look of contempt on his face.

Joe spoke a few cool words to Griselda, who suddenly seemed to go limp. He made an indecisive motion, as if to order Joe from the stand, then stood glowering. Joe returned to the mike. "I agree this is really a ham act I'm putting on, but I figure that since you're the voters you're entitled to know the kind of man you'd be voting for.

"These are the facts. Lee Gervase is an able ambitious man. He sees a big future for himself, he's got his sights set far ahead — maybe on Sacramento, maybe on Washington. Who knows? To achieve these goals, he figured he had to make himself look good in his first public office. What better way than to make the incumbent sheriff and the previous sheriff look a couple of monkeys? Lee Gervase got carried away by his ambition and he let himself in for serious trouble.

"This is what happened. Sixteen years ago a man named Ausley Wyett was sent to jail for the murder of a little girl. A man named Clarence Hacker was a witness against him — and he didn't tell the truth. He probably didn't lie on the witness stand, but there was a great deal he didn't tell, for reasons of his own, which were blackmail. A blackmailer is always scared to death of his victim, and Clarence Hacker made use of the usual system. If he were to die suddenly, a letter was to be sent to the authorities.

"Clarence Hacker died, the letter was sent. It was opened by a woman who had served under Sheriff Cucchinello. She read the letter, she instantly saw how important the letter was, and instead of showing me the letter, she took it to Lee Gervase. This, I imagine, is what she told him: 'Mr. Gervase, Sheriff Bain is about to discharge me. If I show you how to make yourself look real good the first week you're in office, can I keep my job?' To which, so I guess, Lee Gervase expressed interest. Mrs. Rostvolt showed him the letter —"

Lee Gervase said in a harsh voice, "This is a vicious collection of lies. It's slander!"

Joe said, in a mild voice, "Do you think I'd lay myself open if I couldn't prove what I'm talking about?"

"I don't know. Ladies and gentlemen, Mrs. Rostvolt is my client. Today she called me to complain of persecution suffered under this poor excuse for a law-enforcement officer — culminating today when he arrested her and locked her in a jail cell for what was no more than a simple mistake. Thereupon, knowing how hopeless his campaign for re-election is, Bain tries to slander me —"

Joe said, "Not at all, Lee. I'm not slandering you, I'm arresting you. You can't run for Sheriff or be elected because you'll be in jail. The charges are being accessory to murder. Mrs. Rostvolt hasn't any defense, any more than you. And do you know why?"

"I certainly do not know why!"

"Because, big as you please, on the letter is your thumb-print. Remember today when I handed you a glass? I checked your prints with the prints on the letter — and there you are, big as life. You can't get around it, Lee — and neither can Mrs. Rostvolt. If she thought enough of the letter to show it to you, and you read it, and agreed to her terms —

you're both guilty." Joe reached out, deftly snapped a pair of handcuffs on Lee Gervase, who looked down at them in confusion.

Joe motioned to Sergeant Miggs, who stood just below. Miggs stepped up on the dais, took Lee Gervase's arm. "Let's go, boy."

Lee Gervase shook him off, turned to his stunned friends at the back of the dais. "Aren't you going to stop this? Aren't you going to do something about this?"

Griselda said in an odd choked voice, "If his charges are true — there's nothing we can do. Nothing we want to do."

Fred Hatch spoke in a high-pitched voice: "Tell us, Lee. Tell us Bain is crazy. Tell the people this is all a hoax — a monstrous evil hoax."

Lee Gervase shuffled to the microphone. "Ladies and gentlemen — this is a hoax — a monstrous evil hoax."

Joe grimaced, motioned to Miggs, who pulled Lee Gervase away and off the dais. Cole Destin rose abruptly to his feet, stood staring at Joe, then started for the steps. Joe said, "Don't go, Cole, I'm not finished. Not by a long shot."

Cole Destin said, "What do you mean?"

"While I'm here I might as well go into the whole case, unless the people here don't want to hear about it — in which case I'll depart." Joe looked out over the crowd. "What about it? Do you want to hear the whole facts of this case? It's the strangest thing I've ever come on in my life, I'll guarantee you that. All those who want to hear about it say aye."

There was a great chorus of "ayes".

"Opposed?"

Silence.

Joe turned to Fred Hatch. "Do I have your permission to speak?"

Fred Hatch made a helpless gesture, grinning feebly. "You might as well. We don't have any program. We don't have any candidate, it looks like."

Chapter XVI

"To start with," Joe told the audience, "we have to go back sixteen years. Some of you will remember the case. Ausley Wyett was accused of murdering Teresa McAllister. There were five witnesses against him: Clarence Hacker, Charles Blankenship, Willis Neff, Cole Destin and Oliver Viera.

"Ausley Wyett pleaded not guilty, but he was convicted. About a month ago he was paroled out of San Quentin, and returned to the farm where he was born.

"I don't know what he had in mind but Ausley wrote five letters to the five witnesses, to the effect that 'here I am out of jail, where your testimony put me. I aim to do something about it. What do you plan to do to help me?' Maybe not quite these exact words — but to the same effect.

"It was a real ill-advised set of letters. The first I heard about them was when Charley Blankenship came into the office complaining. I checked on the other four witnesses. Sure enough — they all had received letters, and all were angry at Ausley Wyett.

"I went to talk to Clarence Hacker. Right in front of my eyes he had a heart attack. Accident.

"A few days later Charley Blankenship ate some poison mushrooms. He died. Accident.

"A few days later Willis Neff was shot, apparently by an out-of-season hunter. Accident.

"Ausley Wyett claimed to know nothing of these strange accidental deaths. He told me that he was with Oliver Viera at the time when Neff was killed. Before I could check with Oliver Viera, he fell off a ladder into a ravine and broke his neck. Accident.

"By now there was only one of the five left alive — Cole Destin. I warned him to be careful. In fact —"

Cole could no longer contain himself. "A bloody lot of good you did!" he burst out in a harsh voice. "Today Ausley Wyett tried to kill me! And only just missed!"

"That might be slander, Cole — in case Ausley wants to push it."

"Let him try."

"Well, here we were with four people dead — all by accident. I knew that Bus Hacker had a letter he wanted me to see, but I couldn't find it. Somebody else wanted this letter. Whoever it was tried to jimmy Bus Hacker's old safe, and when that failed, he burned down the house, hoping to incinerate the letter.

"I opened the safe — no letter. Bus Hacker had arranged for it to be mailed and so it was. Mrs. Rostvolt read it, and Lee Gervase. If I'd seen it promptly I could have saved the lives of Oliver Viera and Willis Neff. Possibly even Charley Blankenship. What was in this letter? I'm coming to that.

"Even before I read the letter I knew who was causing these 'accidental' deaths, and I worked out some theories as to how they could be accomplished.

"For instance, in the case of Bus Hacker. Everybody knew he had a bum heart. So the man responsible — call him X — set his plans in motion. First he arranged that Bus' car be laid up for a day or two, by putting water in the gas tank. Then he arranged that Bus be called into town on a wild-goose chase, and while Bus was out he made his preparations. Just by a stroke of luck, I happened to be calling on Bus when he returned. He was furious at being fooled, hot and tired and red in the face from the long walk. When he marched up to his front door and keeled over, I wasn't surprised. But just out of habit I checked around. I saw something that puzzled me — not much, but enough that it stuck in my mind. There was a quarter-inch hole in the porch right under the steel mesh foot-scraper. I wasn't able to get into the house, but there must have been another hole just inside the door, close to the baseboard. As I say, this hole didn't mean much to me at the time. There was no reason to suspect anything out of the ordinary. Right after Bus died, I went up and did the same thing he did — walked up the steps, pulled back the screen door, opened the front door — and nothing happened. I think I know how it was worked. Bus Hacker was electrocuted — he was given a big jolt of 220-volt current. Wires were led from the entry box in the basement, one through the hole on the porch to the wire-mesh foot scraper, the other through the hole on the floor to the door handle. How come I didn't see the wires? This is how it could have been arranged. A string wedged under the screen door supported a weight fixed to these wires. When Bus opened the screen door the string came loose, the weight pulled on the wires. But Bus' weight on the mesh held them in place. He grabbed the door handle, and this big jolt of current goes through him. He can't let go, he just holds on; his heart gives a couple of wild kicks, and Bus has had it. He falls off the porch, the wire comes loose from under the mesh, the weight pulls the wires through the holes into the basement.

"That night X breaks into the house, removes the evidence. He tries to jimmy the safe. No luck. He burns the house, thinking to destroy the letter. He just about succeeds. The next day, Cole Destin brought out Walt Hobius and his tow-truck and pulled the safe up from the basement, and the jouncing around didn't help a bit.

"I opened the safe. No incriminating letter. But I found Bus Hacker's ledger, accounting for every cent he spent. One or two omissions I thought peculiar — but with Ausley on my mind I wasn't overly suspicious.

"So Bus Hacker went to his grave — murdered in front of my nose. X sweated it out for a while, but when nothing happened he figured the letter was destroyed and he was safe.

"Next on the program: Charles Blankenship. And X really shows his ingenuity. I don't know where he found the Amanita mushrooms. When I was a kid a lot of them grew up in the wet part of the hills. I guess they do yet. Death-angels we used to call them. Or just plain toadstools. It doesn't take much to kill a man.

"Charley Blankenship was accidentally killed like this. X locates a beautiful clump of good mushrooms, which he digs up carefully, and a few Amanitas. One is enough. They don't look much different from an ordinary mushroom, except for white gills and a death-cup around the stem. Our man colors the gills dark brown, pulls off the death-cup, and he's got just another mushroom. He transplants the lot — mushrooms and Amanita with the brown gills — into Charley Blankenship's pansy bed. The rest is well known.

"Next — Willis Neff. So far this is all speculation. I couldn't prove a thing. There's interesting angles — such as Bus Hacker's ledger, and Mrs. Blankenship being sick with her gall bladder — but nothing definite.

"The death of Willis Neff is different. It's more violent, and more complicated, and it left traces. Still, they wouldn't be noticed unless somebody was extra suspicious. X figured he's worked a pretty smart deal.

"By the time we found Neff's body the doctor couldn't pinpoint the time of death. It was sometime between ten Wednesday night and six Thursday morning. His stomach contents proved he died half an hour after eating bacon and eggs. Then an old pensioner fixed the time for us. He swore that Neff could have driven in only after five o'clock Thursday morning — the time he was gone from his cabin. There wasn't any other possibility until Friday night, when a car had gone in and the same car had gone out again. But this didn't account for Neff's pickup. There it was — and Hill swore on his grandfather's Bible it could only have come in early Thursday morning. So that seemed to fix the time and place of Neff's death. He had arrived at five o'clock, fixed himself breakfast, went to stretch his legs — and somebody shot him. Peculiar thing though. The rear wheels of his pickup were dusty, but not the front wheels. Did Neff maybe start to wash his pickup at five-thirty in the morning?

"Unluckily for X Ausley Wyett put forward an alibi. He was talking to Oliver Viera at seven o'clock Thursday morning. It's not possible that Ausley could have shot Neff at five o'clock, planted evidence on the ridge and rushed back in order to meet Oliver Viera at seven, especially when he didn't know Oliver was coming. If Ausley were actually with Oliver Viera at seven, he's got a substantial alibi.

"By now people are becoming edgy. All these 'accidental' deaths — no matter how accidental they seem — they can't all be coincidences! But if Ausley hasn't killed Neff, then it's highly doubtful that he's killed any of the others and the whole plot falls through.

"Oliver Viera is Ausley Wyett's alibi. Too bad for Oliver. Oliver must go, and fast — before the alibi is official. Also, he is one of the original group of five — which puts the frosting on the cake, so to speak.

"This is how I think Oliver Viera died. I can't be sure, because there isn't a single clue. X is much too cagy. But it could have happened this way.

"Oliver and his family go out for the evening: it was his wedding anniversary. X visits the house, sets up a ladder with a gallon of paint about ready to fall off the top step.

"As soon as Oliver gets up in the morning he sees the ladder and the paint. He starts up the ladder to take down the paint before it falls and makes a mess. Across the ravine, X is waiting behind a tree. He sees Oliver come out of the house, look at the ladder, start climbing. X gets himself set. Oliver climbs to the top. X walks backwards, pulling on the nylon fish-line which runs across the ravine and loops around the top of the ladder. He doesn't need to pull hard. Over goes the ladder, Oliver falls sixty feet, breaks his neck. Another revengeful stroke by Ausley, so it appears, and now Ausley is also without his alibi for Neff's death. Very very clever.

"From the original five, there's only Cole Destin left, and, as he will tell you, he almost got it today."

Joe paused, looked out over the crowd. No question but what he had the undivided attention of everyone. In all quarters were fascinated faces, dark rapt eyes. He turned, looked over his shoulders at the four dignitaries, who had assembled so confidently not an hour before. Howard Griselda sat hunched, defeated and humiliated beyond any previous recollection. Cole Destin stared furiously, every muscle taut. Fred Hatch, who had wandered uncertainly to the seat once occupied by Lee Gervase, stood nervously behind it, as if not quite daring to seat himself in the chair of a man disgraced. Wilfred Mortimer and Dr. Henry Gomez blinked and frowned like men in a dream.

Joe smiled pensively, turned back to the microphone. "So now the big question: what about this man X? I can tell you one thing, he's sweating right now. He's here listening to me, and he's wondering whether or not to make some kind of move. It won't do him any good — so he might as well relax. Unless he wants to give himself up?" Joe waited. But there was no response. "He's still wondering if I really have the goods on him.

"Well, I do. Bus Hacker's letter is pretty definite. Bus Hacker, incidentally, doesn't come out of this business very well. For sixteen years he'd indulged in blackmail — a petty, miserable blackmail, not pushing hard enough to make X revolt. Although something must have happened recently to make X take his chances with Bus Hacker's letter — which Bus had undoubtedly told him about and which he thought was kept in Bus Hacker's safe.

"One more thing. As I see it X wasn't really mad at Ausley Wyett to begin with. But he came to hate Ausley, in the way a man hates somebody he's doing wrong to. A matter of psychological self-protection, I guess. Perhaps it happened directly after the murder of Tissie McAllister. Ausley Wyett, an innocent man, spent sixteen years in jail for a crime he did not commit. I don't wonder that he felt a grievance against the five men who bore testimony against him. But that's not here nor there. It happened that X also had a grievance against at least three of the men on Ausley's list: Bus Hacker, Charley Blankenship, and Willis Neff. Oliver Viera had to die for the reason I mentioned: he was Ausley's alibi, and his death made things look even worse for Ausley.

"That's the background. If this man X wants to say something, I'll be glad to let him use the microphone... No? Well, I can understand his bashfulness. He's a pretty wicked man — and he knows it. Sixteen years ago he killed little Tissie McAllister, and let Ausley Wyett take the rap. How did Bus Hacker know this? Bus Hacker drove the school bus. Just about the time that Ausley Wyett was showing his new kittens to Tissie, Bus Hacker parked the bus in front of his house. He saw enough to give him a pretty good idea of what went on.

"Now, if you'll excuse me for patting myself on the back a little, I'll give you the clues which led me to X before I read the letter, then I'll read you the letter.

"First, Bus Hacker's ledger showed no money spent for rent or for any automobile expenses. Millie Hacker worked for the Destins thirty years, and Cole explains that the use of the house was a kind of a pension. But how to explain the lack of automobile expenses? No money spent for gas, oil, tires, repairs — it seems too good to be true. Almost as if Bus owned a service station.

"Second, Charley Blankenship hated his nephew Walt Hobius. More accurately, his wife's nephew. One time he shot a charge of rock salt at him. When I was talking to Metty Blankenship, she mentioned that Charley wanted nothing to go to Walt. Today I telephoned her and asked about Charley's will, just to make sure. I found that he left everything to his wife, or in the event that he survived her — which it looked like, what with Mrs. Blankenship's bad gall bladder trouble — his grand-niece in Denver inherited. But Mrs. Blankenship always felt a soft spot for Walt — and with Charley dead, Walt could figure on inheriting a good-size sum, together with forty acres of cherries in the near future.

"Third: a day or so before Charley Blankenship died, I noticed some brown stains on Walt's fingers. I thought they were nicotine. Walt should have kept his mouth shut, but he wasn't thinking and blurted out the truth. He said the stains were from iodine or brown ink or 'something'. At the time I thought this was pretty peculiar for a man not to know what his hands had been in. But Walt, experimenting with the Amanita, trying to color the white gills, had fooled with both, and maybe other brown colors as well.

"This is what put me on the track. I'd figured out the method of Bus Hacker's death, but it didn't give me any line on who. But as soon as I asked 'How would I get someone to eat an Amanita?', and answered, 'I'd make it look like a mushroom by coloring the gills brown', I thought of Walt's fingers. And after that everything began to fall into place.

"Fourth: the front wheels of Neff's pickup were clean. Neff might have been killed almost any time Wednesday night or Thursday morning. But the evidence pointed to Monterey County, at five o'clock Thursday morning — unless he was killed somewhere else and brought in. But this was impossible. Hill told us only one car had come and the same car had gone out on Friday night — hence Neff must have driven in just before he was killed. Unless Neff and his pickup were brought in together Friday night. Pretty hard unless you own a tow-truck. Pretty hard unless you have a garage where you can hide a pickup and a body for a day. A pickup which was towed would have dusty rear wheels, but clean front wheels.

"That's how my theories went. Another small matter. The day Bus Hacker died I talked to Walt. He was reading a newspaper, in no hurry to repair Bus Hacker's car. I thought nothing about this at the time, of course. Well, I finally saw the letter from Bus Hacker which Irma Rostvolt and Lee Gervase had conspired to hide from me." Joe took a paper from his pocket. "This is how it reads:

To whom it may concern:

This letter reveals me for what I am, a man troubled by his conscience and in fear of God Almighty for his sins on this earth.

For many years I have wondered what to do. I have no certain proof that Walter Hobius abused and killed Teresa McAllister on the 22nd day of May, 1946, but for all these years he has paid me for my silence, and I believe that he and not Ausley Wyett should have paid the penalty for the crime.

I cannot be dead certain. If I were, no power on earth could force me to silence, for I am not a man bereft of morals.

On the afternoon of May 22, Walter Hobius rode home from high school on my bus, rather than on the Route 1 bus, which he normally rode. The reason for this was that the bus was giving me trouble and I was hiring Walter to make the necessary repairs. He listened to the engine and told me I needed a valve grind, which he would do the next day. If I wanted to save a few dollars, I could remove the cylinder head myself.

I parked at the corner of Destin Lane and Mitre Canyon Road. We got out, raised the hood, looked at the engine, whereupon I decided to let Walter do the whole job, as I am no mechanic. Cole Destin drove past in his car. Walter started to walk toward Marble-stone. In my testimony, after taking an oath before God, I could not tell an untruth, as I am not and never have been a perjurer nor an oath-breaker, I swore that I had seen no one pass. This was absolutely true. Walter Hobius did not pass. He walked away from me.

After a while I looked down the road, and saw Ausley Wyett leave the barn and walk away toward the pasture. I saw Walter stop and talk to Teresa. She indicated the barn and now I believe that she was telling him about Ausley Wyett's kittens, and asking if he wanted one.

I saw Walter hesitate. Then he and Teresa walked to the barn and went inside.

This is all I saw, for at this time I went into my own house.

When I learned of the murder I was sorely distressed. But Ausley Wyett's attempt to dispose of the body led me to believe that he was guilty, for an innocent man would not have acted in this way.

Walter Hobius started to work on my bus the next day. He was nervous and ill at ease. I told him that I had seen him go to the barn with Teresa, and he asked me to say nothing about the matter. He assured me that he had not molested the girl, and that if I mentioned his presence, it would only embarrass him, and introduce confusing factors into an otherwise clear-cut case. In which case he might not be able to finish his work on my bus. He said he wanted to do a good job, to change the piston rings and the bearings, in short a complete overhaul, for which he would not charge me a cent, but if he were called as a witness he would not be able to do this.

So here, and I pray forgiveness from our Heavenly Father who understands all, I agreed. It seemed as if the case were already definite against Ausley Wyett, and I would only be confusing the issue.

Walter Hobius overhauled the bus. Whenever I needed further work, I told him and he did the work. I felt no qualms using him in this fashion. If it were not for my cooperation he might have fared far worse. As the years went on, Walter Hobius maintained my automobile for me and occasionally supplied me with gas and oil. I feel no remorse. He only partially recompensed me for the agonies of conscience I suffered over the years. It is right that he should be penalized, to some degree, for the crime I am not sure he committed.

I swear, by my hope of eventual salvation and by my fear of God's wrath, that this letter contains the exact truth. If I were less weak I would appear before the authorities and make a statement, but I am old and ill, and I want to live my life out in peace.

If I have erred, I pray forgiveness and understanding. The above is the truth.

CLARENCE J. HACKER

Joe looked up, across the crowd. He pointed. "When I began talking, Walt Hobius was standing over there, near the coffee booth. I was watching him. So were three deputies. He listened a few minutes, and then decided to leave. The deputies followed, and made the arrest on the sidewalk.

"Walter Hobius is now in jail."

Chapter XVII

WALTER HOBIUS TALKED FREELY, making no attempt to deny or gloss over his guilt. Indeed, he seemed to display an inordinate pride in his own cleverness. He showed no hostility to Joe, and even less to the newspaper reporters who converged from all parts of the state. Toward Bus Hacker Walt evinced acrid hate. "You know something? The only thing that bothers me is that I didn't do for that miserable old cur sooner. All these years he's been sucking my blood — gas, oil, tires, repairs. Why should he buy a new car, when I'd patch up his old heap? Then, just before Ausley was paroled, he told me he wanted four new tires, and a paint job. I told him I didn't have that kind of spare money. One time when I was at his house he showed me the letter which he'd written and kept in his safe; now he reminded me of the letter and warned me that I'd better cooperate. I told him okay, but then and there I decided to fix his wagon. Ausley getting out of jail only pushed matters along... What? Ausley? Yeah, Ausley the chump. Why shouldn't he stay in jail? Living outside of jail never did him no good. Girls didn't like him, he was just a big clown. Jail was a good place for him...Joe was just about right how I put away Charley. Another mean old bastard who didn't deserve to live. But Joe missed a bet. I was nervous he'd catch on. The toadstool I found, but the mushrooms I had to buy. I couldn't find any. I bought them at a mushroom farm in Santa Cruz. If Joe had thought to ask around, the jig was up...

"On Wednesday night Neff visited the cat-house in San Rodrigo. He left off his spare tire and told me he'd call back for it. I told him I'd wait — no matter how late. I'm a patient son of a bitch. That's another bet Joe missed. He saw Neff drop off his spare; in the back of the pickup,

— 182 —

there was the spare. Neff must have come back to the station for it. If Joe had thought about that, the jig was up again. So Neff went to San Rodrigo, visited his woman, and I guess he ate somewhere, then he came back about eleven o'clock. I took him out into the garage and shot him, using a silencer on my gun. I'd been to this meadow in Monterey County a few months back, so I just laid Neff out in the pickup, closed the doors on the garage, and Friday night towed the whole shebang to location…Nope, I don't regret it. I don't regret anybody but Ollie, who wasn't a bad guy. But he had to go. It was him or me. One man's gain is another man's loss: that's the way life goes. I don't regret a thing. I've really lived this last month. None of you guys know what it's like to go full out. And I'll tell you something. I'd have got Cole Destin next. Why? To make everything pretty, so that everything came out exactly right. Cole had to go. Yep. He would have been next. Five witnesses, five letters, five accidents. See what I mean? It's beautiful, when you stop to think about it…And it's only by miserable poor luck I was caught. I didn't deserve to get hung up. I'll get out of it yet, wait and see…"

Ausley Wyett looked into the sheriff's office the day after election. There were three men in Joe's private sanctum, and the air reverberated with congratulations and well wishes. Joe excused himself, stepped out into the hall. "Ausley, old man! How's it going?" Joe spoke in a somewhat slurred voice. He had been forced to drink a number of toasts: to a successful term in office, to the future of San Rodrigo County, even to the venerable courthouse, which after a resounding defeat of the bond issue had assumed the status of a local monument.

"Things are pretty good," said Ausley. "I happened to be in town and I thought I ought to thank you once more for getting me out of a hole."

"Don't thank me, Ausley, it's in the line of duty. Helping you, I helped myself. I'm glad things turned out the way they did for both of us. How are folks in Marblestone treating you?"

Ausley smiled wanly. "Not bad. Nobody's really friendly. I guess I still carry a reputation — even if I didn't do anything."

"It'll wear off — hey! What's this?" Joe examined the broad gold band on Ausley's third finger. "Don't tell me you went and made the leap?"

"Yeah." Ausley grinned sheepishly. "Somehow I convinced Ellie I'd make her a good husband, knowing the ranch business and all that. We got married this morning."

"Well I'll be horsewhipped!"

Ausley gave him a look of mild reproach. "She's out doing some shopping — clothes and stuff like that. We're heading for Los Angeles for a week or two."

Joe drew a deep breath, shook Ausley's hand. "Congratulations, Ausley. You got a real good girl, about the nicest one around."

Ausley shuffled his feet. "I think so too…Well, I better go pick her up. We got a long drive ahead of us."

"Give my regards to the bride!"

"I'll do that, Joe. So long."

"So long, Ausley. Have a good time."

The tall shape moved down the hall and out into the sunlight. Joe shook his head. "That's the way it goes. If a man sits back, dilly-dallies, pretty soon he finds he's left behind. Way behind…Oh well, I can't complain. It's Sheriff Joe Bain now, for real…I feel like taking off a week or two myself."

JACK VANCE was born in 1916 to a well-off California family that, as his childhood ended, fell upon hard times. As a young man he worked at a series of unsatisfying jobs before studying mining engineering, physics, journalism and English at the University of California Berkeley. Leaving school as America was going to war, he found a place as an ordinary seaman in the merchant marine. Later he worked as a rigger, surveyor, ceramicist, and carpenter before his steady production of sf, mystery novels, and short stories established him as a full-time writer.

His output over more than sixty years was prodigious and won him three Hugo Awards, a Nebula Award, a World Fantasy Award for lifetime achievement, as well as an Edgar from the Mystery Writers of America. The Science Fiction and Fantasy Writers of America named him a grandmaster and he was inducted into the Science Fiction Hall of Fame.

His works crossed genre boundaries, from dark fantasies (including the highly influential *Dying Earth* cycle of novels) to interstellar space operas, from heroic fantasy (the *Lyonesse* trilogy) to murder mysteries featuring a sheriff (the Joe Bain novels) in a rural California county. A Vance story often centered on a competent male protagonist thrust into a dangerous, evolving situation on a planet where adventure was his daily fare, or featured a young person setting out on a perilous odyssey over difficult terrain populated by entrenched, scheming enemies.

Late in his life, a world-spanning assemblage of Vance aficionados came together to return his works to their original form, restoring material cut by editors whose chief preoccupation was the page count of a pulp magazine. The result was the complete and authoritative *Vance Integral Edition* in 44 hardcover volumes. Spatterlight Press is now publishing the VIE texts as ebooks, and as print-on-demand paperbacks.

Colophon

This book was printed using Adobe Arno Pro as the primary text font, with NeutraFace used on the cover.

This title was created from the digital archive of the Vance Integral Edition, a series of 44 books produced under the aegis of the author by a worldwide group of his readers. The VIE project gratefully acknowledges the editorial guidance of Norma Vance, as well as the cooperation of the Department of Special Collections at Boston University, whose John Holbrook Vance collection has been an important source of textual evidence.

Special thanks to R.C. Lacovara, Patrick Dusoulier, Koen Vyverman, Paul Rhoads, Chuck King, Gregory Hansen, Suan Yong, and Josh Geller for their invaluable assistance preparing final versions of the source files.

Digitize: Richard Chandler, Mike Dennison, Billy Webb, Dave Worden; Diff: David A. Kennedy, David Reitsema; Tech Proof: Hans van der Veeke; Text Integrity: Patrick Dusoulier, Paul Rhoads, Steve Sherman; Implement: Donna Adams, Derek W. Benson, Damien G. Jones; Security: Paul Rhoads; Compose: Andreas Irle; Comp Review: Marcel van Genderen, Charles King, Bob Luckin; Update Verify: Rob Friefeld, Robert Melson, Paul Rhoads; RTF-Diff: Deborah Cohen, Charles King; Textport: Patrick Dusoulier; Proofread: Kristine Anstrats, Mike Barrett, Deborah Cohen, Greg Delson, Patrick Dusoulier, Rob Friefeld, Charles King, Roderick MacBeath, Michael Mitchell, David Reitsema, Steve Sherman, Suan Hsi Yong, Fred Zoetemeyer

Artwork (maps based on original drawings by Jack and Norma Vance):

Paul Rhoads, Christopher Wood

Book Composition and Typesetting: Joel Anderson

Art Direction and Cover Design: Howard Kistler

Proofing: Steve Sherman, Dave Worden

Jacket Blurb: John Vance

Management: John Vance, Koen Vyverman

www.ingramcontent.com/pod-product-compliance
Lightning Source LLC
Chambersburg PA
CBHW020633180626
46816CB00003B/937